The years all end

Elysia Nates

Content Warning

This book contains content and themes that may be sensitive to some readers, including suicide, death, mental disorders, profanity, family violence and underage drinking.

The lovely feeling of being family is made up of thousands of very little, seemingly insignificant things which are going on around us all the time. When you look back in years to come, you will most likely remember the high points and the low points. And all the rest will be lost in a blur of nice, comfy, family feeling. It is important to remember that this feeling of family means that each person recognises the bond and the strength of the family unit, but also recognises the importance and the individuality of each member.

Gregory Nates

Playlist

On the Road Again *Willie Nelson*

Golden Brown *The Stranglers*

Please, please, please let me get what I want *The Smiths*

Used to Be Young *Miley Cyrus*

Sorrento Moon *Tina Arena*

Down So Long *Jewel*

Buses and Trains *Bachelor Girl*

Big, Big World *Emilia*

You Learn *Alanis Morissette*

1000 Miles Away *Hoodoo Gurus*

The Show *Lenka*

I'll Remember *Madonna*

It's Okay *Nightbirde*

Live and Die *Orchestral Manoeuvres in the Dark*

Liam's Song – **I Took a Pill in Ibiza** *Mike Posner*

Part One

New Year's Eve 1991

Dad blurts out some word that I'm not supposed to know and slams on the brakes, hurling my brother and I forward. Eric's arms instinctively brace against the back of Mum's headrest and I clutch at the seatbelt as it suddenly tightens against the base of my neck. I dab my finger to my stinging skin and look down at my hand, expecting to see blood.

Mum turns around, fretting. "Everyone okay? Jesus, Mitch!" My bottom lip trembles and tears prick my eyes. "Ouch, let me see, baby." Her voice is gentle and protective, just like she is. "Did you get a bit of whiplash?"

Eric pats my knee reassuringly. "You're okay, Buzzy."

Mum studies my neck and forms a theatrical sad face. "Ouch! My poor little Bea. It is a bit red actually. We'll put some ice on it when we get to the cabin. Not much longer now, maybe half an hour."

Dad honks the horn hard and prolonged, shouting that word again that I'm still not supposed to know. The koala sitting in the middle of the road is unfazed by the noise, testing Dad's patience. He sticks his head out the window and glares at the stubborn creature, keeping his hand pressed down on the horn. The koala still refuses to move. Dad is becoming increasingly annoyed and Mum is biting her nails. I don't like it when they are stressed and I especially don't like it when I can't help the reason why. I contemplate getting out to shoo the koala away myself but the succession of cars behind us are all honking now, too and the whole world feels so frantic and angry. I can't make a difference. If the koala isn't listening to a grown man with an assertive honk under his hand, he sure isn't going to listen to an eleven-year-old child with a Baby-sitter's Club book on her lap. I strain to hold in my tears but it just makes my throat sting and I want to cry even more. I can never fix things.

Eric notices my demeanour and inches across the seat. "Pity that fucking koala can't speak fucking English," he whispers. "Good thing we don't know what any of those fucking swear words are either."

My rapid breath calms at the sound of his voice and the impulse to laugh takes over the urge to cry. My big brother is a magician: he always makes everything feel better. I wish I could do that, too.

The koala doesn't look particularly friendly. I thought they were meant to be cute and cuddly but this guy looks primed for a fight. He knows full well that he is single-handedly holding up ten cars. Dad blurts out that word a few more times; in front of *off*, *you*, and *sakes* but I'm still not meant to know what it is. I guess I'm allowed to hear it, I'm just not allowed to know what it means.

Dad opens his door and motions to exit the car, sending Mum into a panic. She grabs hold of his arm, frantically reminding him about that article she read in last month's Women's Weekly, about a koala that attacked a family while they were out bushwalking. Dad requests Mum to *hush, dear* and bravely ventures towards the angry creature anyway.

"Hey, little guy! How you going?" I haven't ever heard Dad's voice sound quite so high-pitched before. "You need to get off the road, you're holding everyone up!"

Mum leans her head out her window and Eric and I copy. The koala grunts aggressively and lunges towards Dad. I guess they're not cute, definitely not cuddly and apparently, they even growl! Dad yelps and bolts back to the car, jumping in through the open door. He jigs his knees up and down and tries to catch his breath.

"The fuck is his problem? Since when do koalas attack people?"

Mum sighs.

Seeing Dad panic like this makes everything feel scary again. Eric gently takes hold of my hand. "Don't be scared, Buzzy."

I grab onto him tightly.

The mean koala grunts again and charges towards

the car as if he fully intends to bowl it over. Dad instinctively instructs us to roll up our windows.

Mum pats him on the thigh, a little smug. "Now that you've reacquainted yourself with the native fauna, dear, can we just get to the lake?"

Dad swerves the car past the confrontational koala; poised in the middle of the road, daring someone to take him on. We make this trip annually, and yet somehow, without fail, Dad always manages to anger the wildlife.

We leave home early in the morning on New Year's Eve, to the sound of Willie Nelson's On the Road Again cranked up loud. It takes us just over an hour to reach our first destination: the petrol station next to the rusted old windmill at the bottom of the hill. It's a popular stop for long-haul truck drivers. The adjoined 24-hour diner has the best bacon and eggs in the world. Eric habitually steals my crispy bits and I pretend to mind, but I don't. Dad lets us choose one magazine and one chocolate for the second part of the drive, which is even longer than the first. But Dad has the timing down to a fine art; we always arrive at the lake around lunch time, so we can settle in and go exploring before the big party kicks off. There are fireworks and everything.

We have to drive back home on the second of January, because my grandparents can't handle looking after our Golden Retriever, Gilbert for much longer than that. He demands more attention than they can be bothered to give him. He will be six next year but still runs around like he did when Eric first got him as a puppy. But I think maybe Mum and Dad just use Gilbert and Nanna and Pappa as an excuse to come home because we can't afford to stay for the whole week like everyone else does.

Mum says she and Dad have spent every New Year's at the lake since they first got married fifteen years ago. My earliest memory is whizzing down the yellow water slide cradled between my brother's legs, determined to beat the magnitude of each past splash.

Eric is a little bit older than me. He'll be thirteen in May, two months after I turn twelve. Everyone always asks if we're twins, even though he's skinny and I'm kind of not. We both have hair that's not quite blonde, not quite brown, full faces and matching hazel eyes. Mum says that if she were to only look at our eyes, even she wouldn't be able to tell us apart.

Mr Randall, who lives next door, calls us the *dynamic duo*. He jokes that he only ever sees the two of us together, never one without the other. I like that. Mr Randall's wife died during childbirth, so he raised their son on his own. When I was really little, I remember asking Mum why the old man next door looked so sad all the time. She told me that his son had moved to London for work and so Mr Randall was completely alone here now, after devoting his whole life and sacrificing everything to be a father. Mum sounded different when she said that. Every day when I get home from school, he is pottering around his front garden, tending to a row of yellow and orange roses, with a stumpy glass of dark red liquid on the ground next to him. When he comes up to the fence to say hello, his sips of that dark red liquid linger on his breath, compelling me to scrunch up my nose at the tangy aroma. It smells like cough medicine mixed with vinegar.

I guess he has a right to be sad all the time. Losing your wife and then losing your son, just in a different capacity, must be really hard. No wonder Mum makes an extra bowl of spaghetti bolognaise on Sunday nights and takes it next door to him.

I like it when people gush over Eric and I being inseparable, especially around Liam. He's Mr and Mrs Sanderson's son, Mum and Dad's best friends. They come to the lake for New Year's too but they stay for longer than us, like everyone does. The other day when Liam was hanging out at our house, Mr Randall called out that *the twins have a third wheel today*. Liam scoffed at that. He didn't like it. He gets jealous of my relationship with Eric. I loved that Mr Randall put him back in his place. Eric is *my* brother, *not* Liam's. I hoped Mum would put extra meatballs in Mr Randall's spaghetti that week.

Mrs Sanderson has been Mum's best friend since their high school days. She was married to someone else when I was really little, so I guess she wasn't Mrs Sanderson then. I don't know who she was or what happened to her first husband though. No one ever talks about it and I can't remember him.

Mr Sanderson became Dad's friend out of convenience, or necessity, it seems more than anything else; he's a bit loud and obnoxious and not really Dad's sort of person. He isn't even into music. Dad knows everything about every band, singer and album before 1980 but Mr Sanderson is all about cars and sport. He brags a lot, usually about his new car or the great seats he got for the latest game. I don't think Mum particularly likes him either. I wonder why adults are friends with people they don't even like.

My parents have always been popular. They are the core of a wide social circle and I'm expected to prefix everyone in it with *Uncle* and *Aunty*. We're always going over to someone's house for a Saturday night barbecue or someone is always coming over to our house for a Sunday afternoon drink on the patio. And the Sandersons are always wherever Mum and Dad are.

Eric and Liam were born within a couple of weeks

of each other, so they were destined to be best friends, just like their mums. But Liam is an only child so there is no one for me to play with when his family come over or we go to their house. Eric lets me follow them around but Liam would rather I rack off and make my own friends.

Liam always tries to take Eric away from me, especially when we stay at the lake. They meet up with Ant and the other guys in the games room but Liam insists that you're only allowed in there if you're over twelve. And a boy. I've never seen a sign that says that, and I've looked all the way around the building. I checked the pamphlet next to the cabin's phone but there was no mention of any rules like that. Even when they ride their bikes around the resort, Liam deliberately speeds up so I can't keep up with them. I trail along behind them on my purple scooter but I always lose them and end up on my own, exploring the lake for new rocks for my collection. I try to find smooth ones, because they are the best ones to paint. That's what I do when I can't be with Eric.

The resort books out at New Year's with an even mix of regular and first-time guests. The swimming pool and water slides are the most popular attractions but I like the lake the best. Mum takes me kayaking and Eric and I jump off the jetty. Dad taught me how to swim in that lake.

The atmosphere at the holiday park is the same every New Year's; a familiarity as comforting as a hug from my parents. It's like someone took a recording of the year before and just pressed play the year after, like time stood still. Like life in-between didn't even happen.

When the first cork of the day is popped, everyone cheers. Dad props up his ghetto-blaster by a tree and proudly showcases his envied collection of CDs, featuring a succession of singers predominately named Johnny or Bobby. There are sack races and fishing, water pistol fights and croquet. New friends. Old friends. As the evening creeps in, the air begins to smell like mosquito coils and we all smell like Aerogard. There are sparklers and rounds of limbo. The dads cook chicken shashliks and stuffed potatoes on the communal gas barbecue for everyone to share. There's always so much food.

New Year's at the lake makes strangers feel like family. People you've never seen before, some you'll never see again: family for the night.

"Are we there yet?" Eric moans. "I gotta pee."

"Twenty minutes," Dad answers. "Providing we don't run into any more fucking koalas."

Eric scrunches up his face and cups his hands over his private area, jiggling his knees to make me laugh.

Mum turns around and scolds him. "Eric, don't be gross."

Six Willie Nelson songs later, we drive through the gates of the resort and into a whole new world. Parents don't worry about the electricity bill being two months overdue here, or fight about the mortgage when they think their kids are asleep. Teachers don't send notes home about your lack of social skills and inability to relate to your peers. It's just far enough from home to feel *far away*.

Dad parks next to Reception. We wait in the car while he checks us in and collects the keys.

"Looks like the Sanderson clan are already here," he announces when he gets back. "It's a full house; ours were the last keys on the board."

Dad is right: the holiday park is completely booked out. Most people are still unpacking their cars, stretching their arms to the sky after the long drive. Warm greetings abound as everyone reacquaints themselves with their traditional New Year's neighbourhood and the first-timers check out the surroundings.

The grassed areas are a vision of fold-up deck chairs and patterned outdoor umbrellas that try in vain to offer shelter from the relentless summer sun. There is a dense population of tents, and caravans with faded blue or yellow stripes. I spy my favourite one as we drive past on the way to our cabin: it is silver, wrapped in a thin chocolate-brown decal and the curtains are orange, as if surely owned by a little old lady. But actually, two women a bit younger than my mum drive it up here every year. They usually park it across from the big barbecue.

I guess they must be sisters, because they dress the same, just like my brother and I do. Cowboy shirts tucked into high-waisted dark denim jeans and hair flicks that frame their faces just like the Charlie's Angels. They wave at me, as if they know me personally, or just recognise me fondly. I don't know what their names are but I think of them as Pat and Joanie.

The road is smooth, as if no one has driven on it since last New Year's. It is bordered by a gravel footpath and winds through the commune of parked caravans, tents and established log cabins which overlook the naturally unkempt grass leading down to the lake.

Dad slows the car as the cabin numbers get higher. "Keep a lookout for number 22."

Disappointment grabs hold of me. I refrain from blinking so the tears coating my eyes don't gush down my face. I was hoping we would be in cabin 16 again this year, not 22. Cabin 16 has a special secret spot, right on top of the wardrobe. You can climb onto it from the top bunk. I put a pillow and a blanket up there last year and read my newest The Baby-sitters Club book, because Liam was constantly trying to keep Eric all to himself. I could cry freely in my secret spot, and I did. I cried so much up there. I cried about how mean and selfish Liam was and how much I hated him, until Mum came looking for me because the countdown was about to start.

I guess number 22 is pretty cool too, in its own way. It has a deck that goes all the way around it like a giant hula hoop. I hope I can climb up onto the wardrobe. I liked having a secret spot like that. I liked having a space where I could cry.

Dad parks the car and we all hop out.

Mrs Sanderson rushes up to hug Mum. "We just got here, too! We're right behind you in number 8!"

They gleefully sway side to side in their embrace. I half expect them to topple over.

"Has Bea put on a bit more weight?" she whispers to Mum, 'subtly' examining my figure.

I reach into the car to retrieve my overnight bag,

resting on the middle seat. I pretend it's stuck on the seatbelt so I've got a few seconds to shake off the humiliation. Mum is kind, warm and nurturing. She knits blankets for all the cats and dogs at the animal shelter. Whatever the opposite of all that is, that's Mrs Sanderson. I will never understand why Mum is friends with her.

"It's just baby fat, she'll grow out of it," Mum quietly assures Mrs Sanderson, quickly trying to brush her off.

I slide back out with my bag in tow and a smile on my face, but the usual commentary about my weight lingers in my mind. I lean back against the car, subconsciously waiting for Eric to come fix me, because he likes doing that. I fan my baggy t-shirt out from my tummy, slump my shoulders forwards and let the long strands of my straight hair drape over them.

Eric winks at me as he makes his way over. "Has Buzzy put on a bit more *fabulousness?*" he jokes quietly, mocking Mrs Sanderson's whiney voice.

My smile feels more natural again now.

Mr Sanderson helps Dad unload the rest of the bags from the boot. He asks Dad about the mileage and brags about how he could get him a good deal if he is ready for a trade-in.

Liam and Eric greet each other affectionately with their special handshake. I'm only Eric's dorky little sister so I'll never be cool enough for them to do it with me, even though I know it off by heart. I practice it in front of the mirror every day. Just in case. It's hard doing it on my own, but I've got the timing perfect, so if they ever do include me, I'll be ready.

Liam frowns at me, perpetually annoyed by my mere presence. "Hi," he mumbles, before turning his attention back to Eric. "Do you and Beatrice have any more bags?"

Liam always calls me Beatrice and I hate it, which I bet is why he does it. He thinks he's so grown up compared to me just because he's a year older. He forgets that he's just as much of a child as I am. Whenever he is around, I am suddenly inadequate. It's like we're in competition with one another, and no matter how hard I try, I'll never be able to beat him, whatever it is that we are actually competing for.

Eric motions to the bags at his feet. "Just these."

Liam is wearing a yellow t-shirt with a picture of TV's ALF on it and dark denim shorts that sit just above his knees. He wears that top a lot, even though I don't think he watches the show. His glasses are folded in his short's pocket; he self-consciously pushes them back in when he feels them peeking out.

Dad ruffles up Liam's unruly mop of copper hair. "Good to see you, Liam."

Liam's cheeks blush and his torso stiffens like a cat that just got stroked the wrong way. Mr Sanderson rolls his eyes and makes a humph noise before following Dad up the two steps into our cabin, trailing off about the footy ladder. It's hard to believe that a father could dislike his own son and I feel guilty for thinking it, but that's always the impression that I get when Mr Sanderson looks at Liam.

Liam stays over at our house a lot. I've overheard

Mrs Sanderson telling Mum that Mr Sanderson is 'too hard' on Liam but it's just because he wants to 'toughen him up'. I feel kind of bad for Liam; even though I still think he's a jerk. But it's not like he can strip his shyness off like a coat and just hang it up in his wardrobe.

We all went to the same primary school but Eric and Liam are starting a boy's only high school when we go back at the end of January. It will be a year of firsts and lasts for me: my last year of primary school and my first one without my big brother there. I'm dreading it.

My Year 6 teacher, Miss Blunt, encouraged me to make my own friends, like it was her mission to bring me out of my shell. She said it wasn't healthy that I only ever sat with my older brother and his friend at recess and lunch. She asked me what I would do with myself when Eric went off to high school. I shrugged my shoulders nonchalantly, as if that wasn't something that I even needed to consider. I guess I did need to though.

I have had friends before, well, *a* friend. Mindy and I

were the best of friends for a few years, since the start of school. She loved The Jetsons and Scooby-Doo, and only ever ate pink marshmallows for recess. Mindy's hair was so blonde it was almost white and she wore it in two plats that hung just below her shoulders. Almost overnight, we just didn't seem to like each other anymore. Nothing happened; we didn't have a fight or anything. We stopped hanging out together because she wanted to play Four Square with Bess and Anna and I just wanted to go find Eric.

Liam fetches one of Eric's bags, ready to take it inside for him. He seems a bit withdrawn now.

"Interesting that you picked that bag, it's got my notebook in it." Eric's voice is overtly laced with excitement. "I've got a new story idea!"

Liam's instant smile vanquishes the sadness that had engulfed him. "I've been working on some new designs for the Lake Monster!"

Eric is a superhero. He saves everyone.

As much as he tries to include me in their friendship,

Eric and Liam are best mates and there are just some things that I will never be able to be a part of. They are writing a graphic novel, which they are hopeful of turning into a three-part series. Eric is forever conjuring up fanciful stories and Liam brings them to life with his illustrations.

I'm jealous that Eric and Liam have their secret things and plans and experiences that I don't get to share, like their upcoming first year of high school. The special handshake, the sleepovers, the stories, the dream to go on book signing tours and negotiate a million-dollar contract for the eventual movie adaptation of their series: that's just the two of them. Eric pretends that I am a part of it all to keep me happy, but that's his life with Liam, not me. I'm just his annoying kid sister who doesn't have any friends of her own.

Eric and Liam know exactly what they want to do when they grow up and they are already doing it. I just paint rocks and read.

The cabin opens to a quaint living area with a sofa and two recliners. The walls are painted light green.

A painting of the lake adorns the space above the tv and there is a single cabinet filled with an extensive VHS collection of Disney movies. A dining table and cramped kitchen are adjacent. Past the entrance, a short hallway connects two bedrooms, a bathroom and a separate toilet. It's such a tiny little home but it feels like I'm stepping into a mansion.

Liam follows Eric and I into our room. The walls have dark wooden panelling the same colour as the wardrobe. I suck back my tears at the sight of the wardrobe: it goes all the way up to the ceiling.

A bunk bed is pushed against the far wall beneath a small oval window that looks like it belongs in the cabin of a boat. I climb up to the top and peer over the railing. Below, Liam and Eric gleefully ogle the completed pages of their story, as if they don't do so every lunch break anyway.

"Let me show you the stuff I've been working on!" Eric beams, rummaging through the bag next to him to find his notebook.

Eric is so good at making up stories. Liam and I both tell him that he is going to be a mega famous writer someday. When I scraped my knee after falling off my purple scooter in the backyard, Mum sat me down on the edge of the bath and dabbed Dettol on the wound. It stung so badly but I didn't cry because Eric distracted me by telling me a story about a triple-headed alien from Planet Mashoo. I didn't even notice when Mum put a band-aid over it.

They still haven't settled on a name for their graphic novel but I believe The Monster in the Lake is the latest. It comes after they trialled Beneath the Beach, Swim for Your Life and A Monster Ate My Bathers. Eric tells me it's a horror story for kids. I thought horror wasn't meant to be for kids, but I don't tell him that.

I get a bit sick of hearing about it, really. Last Saturday night when the Sandersons came over to our house, the boys went on and on about what colour the monster should be. I had lots of new rocks to paint, but I still felt left-out and lonely. Eric has a best friend, and they do lots of best friend things together. My brother is my best friend, but I'm not his.

I didn't realise there was enough colours in the world to warrant an hour-long discussion but evidently, it's serious business deciding what colour skin a monster should have. Liam promised me that I could be the leading lady when their book gets turned into a movie one day, just as long as I *shut up now* and leave them *alone*. I told him that actresses have to be pretty and he mumbled that I was pretty but then Eric made a vomiting noise and Liam punched him in the arm.

I don't know what I want to be when I grow up. I probably can't make a living out of painting pink flowers on pebbles or reading books. Making up stories is Eric's thing. I guess reading is mine. Maybe I could be Eric's own personal proof reader when I grow up. At school, Mrs Avery says the library will run out of books for me soon.

Mum and Dad will never boast to their friends about me the way they do about Eric. But I understand why they proudly tell everyone about him and all the amazing things he is going to achieve. I would tell my friends the same, if I had any.

You should hear his stories, he's really good!

Our boy is the next Paul Jennings!

Eric's books will be Aussie classics one day!

He'll be more famous than May Gibbs!

Oh, Bea you ask? Um, well yes, she is a bit chubby but she has such a sweet nature and she loves her brother. I haven't actually heard Mum and Dad say that but I'm not sure what else they would be able to say about me, really.

I sit cross-legged on the top bunk and peer through the window, looking out over the lake. It is the sole window in the room and it is only accessible from the top bunk, which means it is mine. It is my window, so I own the view that comes with it. The lake belongs to me.

I smile contentedly at a lone tree, close to the edge of the water, separate from the rest. Strong enough to stand on its own. The trunk is bendy and the branches twist like someone stretching after they've just got out of bed in the morning. It is the easiest tree to climb here; each branch is just a big step up from the next. *Nature's Ladder*, I call it. I love that tree. It's the first one I look for when we get here.

I'm excited that I get to stay up late tonight because of the New Year's Eve celebration. The lake looks so different after the transition from day to night. It kind of fascinates me. When darkness comes, the surface is suddenly still and sombre, as if it is mourning the loss of the sun for just a brief moment, wondering how it will continue to exist on its own. But then the light of the moon showers the whole lake in glitter and it is new again, or just still alive perhaps. It curls up onto the grassy shore, able to go on just the same without the sun, but somehow just a little bit different.

For now, it appears motionless, not a ripple in sight. The sun shines without a cloud in the sky. A lone ibis strolls along gracefully. Families ride go-karts and men sit with fishing rods on the old, rickety jetty. Kids in bathers rush past my window, racing each other to the pool. The holiday park's soundtrack plays again: a familiar mix of magpies yodelling and radios all playing a different song. Yet together, it all seems to harmonize.

My teachers tell Mum and Dad that I'm *too sensitive* and *emotionally fragile. Inattentive. Always distracted.*

Beatrice doesn't seem interested in any of her school subjects, or in making friends with her peers. The unhealthy attachment to her brother prohibits her from coming out of her shell and connecting with anyone her own age.

The thing I love the most about here is the contrast: if you look out across the water, everything is calm. Quiet. Peaceful. But if you close your eyes and listen, everything is buzzing. Loud. Energetic. Two worlds existing at the exact same time.

And the other world waiting back at home doesn't exist at all, for just a couple of days.

New Year's Eve 1992

Dad pays for breakfast before a noticeable tension settles over everyone but me it seems.

The cashier kept staring at Mum's black eye, and then back to Dad with disapproval stamped all over her face. I wanted to yell at the lady to stop staring, but I know Mum is big on not making a scene. She just likes everything to be okay and everyone to be happy. So even though Mum simply tripped over the broom last week when she was sweeping the kitchen, I didn't even give the cashier lady daggers for insinuating bad things with her judgemental eyes.

We head back to the car, weaving between the huge trucks that are parked horizontally across three or four spots. The festive vibe of our traditional New Year's road trip to the lake seems to have been replaced by anxious glances and uneasy silence.

"It wasn't that expensive last year, was it?" Dad asks Mum softly, as if trying not to let Eric and I hear.

I can't wait to get to the lake. Mum and Dad don't worry about money there. They don't trip over brooms because they're tired.

I hop into my seat, loaded up with my new TV Hits magazine and Kit-Kat, and grab my seatbelt by the buckle, but it's burning hot so I drop it instinctively, shaking my hand about furiously to cool the sting.

"Silly Bea," Eric soothes me, picking up my seatbelt by the strap. "Don't touch the metal, it gets hot in the summer, see?"

He dabs the buckle on my knee and I gasp at the shock of the burn. "Ow!"

Mum quickly turns around. "What happened?"

"Nothing!" Eric moans. "I'm just clicking in Bea's seatbelt because it was too hot for her." He blows on my knee and tears open my Kit-Kat. "Here, let's see who can eat all the chocolate off their bar first without making the wafer snap."

After our chocolate race, which I win, Eric buries his face in his notebook for the rest of the drive, writing so fast his hand can barely keep up. He must have a great new story idea he wants to work on. His notebook is getting full; the pages are fanned out from the weight of all the words he has been frantically filling it with lately.

I flip through my magazine and then devour the new Sweet Valley High book I brought along. Mum and Dad listen to the same Willy Nelson cassette tape a million times over.

When we finally make it to the resort, Dad collects the keys from Reception while the rest of us wait in the car.

"Doesn't look like the Sandersons are here yet," he announces when he climbs back in and drives us down to Cabin 11.

Mum turns the key in the front door, dramatically slowly. Dad makes a drum roll noise with his tongue. I giggle at how silly they are sometimes but Eric just rolls his eyes. He's in a bad mood all of a sudden. Seems to be a standard thing for boys once they turn thirteen.

But Mum and Dad are in a good mood now that we're here. It's nice to see finally.

I know a secret about grown-ups: happiness and groceries are directly correlated. If there is ice cream in the freezer and bacon and eggs on the table on a Sunday morning, I won't overhear Mum and Dad arguing when they think Eric and I are asleep in our rooms. If Eric and I come home from school to a chocolate doughnut and Dad cooks steak on the barbecue for tea on a Friday night, I know that my parents are happy. But if it's been a few weeks and the cupboards are still dominated by tinned spaghetti and baked beans, and if Mum has been pretending to like the Home Brand coffee for her evening cuppa and Dad has been rolling his own cigarettes, there won't be much joking around or jovial banter at home. And I'll overhear them shouting at each other late at night.

Their last argument was about the dog. They didn't

know how they were going to afford Gilbert's vaccinations. Dad got mad at Mum because she was the one *who wanted to get Eric a dog in the first place* and Mum got mad at Dad because she was the one *raising two kids and looking after the home* and now, she *has to work Saturdays at a drycleaner.* I tiptoed into Eric's room across the hallway and got into bed with him. He comforted me with a story about a friendly goblin named Bogart who desperately wanted to be friends with the prettiest fairy in the land. I'd heard it lots of times before.

Mum and Dad must have argued all night long, because Mum was really tired for the rest of the week and ended up tripping over the broom and giving herself a black eye. I overheard them yelling the night after Mum got her black eye and tried to go into Eric's room but my bedroom door opened to the linen cupboard blocking the entrance. That's how tired Mum is: she must have shifted it in front of my door when she was sweeping up after saying goodnight to me, and forgot to move it back.

But soon enough, Gilbert got his yearly shots, Mum

bought the good coffee and she and Dad loved each other again. Eric even got to take up piano lessons.

This cabin is bigger than the ones we usually stay in. Mum says I'm too old to be bunking with my brother now. She says growing young ladies need their privacy. So, Dad booked a three-bedroom cabin this year. I do like my room. It just feels weird having my own here. Lonely.

The Sandersons soon come knocking and Mum and Dad greet them as if they are long lost friends, even though they were over at our house just a few days ago.

"Liam forgot his reading glasses and of course only realised when we were half-way here," Mr Sanderson complains. He is visibly cross. "We had to turn back to get them," he grumpily continues, even though Liam is standing right next to him with his head bowed.

I don't understand why Mr Sanderson is so annoyed. Liam wears his glasses when he's working on his illustrations, so he obviously needs them. It's not his fault he can't see properly. I'm pretty sure he's meant to wear them all the time, but he doesn't for some reason.

Mrs Sanderson squints, as if trying to zoom in on Mum's black eye. "Have you been using that concealer I gave you? It doesn't seem to be doing much in the way of cover up."

"It's fine, love," Mum brushes her off.

Mr Sanderson looks even more annoyed now. "We've got champers in the fridge. Let's go."

My parents leave with the Sandersons while I change into my bathers in my room and the boys get ready in Eric's.

Heading out, I wrap a towel around my body, double-checking that it is tightly secure and won't slip down, but I'm surprised to see the door to Eric's room is still closed. They normally get ready faster than I do.

"Are you guys coming?" I impatiently ask the closed door.

They don't answer, which instantly frustrates me. I

bet they're just hanging out working on their stupid Lake Monster while I'm standing here waiting around in *bathers* and a towel: fodder for Mrs Sanderson's whispers.

I aggressively push the door open. "Hurry up!"

Greeted by a suffocating smell of smoke, Liam leaps up and pulls me into the room, frantically shutting the door behind me. He is wearing his glasses. He wasn't when he got here. I hardly ever see him wear them.

I pull the knot of my towel up to cover my nose. "It stinks in here! What are you two doing?"

The boys shush me in unison. "Nothing!"

"You guys are going to get in so much trouble! If Mum finds out you've been smoking, she'll kill you both."

"Mum won't find out, will she Buzzy? We're not smoking, we're just chilling."

Eric must think I'm such a baby sometimes.

"Why does it smell so bad? That's not what Dad's

smokes smell like."

The same sheepish expression finds them both.

Eric's giggle is reminiscent of a toddler impressed by his mum playing Peek-a-Boo. Poorly attempting to compose himself, he assures me that "it's just a different brand."

Liam ungracefully plops himself down on the floor, resting his back against the bed. He brings his knees up to his chest and drapes his arms over his knees, his sudden burst of laughter so consuming that it fogs his glasses.

Eric slumps down next to him in an identical pose and perpetuates his nonsensical behaviour.

The hilarity is lost on me. "You guys are idiots and I'm not waiting for you! I'll just meet you at the water slides."

Liam thinks he's so special because he's doing something with Eric that I can't be a part of. Stuff him; I'll go to the pool without them. Storming out of the cabin barefoot, I aggressively kick the blades of grass with each stride as tears prick at my eyes.

A few doors down, Mum and Dad are having a drink on the front deck of the Sanderson's cabin.

"Bea!" Mum calls out. "Where's your brother?"

"Oh, um, he's coming down in a minute. He's just getting ready with Liam. I said I'd meet them there," I yell in return, intentionally trying to make my voice sound upbeat.

"You know you're not allowed to go to the pool on your own. Go on, go back and wait for the boys, they won't be long."

Dad takes a puff of his cigarette. "Your mother's right, Bea. You shouldn't go to the pool on your own. If they're busy, come sit with us or collect some new rocks. Just don't go too close to the lake." A roaming pelican approaches the raised deck and swipes its huge beak under the railing at Dad's foot.

"Fuck me!" he panics.

Mr and Mrs Sanderson are amused.

Mum shakes her head. "Jesus, Mitch. Don't provoke it!"

"I'll go wait," I sigh, turning back towards our cabin.

"Oh dear, Bea really is filling out now, isn't she?" Mrs Sanderson 'whispers' to Mum. Her whisper is the same volume as her normal voice.

I grip the knot on my towel. I shouldn't have wrapped it around so tight; it clearly didn't hide my shape well enough.

When I get back to the cabin, the boys are still giggling behind the closed bedroom door, so I lie on the couch and flip through the channels, catching the last half of Blossom before switching over to Valerie. I want to marry Jason Bateman when I'm older. Or maybe Joey Lawrence, actually. I haven't chosen between them yet.

Eric and Liam finally emerge, just as I'm about to get involved in another show I've already seen twice before. I want them to feel guilty for making me wait around for them. It's not fair that I can't go to the pool on my own. In three more months, I'll be a teenager: I'm old enough now. And clearly more responsible than Eric. But no matter what he does, he's the perfect one. And yet somehow, even when I know he's not, he is to me, too. He has to be. Everything is okay that way.

"Finally! Have you got all your brain cells back again now?" I scoff.

Eric settles next to me on the couch. "Sorry, Buzzy. We were just letting off a bit of steam."

"You mean creating steam!"

Liam stands stiff next to the recliner. Whatever it was that made him so relaxed obviously isn't working now. He's also not wearing his glasses anymore. "We opened the window. It's all clear. Thanks for not ratting on us."

"As if I'd do that," I scowl.

We head for the pool side-by-side, bare foot. I don't notice a muddy patch until it's too late; clumps of mud coat my foot and splash up my leg.

"Ewwwwwwww!" I cry; embarrassed that of course I was the only one who didn't manage to avoid the mud. I feel the familiar sting in my throat and my eyes involuntarily produce more tears than I can hold in.

Eric jumps into superhero mode. "It's okay, Buzzy. Look, see, there's a hose right over there."

I limp to the hose, coiled up on the lawn in front of the cabin next to ours. I hold my leg out as Eric aims the end of the hose and turns the tap on. Water bursts out directly onto my skin, but it is burning hot.

"That's hot!" I gasp, jumping back, away from the water.

"It's okay, Bea. The hose has just been in the sun, that's all," Eric assures me. "It should be okay now, try it again."

I apprehensively put my leg under the stream but it has yet to cool down and scorches me again.

"Geez, that must be hot! You were right, Bea."

Liam comes over, impatient that we are taking so long. *Now* who doesn't like waiting? The water has finally cooled so I let it run over my leg and watch the mud slide away, relieved.

The three of us continue on our walk to the pool. I am in the middle for only a couple of steps before Liam lingers back and shifts himself so he can walk next to Eric, instead of staying next to me. Now Eric is in the middle, as if Liam intentionally made it so that he could walk next to him. He always tries to hog *my* brother.

Passing the Sanderson's cabin, they all raise their champagne glasses as if in toast. I make sure my towel is tied up loose enough to disguise my shape.

"She's about to start high school, you don't want the other girls making fun of her," the whisper goes again. "A friend of mine joined a weight loss group; I can help you look around for one."

Down at the pool, I wait until Eric and Liam have their backs facing me, drop my towel and quickly jump in before they can turn around. Thankfully there are only a few other people swimming today. I'm already planning how I'll be able to get out of the water without being noticed.

Eric and Liam will be starting Year 9 when school goes back at the end of the holidays. Eric wanted

Mum to make an official complaint to the headmaster because he and Liam aren't going to be in the same homeroom, for the first time ever. Mr McIntosh reported that they talk too much and distract each other during lessons.

Eric got really upset about it. "Mr McIntosh just has it in for me!"

Mum tried to be understanding but said there was nothing she could do. "You'll see Liam at recess and lunch anyway."

"I don't care about school! It sucks! It's not like you can make me go!"

"There's no need for dramatics, Eric. You have to go to school, that's the way it works."

Eric didn't seem to think so. He stayed in his room that evening and didn't come out for dinner, even though Mum bought Neapolitan ice cream for dessert. She even got Ice Magic. Eric sulked for days but Mum and Dad didn't mind; they cuddled on the couch each night, contentedly watching TV while I enjoyed my evening bowl of ice cream. I even heard

Mum whisper to Dad; *he's just a normal teenager, sulking because he can't get his own way.* Getting the good groceries really does make Mum and Dad so much happier.

It was the worst year ever for me. Everyone's friendship groups were already set in stone, there was no hope for me to infiltrate one in my last year of primary school, just because I was suddenly in need of one now that my brother had left. I didn't know what to do with myself during recess. I ate my muesli bar sitting on the toilet and hid in there until the bell went. Lunch time was always easier because the library was open.

But now it's my turn to start high school. It will only be a five-minute walk along the main road to Eric's school, so I don't care if I make friends or not, because I'll be able to run down to Eric the second school finishes and then we can walk home together. Maybe at my high school, the library will be open at recess.

The boys tread water while deciding who the lake monster's first victim in their second book will be.

Eric wants it to be a chubby teenage girl with mousey brown hair. Liam's trying to persuade him; he thinks it would be scarier if the attack falls on a frail old lady, but he'll settle on Eric's idea as long as the girl is a boy and he has black hair instead. Colours really do seem to be their biggest discrepancy.

They finished the first book just before Christmas and now plan to save up their allowances so they can make copies to sell at school. They have envisioned a trilogy. Eric may have got a D in Maths but Mr McIntosh will feel pretty silly when my amazing big brother inevitably becomes a rich and famous bestselling author.

"Hey, Buzzy!" Eric calls out from the deep end of the pool. "We're going to the water slides. You coming?"

I guess Liam has decided that I'm allowed to spend time with my own brother now.

They climb out up the ladder as I swim down to their end, taking a quick scan around the pool to make sure I'm safe to get out, too. The two kids behind me in the shallow end are facing away from me. The other couple are close by but they are belly-flopping in and out. The second their bodies slap the water and disappear underneath the splash, I bolt up the ladder, hoping to be out before they resurface. I self-consciously fold my arms across my tummy and trail along behind Eric and Liam over to the water park.

Three water slides connect to the one square platform. The yellow slide is just a normal, plastic slippery dip. I don't go on that one anymore. I used to with Eric when I was just a toddler, but now I'd probably make it collapse. The two enclosed red slides seem sturdier, like they'd be able to handle my weight more.

The slides end in a shallow pool of water, just deep enough to cover your thighs. That's my favourite part: even a little water is enough to make a splash. Like it doesn't matter how small you are, or how insignificant you might feel, you can still make a difference in the end just by being there.

We race down our designated slides and then run up

one of the three stairwells, meeting at the top. I'm always the last to get back up. Eric is always the first. But I'm pretty sure Liam would be the first if he didn't seem to deliberately fall behind a bit.

I get distracted by a lone ladybug sitting on the edge of the bottom of my slide. I nearly splashed her so I'm relieved to see that she is okay.

Eric calls down to me. "Hey, slow poke! Where'd you go?" He and Liam have already made it back up to the top.

"I found a ladybug!"

They laugh at me as if to say *great* and then rush back down the stairs.

I delicately place my palm down next to the tiny red beetle. She briefly flutters upwards and then lands on my finger. My eyes widen with glee. "She landed on me!"

Eric and Liam crouch over the side of the slide. I quickly cover my tummy with my free hand.

"Pretty cool, Buzzy!"

Liam looks fascinated. "She must like you. It's good luck if a ladybug lands on you. You have to count how many spots it has, that's how many years you'll be protected for. They're like a shield."

Although I am cynical, the notion is nonetheless comforting. I quickly total nine tiny black spots and ask the pretty creature in whisper, "will you really keep me safe for nine years?"

"Hey, look!" Eric brings his face closer to the wet rubber ground. "There are millions of them here!"

I carefully stand, trying so hard not to move my hand too much and frighten the ladybug away. Eric and Liam scoop up the beetles that are on the cusp of drowning in the shallow puddles.

I gasp at the thought that maybe the magnitude of my splashes is to blame. Maybe the puddles I caused were just too deep for the poor creatures to withstand. The one on my finger flies away, as if celebrating her triumphant survival. I drop to the ground in desperation, determined to save as many as I can. I'm so heavy I slaughtered a whole bunch of ladybugs.

We run back and forth to a dry corner, releasing the ones we have managed to save from our cupped hands. There must be hundreds of ladybugs; we will never be able to get to them all in time.

My bottom lip trembles and my throat suddenly stings, as if someone is pressing their thumb into my neck. The ladybugs are dying because of me. They are dead because of me. I give in and let the tears crash down my cheeks freely.

Back at the start of the year, Miss Nolan sent a note home to my parents. I had dropped my papier-mâché volcano in her science class and it pretty much splattered on the floor, because the glue hadn't hardened yet. It was ruined. There was no way I was going to be able to fix it. I sneakily retrieved Miss Nolan's note after Mum aggressively threw it in the bin.

Beatrice really is too old to be crying in front of her peers now. Perhaps she requires extra support with her emotional regulation or has an unmet need at home. I can recommend a good child psychologist if you would like. She isn't connecting with anyone her age. If you don't mind me saying, I feel that

Beatrice is internally harbouring something that needs addressing.

"It's my fault," I sob, "the ladybugs are dying because of me! I can't save them!"

"It's okay, Buzzy," Eric tries to comfort me, "they just overestimated the water, that's all. Look, most of the ones we brought over here are okay now. They're just going to have a little rest, shake it off and then fly away back to Ladybug Land!"

"Except that dude," Liam chimes in. "Pretty sure he carked it."

"Because of me!" I cry loudly.

"But like, he'll come back to life, no doubt," Liam lies. "He always wanted to be a ghost bug."

Eric's face lights up. "That can be our next book, The Ghost Bug!"

Liam holds his palm out, face down, initiating their special handshake. I don't have any tears left now so I let myself chuckle, wishing that they would do the special handshake with me, too. I hold onto my neck as if clutching an invisible necklace, purposely trying to stop my hands from involuntarily doing the actions along with them. But one day it will happen. They will let me join in and I'll be ready. I know the actions even better than they do.

Their fists mimic fireworks: the last step in the special handshake. Eric's eyes twinkle with inspiration. "We'll have to come up with a cool way for The Ghost Bug to die! He could fly head-first into a semi-trailer, or get sucked up by an anteater, or maybe he'll get doused with fly spray!"

Liam matches his enthusiasm, leading Eric away from me. I guess he's had enough of sharing his time with *my* brother. "Okay, buddy. You write the story and I'll draw it!"

That night, the reserve by the lake is a beacon for the celebration of the fast-approaching new year. Deck chairs are scattered around the trees, eskies brim with cans of beer and Halls lemonade. Casks of red and white wine rest atop the railing on the decks of the cabins.

Dad tends to the barbecue with Mr Sanderson and

some other man I know as Uncle George. He turns the sausages, lovingly admiring Mum as she sits barefoot on the grass with a group of her own friends. They sing along loudly when an Elvis Presley song plays from the ghetto blaster propped under the closest tree. It only ever plays songs that all the parents seem to know off by heart.

Kids run back and forth, topping up their paper plates with second and third helpings. The little ones sleepily ask their parents *how much longer, how much longer* but Mum or Dad just scurry them away. *Less than half an hour, go and play.* They started saying 'less than half an hour' at nine o'clock.

Next to their silver caravan with the chocolate-coloured stripe and orange curtains, Pat and Joanie slow dance under a string of dim fairy lights. They don't really mingle with anyone else. Mrs Sanderson often whispers about how gross they are but I don't get why. Maybe she thinks sisters shouldn't dance together.

Eric and Liam skip pebbles along the surface of the lake and try to teach me but mine just sink straight to the bottom. Liam is by far the best at it. His bounce two and sometimes even three times before diving under the water. Eric's personal best is one skip but that's still better than I can manage.

"Here, Buzzy," Eric demonstrates, "like this. Stick your bum out, bend your knees down low and chuck it at an angle so it just skims the surface." He hurls his pebble and it skips once on the surface and then sinks.

I try again but mine instantly plops to the bottom.

Liam stands behind me and places a new pebble in my palm, outstretched to the side. He manoeuvres my hand so that it turns over in his. "Like this." He pulls my hand back then thrusts my arm forwards, softly uttering "let go" close to my ear. His warm, shaky breath tickles my cheek. The pebble skips once on top of the water and then slips under, just like Eric's did.

I open my mouth wide in disbelief. "I did it!"

Liam smiles. His face is rectangular but when he smiles, his cheeks puff out and change its whole shape. "You did it!"

Sometimes, he doesn't seem to mind me hanging around them so much.

Just as I'm about to thank Liam for helping me, Eric punches him in the arm and they tackle each other to the ground, play-fighting on the lake's grassy shore by the light of the full moon.

Next year will be my first year of high school. Eight years of education and I have yet to form a friendship like they have. My teachers say I can't connect with my peers. They say it in private notes sent home to my parents, in whispers on yard duty, and in subtle heart-to-hearts about growing up before I rush out the door to go find Eric at recess. But I know something they don't know: I only need my brother. I don't need friends.

I stare across the water; the ripples of our pebbles still evident on the surface. None of that stuff applies here. None of it is an issue. Here I'm not Bea, the anti-social girl who never fits in and doesn't have any friends. Here I'm just Eric's little sister and I can be with him all the time. Even though Liam gets in the way sometimes. At the lake, we're not separated by year levels, or schools. I'm his sister, and we're together. That makes everything feel okay.

My brother's sister is all I've ever wanted to be and everything I imagine I will always want to be. Eric is my brother. And he will always protect me.

"Kids! Come quick!" Mum calls out.

The boys leap to their feet and we sprint up the hill together. The whole resort has gathered. Dad's arm is loosely looped around Mum's shoulder, giving her room to shimmy her hips in time with the crowd's countdown.

10! 9! 8! everyone shouts enthusiastically.

Pat and Joanie are still swaying in their embrace next to their caravan; arms draped around each other, gently laughing and counting along even though they're separate from everyone else.

7! 6! 5!

Eric and Liam each mount a deck chair, wobbling them back and forth under their feet like they're standing on surf boards.

4! 3! 2!

Mr Sanderson shoves half a shashlik in his mouth, pulling off several chunks of meat in the one obnoxious bite. Mrs Sanderson stands next to him with a look of repulsion before quickly glancing at Mum, as if paranoid that Mum might have seen how grotesque her husband is. But Mum and Dad are caught up in a passionate kiss, oblivious to everything around them. Mum's black eye isn't the foremost thing on their mind now.

1! Happy New Year!

Cheers and applause resound in abundance. Dad hands out sparklers to the kids and I write my name in the sky with mine.

I love it here.

Everyone is happy.

Everything is okay.

Nothing bad ever happens at the lake.

Nothing bad could ever happen here.

New Year's Eve 1993

Mum's prolonged scream echoes across the lake. The world trembles at the reverberation, as if being recorded by a shaky hand-held camera. But Eric is still.

So still.

He hangs from the tree, motionless. Stiff.

Nature's Ladder.

It is five o'clock in the morning. The adults are traditionally hung-over and sleep in on New Year's Day. But Mum's scream has alarmed them and they emerge from their cabins, tents and caravans wide awake, concerned, confused.

Everyone must be so tired.

It was close to 2am when the celebrations began to

die down. It happened just the way it always did; *5! 4! 3! 2! 1! Happy New Year!* But instead of signalling the end of the night as custom, the countdown rejuvenated the festivities for a couple more hours.

I had fallen asleep on Dad's lap during the biggest New Year's Eve party that I could recall. I stirred when he carried me into the cabin but was already asleep again by the time he laid me down in bed. I woke up in a panic sometime later because Eric *had* to tell me all about his great new idea for that goblin he'd made up, Bogart.

The holiday park must have done a big advertising campaign because there are more people than ever here this year. The communal barbecue sizzled all night long in constant demand. Dad had to put a new CD in maybe 3 or 4 times. No one wanted the party to end.

And Liam wanted Eric all to himself.

I'd tried so hard to keep up with them during the afternoon. They rode their bikes around the resort, lap after lap, round and round, over and over again, but the miniature wheels on my purple scooter just couldn't go as fast as their BMXs. *I* just couldn't go as fast as *them*. I heard enough to figure out that they were discussing Eric's new story ideas but every time I got close enough to hear more, Liam deliberately sped up, forcing Eric to chase after him and leaving me trailing way behind. I lost them all together after my third trip past the lake. I don't know where they rode off to; somewhere I couldn't keep up, just as stupid Liam intended.

Everything felt out of my control.

I hadn't made any friends at my new school yet. It seemed that high school teachers sent just as many notes home to your parents as primary school teachers did. Term 1: *Has Bea ever received any additional support for emotional regulation?* Term 2: *Please phone the office to organise a suitable time to discuss Bea's disinterest in her school work.* Term 3: *…mentally distracted and unable to focus on tasks.* Term 4: *…poor attitude when it comes to responding to the offer of friendships.*

Fed up, I parked my purple scooter against Nature's Ladder and hunted for new rocks along the muddy shoreline. The barbecue would be starting up soon.

Everyone would come together, but I felt completely alone. Eric and Liam were growing up faster than me and only talked about scary horror stories and comics and girls and when they could sneak in a smoke. I'd heard Bogart's name more than my own lately.

I found four smooth rocks, perfect for painting. I planned to make an animal series out of them, starting with a zebra. I washed the rocks in the lake and tucked them in the pocket of my hoodie to dry, just as Mum spotted me from the balcony of our cabin.

"Time to come back now, Bea. The barbecue won't be long. Where's your brother?" she shouted across the summer breeze.

I shrugged to indicate that I didn't know and started to head back up the hill. That's when I finally saw where Eric and Liam had sped off to.

They sat cross-legged over on the jetty, silently, in mutual reverence of their surroundings. The sun settled right between them, as if held in place by their shoulders; its blinding golden glow casting the boys' bodies in shadow. It was a mesmerising sight. I almost wished they could see it too, outside of themselves.

The sun slipped down their arms ever so slightly, as if they had purposely let it go. Liam held out his hand palm down, prompting Eric to put his on top. The start of the special handshake.

In the background, invisible on the fringe of the lake, I joined in. I clicked my fingers, slapped my knee and hi-fived the air in time with them, then quickly ran back to the cabin before they could see me; my fist opening like a firework as I did. I hoped they'd get into trouble for not coming back when Mum wanted us to.

Dad rushes to the tree and frantically wraps his arms around Eric's shins, hopelessly trying to hoist him up. He strains, trying to muster enough strength but evidently a teenage boy's lifeless body is too heavy to manoeuvre on his own. Two men bolt out of nowhere as I watch on. My legs render me useless and prohibit me from going to help. I stand on our porch, frozen. Where Mum found me right before she screamed.

The men relieve Dad, freeing him to climb onto the lowest branch, just a low jump up from the ground and then up to the one with the blue rope wound around it several times. The men crowd Eric's dangling legs and heave his body upwards while Dad desperately tries to undo the branch's lasso.

Eric's feet are stretched downwards, painfully close to the ground, as if he was trying to reach it and be safe once more. He didn't put his shoes on. He faces the lake; his back forever turned to his family in the cabin a short distance behind him. I wonder if his eyes are open.

The rope slips off the branch. Dad swiftly climbs down while the men lay Eric's body on the grass, cradling his head as if it will actually matter if they drop it down too roughly. The blood drains from Dad's face as he drops to his knees and removes the rope tied in a noose around Eric's neck.

Every blade of grass is delicately decorated with pearls of the morning dew. It really is aesthetically beautiful here. I've never seen the lake this early in the day. It sleeps under a blanket of mist.

Dad breathes heavily through Eric's shrivelled lips, void of their usual pink hue and holds his pale, limp hand in his, bouncing it up and down as if trying to shake some life back through his veins.

Mum clutches onto Eric's jeans and drapes her torso across his rigid knees. "What have you done?" she sobs hysterically. "Oh my god, what have you done?"

A crowd has formed but nobody moves or makes a sound. Even the magpies are silent. Everyone stands collectively waiting. Waiting for him to sit up and cough, like a kid pulled out of the water in the movies. Cough, Eric. That's enough now. It's time to cough.

Liam is suddenly standing just below me on the gravel driveway that leads to his own family's cabin. Arms stiff by his side, he doesn't blink. He stares ahead at the scene, blankly. I'm not sure I recognise the emotion on his face. I wouldn't even know what to call it. "Breathe," his lips mime.

Dad blows one more time into Eric's mouth before

sitting back onto his feet, defeat and realisation washing over him so vividly I swear I see his skin turn grey. He looks down at his son and produces a noise that I have never heard before; somewhere between a scream and a howl. It doesn't sound human. His eyes scan the crowd. The lady from cabin 24 buries her face in her husband's protective embrace. An elderly man shakes his head in disbelief and Mindy, the girl I was once friends with for just a little while, covers her mouth with both hands, maybe trapping a cry. I didn't realise she was here this year.

Dad chokes on his words. "Can someone call an ambulance?"

Mrs Sanderson sprints to the tree and drapes her body over Mum's arched back. Their bodies rise up and down in unison, like a choreography to the sound of their inconsolable wailing.

Dad's trembling hand touches Eric's face, patting it, stroking it. "You should have come to us. Why didn't you come to us?"

Pat and Joanie emerge from their caravan, sleepy-eyed and anxious to find out what is going on. Their eyes dart to my grieving parents, cocooning Eric's body as if trying to trap any remaining life inside it. Joanie lowers herself to the ground and buries her face in her chest. Pat rests her unsteady hand on Joanie's shoulder and mouths Dad's favourite word, the one that I'm still not meant to know the meaning of.

I am just over two months shy of turning fourteen.

My brother turns fifteen in May. Right now, right in this moment, he's fourteen.

I don't know why, but that's all I can think about. I am growing older than my older brother. Because from this moment on, my brother isn't growing older at all. He never will.

I love that tree. Eric knew I loved that tree. And now I can't love it anymore.

I need someone to tell me everything is okay. But that someone has always been Eric. I expect to cry but the tears don't come. Not even the sound of my parents' shattered sobs or the sight of them clutching onto the dead body of my brother is enough for my tears to accept the open invitation to fall. Maybe it's just not possible for your heart and eyes to cry at the same time.

Mum and Dad must be so confused. They weren't prepared for this. They had no idea.

Liam slowly turns away from it all and treads back up towards his family's cabin. He doesn't look back at me.

My gaze drifts to the lake, so still and peaceful, as if it is showing its respect.

I step off the deck and lower myself to the ground, picking at the blades of grass that itch my legs: helplessly waiting for Mum and Dad to come comfort me.

But they need to be with Eric.

I'm sure they'll come to be with me soon.

They are going to be so mad at me.

Part Two

New Year's Eve 1994

We drive up to the lake in silence.

I had assumed that Mum and Dad wouldn't want to go this year but maybe they just need the tradition to stay alive. I personally think it's a huge mistake.

They didn't bring the Willie Nelson tape.

A koala sits in the middle of the road. Dad speeds up, seemingly with the intention of running it over but I'm relieved to watch the disgruntled creature rush off into the safety of the trees. Dad sighs, as if in disappointment.

When we arrive, we pull into the car park like always, but Dad makes no attempt to exit the car. He and Mum sit in a stupor, blankly staring at Reception. The world seems extra quiet and the engine left running seems extra loud.

I wait a long minute before deciding to go in myself. I guess I'll collect the keys.

"We're in number 7," I let them know when I return. They don't answer.

The resort doesn't seem particularly full this year. Half the keys remained uncollected on the board and there are noticeably less caravans and tents set up. I guess our family ruined a favourite holiday spot for a lot of other families. Including our own, yet for some reason I've yet to figure out or understand, here we are. Driving along the same road, next to the same lake, past the same trees and cabins, on the same holiday that my brother chose to be his last ever on this planet.

Pat and Joanie are here though, with their matching layered bangs and embroidered denim shirts, as content as ever fussing over their beloved silver caravan with the brown stripe and orange curtains. It's strangely reassuring to see them. They wave at me as we drive past, like it's strangely reassuring for them to see me, too. I wonder what they call me in their own narrative. Maybe I'm Rachel to them. Maybe I'm Tallulah. Maybe before, I was just the girl who followed her brother around on a purple scooter, and now I'm just the girl whose brother killed himself. Maybe one day I'll tell them my name is Bea, and they'll tell me their names are Michelle and Sandy. But I hope they really are Pat and Joanie.

Mum opens up the cabin door, turning the key just as she would when opening the front door at home. Dad doesn't make a drum roll noise. No theatrics this year. The robotic mode my parents have been living in for the past year evidently doesn't wear off just by driving through the gates of the holiday park. The bad stuff isn't meant to exist here; it's not meant to come with you, it's meant to stay at home. But I guess the lake could only keep everything and everyone together for so long before it was all just too much and everything fell apart right in front of it. The healer became the catalyst.

I take my overnight bag to my room, gently close the door behind me and climb straight up onto the top bunk, careful not to step on the bottom one. I will never sleep there. That's where Eric slept.

I sit with my head close to the ceiling and concentrate hard on my breathing. But maybe my breaths are too shallow: my head suddenly feels too heavy for my neck to support and I feel like my whole body is going to topple over. A pulsating urge to run away grabs hold of me, compelling me to navigate my way down the ladder in haste. I lower myself to the floor, curling up my body on the low pile turquoise rug laid over the stained floorboards. Maybe I should sleep here tonight, instead of the bunk bed. I rock my body in gentle rhythm, willing my body to restore calm. I wonder if we can request *no bunk beds* with our booking next year.

A million deep breaths later, I venture out of my room to find Mum and Dad sitting at the table, each having a cup of coffee. It's past midday but they haven't popped the champagne yet.

"I'm going to go for a walk along the lake."

"Wait for your broth-" Dad's warm smile quickly fades. His eyes close in a quiet moment of mental rejuvenation. "Your mum will go with you."

"I'll be fine on my own. Promise. I'm only going for a walk."

"I want to come," Mum insists. "I could do with some exercise after sitting in the car all morning. We'll go for a walk together. Give me five minutes."

Dad nods approvingly.

"Okay, Mum, sounds nice."

Back in my room, I lay on my tummy on the rug now designated as my bed and read a few pages of Looking for Alibrandi, waiting for Mum to finish her cuppa.

I don't understand why they wanted to come back here. I'm not sure they really thought it through. Did they even consider how they'll cope when they see the tree? The tree that supported my brother as he climbed it, held him while he tied a rope around it, and then refused to let go as he dangled from his neck to his death. *Nature's Ladder* became *Nature's Gibbet*. My most favourite tree in the world turned out to be a murder weapon.

No one knows at school. I guess that's one good

thing about starting over at high school. Mindy and I were the only ones who came from our primary school. We've just finished Year 9 and thankfully we haven't been in the same homeroom yet, but I do still see her around. It's awkward between us. She looks at me from across the courtyard or when we pass in the hallways, almost as if she is scared of me, or wishes I had gone to a different high school. She acts as if she doesn't know me. And doesn't *know*. Except that she does know me, and she does know. We are both very aware of that. She is the only person who knew me both times: before and after. It's uncomfortable. And given the way she quickly looks away should I catch her eye, it is for her too.

When high school started last year, most people were in the same situation; needing to start again and form their teenage clique from scratch. But they did it. I didn't even try to make friends, or respond to anyone who for some strange reason wanted to make friends with me.

Mine was a technically lonely start to my secondary education, but I didn't mind so much; I was just in a hurry for the day to end so I could meet Eric at his school for our walk home together.

Back in primary school, the teachers labelled me as emotionally and socially stunted and my peers pegged me as a loner and a cry-baby. By the end of my first year of high school, the opinions were much the same; my teachers thought I had a bad attitude and my peers just thought I was a bitch. But I didn't care. The very second the three o'clock bell sounded, I raced around the corner down to Eric's school. The hours leading up to that meant nothing to me: I anxiously watched them tick away so I could get to Eric. I hated being separated all day. If I had known it would be my last year with him, I would have waited outside his school all day and not even bothered to go to mine.

But it was my last year with him.

And now I've endured a whole year without him.

Life carries on as normal no matter what you are going through. No matter how broken, damaged, hurt or lost you are, it is relentless and won't offer you a moment of grace so you can figure out a way to keep going. You can't devise a plan of attack or fine-tune a way to move forward. Mornings come every day; sleep comes every night. Time still passes. Whether you're okay or not. Maybe that predictability, that certainty is the plan of attack life creates *for* us. Independent of whether we are okay, life will still go on; dragging us along for the ride until we can start functioning again and hop in the driver's seat.

Amazingly, Year 9 brought with it a new friend. Ebony and I bonded over a mutual love of books. She had a falling out with her group, because she likes to be in charge. I was functioning purely on a robotic level, mindlessly maintaining routine, so unlike her previous friends, I was cool with her calling all the shots. And because Eric wouldn't be there waiting for me after school, I tried (insincerely) to reciprocate her interest in getting to know each other. Turns out that making friends really isn't that complicated; you just have to *want* to get to know someone other than your brother.

I confided in her straight away that Eric had recently

died, basically excusing myself for not being overly good company. Her response was to rush us off to the library, because *books let you have a different life.* I didn't really like her, but I did like talking about books. She scoffed when I introduced her to my favourite and insisted that sci-fi and fantasy books were the only ones worth reading, so I agreed with her, even though I really just like books about real life and people. She searched through all the titles in the fantasy section, and I pretended to know them, pretended to like them. Maybe if I had been more agreeable with Mindy and played all the games she wanted to play, she would have stayed my friend. So far, I've read three books I really didn't enjoy, but I've managed to keep Ebony's friendship for the whole year. I hope we'll still be friends heading into the tenth grade. I don't know if I genuinely mean that but if I am a good friend, I probably should.

Ebony lives with her grandparents by order of the court because her parents are drug addicts. Her long, charcoal, curly hair gives her an accurate air of authority and confidence. She is hyper-critical of herself and has an insatiable need to plan and control everything. That kind of suits me. I don't have a mind of my own, I just exist. It's easier to keep up with the normal pace of life post-trauma if you've got someone else pulling you along.

Mindy, meanwhile, became the most popular girl in school after winning a radio competition to get some local band to play a concert at assembly. She hangs out with Eva and Simone, who are just as pretty and as perfectly skinny as she is. Even all the Year 12 girls chat to them. They all wear high pony tails with scrunchies made from the same fabric as the uniform, styled with a smooth strand of hair framing their face on either side. They're straight A students without even trying and always have money for the canteen. They know the answer when the teacher calls on them with a question, unintimidated, even if he was trying to catch them out because they didn't have their hand raised.

They catch the 452 bus home, with all the other popular girls. The bus stop is right outside school and heads to Eric's school next, so the subsequent morning's classroom chatter always revolves around boys and who has a crush on whom. Some guy named Will has all the girls fighting over him. I wonder if he is aware of that. Apparently, Alex isn't as cute now that he's cut his hair and rumour has it that Jimmy has the hots for Simone but he's too shy to ask her out. I wonder if Alex, Will or Jimmy know Liam. I wonder if they knew Eric.

I don't experience the bus gossip first-hand. Mum picks me up right outside the gate these days.

The last time I walked home from school was with my brother.

Life will forever be divided into two: before he died and after he died. Before Eric died, I was defined by my relationship with him: Bea was Eric's chubby little sister who tagged along with him and his best friend, Liam. I had no identity of my own. Even my hobbies had revolved around Eric: I collected and painted rocks only to kill some time when I couldn't be with him. When he died, the girl I was still tagged along just like she'd always done, and followed him to wherever he happened to go.

The girl in her place now is a stranger to me. Maybe

our bodies just get rented out by different versions of ourselves as the real estate of life grows and changes. Just because you're the landlord, doesn't mean you know anything about the person renting your body, your home. The real estate industry is fickle; you never know when your lease is up.

Eric's bedroom door is permanently closed but I can tell that the blinds are still open in there. I see the sunlight shining underneath the door. I forget and almost go in there sometimes. But light isn't always a sign of life.

It's a whole year tomorrow. A whole year.

I keep my collection of painted rocks in a shoe box at the bottom of my wardrobe, lost underneath a pile of clothes that don't fit anymore. I'll chuck the rocks out one day. I don't know why I haven't yet. It was stupid, really. I just never knew what else to do when Eric was busy.

I guess I still don't know what to do with myself. I go to school, do my homework and watch TV with Mum and Dad. I kind of skipped that part of growing up where you figure out what you do and don't enjoy doing.

I miss Eric. I miss him when Gilbert nudges the back of my knee with his wet nose, seeking affection to heal his broken heart, and to offer comfort, sensing my own.

I miss Eric. I miss him when I brush my teeth, eyeing his toothbrush still sitting in the holder. It just collects dust now, never to be used again. I guess the alternative is to put it in the bin, and none of us have been able to stomach that concept.

I miss Eric. I miss him when I overhear Mum and Dad stressing about the overdue notice on the water bill. I still feel compelled to sneak into his room to see if he's awake, listening too. That's when he'd tell me all about a goblin named after a dead movie star, who fell in love with a fairy who played hard-to-get. Everything felt okay then, even when it wasn't, because we had each other. And now nothing will ever be okay, maybe ever again.

I miss Eric. I miss him.

We don't see the Sandersons these days. Dad got into

a fight with Mr Sanderson on the day of the funeral, after grilling Liam. Dad was desperate to know what Liam and Eric's last conversation had been about. Mr Sanderson thought Dad was blaming Liam and told him to back off and it escalated from there. They both threw punches. Liam accidentally got hit in the face when he tried to break it up but it was never clear by whom. He was wearing his glasses and they got knocked right off his face. Mr Sanderson forbade his wife from seeing Mum again, so Mum lost her son and her best friend. I haven't seen or heard from Liam since that day, nearly a year ago. I look for him as we pass their school but I never see him walking home or boarding the bus.

"Knock knock, Bea," Mum cheerfully announces as she enters my room. "Ready? Have you got sun cream on? It's a scorcher out there today."

Mum and I stroll slowly along the lake, holding hands. She asks me if I'm okay. I respond by asking her if she is instead.

"I've got you, my Bea. I'm okay."

I hesitate but ask anyway. "Why did you want to

come back here? We can start a new tradition. We can go to Victor Harbor, or Normanville, Renmark. There are heaps of places. We don't have to come back here."

"I know, and we will go to all those places and more." Her voice strains. "But your father needs to come here. He likes the tradition. He wants us to end and start the year, together as a family, and in his eyes, this is where your brother is now."

Mum's grip on my hand tightens to the point of hurting but I don't mention it.

"I hate it here, Mum."

"I know. So do I, really. But we need to be here. It's important to your father that we're here."

My attention is instantly grabbed by the silver Land Rover speeding towards us.

"You're kidding," Mum breathes. "I can't believe they came."

Mr Sanderson is the sole owner of a car dealership and has access to company cars, so the Sandersons get a new car practically every year. But we still know it's them. Call it a feeling or a vibe, but Mum and I both know, even though we've never seen this car before and the sun is obscuring our view of the windshield.

"Does Dad know they're coming?" I gasp.

Mum shakes her head. "We just assumed they wouldn't. We haven't heard from them since the funeral."

The silver Land Rover races past us, putting on a show. Behind the back passenger window, Liam fixates his intense gaze on me. We lock eyes, both of us refusing to look away first. He looks older. Of course he does. I just didn't think it would be so glaringly obvious. It's almost as if he is bragging about going through puberty. *Look everyone, look how cool it is to grow up. Look how neat it is to be fifteen.*

Mum coughs at the flurry of dirt created by the vehicle's excessive speed and I'm sure I hear a chuckle from the driver's seat.

"We better go let your father know. This isn't going

to go down well."

Minutes later, Dad is adamant that we should insist that they leave. "That prick has no business coming here!"

Mum strokes his arm, smoothing the hairs that have stood to attention. "Don't give him the satisfaction of knowing he got to you. Just let it go, Mitch. We have been coming here for much longer than they have. They wouldn't even know about the lake if it wasn't for us inviting them to come with us all those years ago. You wanted us to be with Eric, well here we are."

It's the first time Mum has spoken my brother's name in nearly a year. It lingers in the room. Uncomfortably.

Mum doesn't talk about Eric. Ever. There is an awkward undercurrent when Dad brings his name into conversation, even if it's just a trivial memory like *Eric loved these chips*. Mum doesn't respond with her own remark or recollection, or even nod in recognition. She either leaves the room or changes the subject entirely.

Dad shakes his head, resigning himself to the fact that he doesn't really have a say in the matter. "Keep him away from me. And Bea, don't even think about going anywhere near Liam. That boy is trouble. Got it?"

"Yes, Dad. I won't talk to Liam."

My teachers have always pegged me as emotionally immature. How appropriate that I now stand in front of my father, telling him what he wants to hear, with my fingers crossed behind my back.

We play Monopoly all afternoon, only venturing out of the holiday park to get a quick meal at the local pub in the main street of town. Driving back later, I watch a young boy scream and run away when his sister squirts him with a hose. I guess the water came out hot from the hose lying in the sun all day. My focus shifts to my own reflection in the window, and I smile sentimentally, listening to the boy's cries.

Having returned to the anti-social confines of our cabin, Dad turns on the TV to drown out the jubilant sound of the small, surrounding New Year's Eve party. But even Jim Carrey's The Mask doesn't bring any laughter to our family these days. Out of guilt, I suppress my amusement when he and Tina dance the Cuban Pete. Mum and Dad are in bed and asleep by 10.30pm.

I wait until the few jovial cries of *Happy New Year* die down outside and then sneak out through the window in my bedroom.

It's so much easier here. Back at home, I have to take out the bottom corner screws and hold the screen out as I squeeze my body through, so it doesn't make a bang when it falls back into place. Here, the window just slides open like a patio door.

I developed a habit for sneaking out right after the funeral. It was impulsive; I was lying in bed, wanting to cry but the tears still hadn't come. Why hadn't my tears come yet? At school, everyone had always called me a cry-baby. I cried over everything, over the most ridiculous and pathetic things. It made no sense that I couldn't cry over losing my brother. *That* was *worth* crying over. Eric took his own life; he left me. I had every reason to cry. But two weeks had passed and I still couldn't make it happen, and I really tried. So, I went for a walk at one o'clock in the morning, unintentionally looking for my tears.

I haven't found them yet, almost a whole year later. I can't cry for him. I can't cry for my brother. I want to, so desperately. But when I think about him, my mind just kind of shuts down and refuses to let me carry on with my thoughts. My own mind blocks me.

Eric lay in bed one morning too, and left it with the sole intention of ending his life. Or maybe he just got up to sit by the lake and plan his next book, and just happened to find a blue rope near a tree. I will never know why. I will never get to know what changed, what made him to decide to leave me. Dad needs to know too, but he went to the wrong person for his answer: Liam doesn't have any closure either. He and I never will.

A few weeks ago, I was playing squash against the side of the house, just on my own as I do, and darted for a ball I should have regarded as a miss. I only just nipped the side of it with my racquet but it was enough to send the ball back to the far side of the wall, right through the laundry window. I cried when

I told Mum because I knew it would be an added stress on their already strained finances to get the window repaired. But Mum just held me and said it was okay. *Just cry, baby. Let yourself cry. Get it all out.* I really was crying because I felt bad about the window. Despite what Mum might have thought.

I aimlessly wander the darkened streets for hours back at home. Mum and Dad are asleep by 9.30pm and I'm out my window by 10pm. It has become an addiction.

Most nights I just walk around on my own, but sometimes on a Saturday night, I meet up with a couple of older girls in the car park at Hungry Jacks. I tag along with them on their escapades, which typically involves shoplifting chocolate from the petrol station and taking sips from a shared bottle of wine. I don't tell Ebony about them. She wouldn't like it.

Cat is the leader. She will be in Year 12 when school goes back, continuing at an elite private college that takes her Mum forty-five minutes to drive to. It's co-ed, and Cat really likes boys. Some of them even board there. Cat got suspended last year for sneaking into one of the dorms.

Her dresses look like silk nighties and swarm her bony frame, which she likes to emphasise with a fluffy white cardigan worn intentionally slipped off both shoulders. Her petite features are swallowed by heavy make-up and her husky voice makes her seem older than she really is. Her parents are rich, she tells us. They give her everything she could ever want and everything she wasn't even aware that she wanted. They bought her a convertible blue Volkswagen for her sixteenth birthday, just as inspiration for her to go for her Ls. She has nothing to rebel against and it pains her because she wants to be a musician, but I don't think she plays an instrument.

Pippa goes to the same school as me but she acts like she doesn't know me during school hours. Like Cat, she'll be in the twelfth grade when we go back at the end of January and I'll only be in Year 10: I'm hardly cool enough to have a senior acknowledge my existence. Pippa is by far the most annoying person I have ever met. She constantly complains and tries to steer the conversation so that it is always about her. She wears black jeans with flannelette shirts, a choker with a crucifix on it and silver rings on every finger, like she's trying too hard to look tough. She laughs a lot, sometimes about nothing. She can't seem to end a sentence without a typically ill-fitting *ha-ha*. She doesn't like it at home because her mum remarried, and now she has two siblings. I don't think she gets the same amount of attention as she had become accustomed to when it was just her and her mum.

On the night we all met, my customary mindless walk had led me to Hungry Jacks. The aroma of salty fries in the air induced a frenzied sensation of starvation. It was 11.45pm, and I'd had my dinner hours ago with Mum and Dad. I had exactly $2.70 in my pocket, more than enough to get a packet of fries but Cat was behind me in the line and eagerly jumped in to pay for my order. Cat and I were Pippa's last customers before her shift finished, so we all wound up hanging out in a corner of the car park, watching the late-night traffic on the main road, eating fries and getting to know each other.

I mumbled that my name was *Bea as in Beatrice* when they initially asked me but beyond that I let Pippa dominate our first heart-to-heart. I declined Cat's multiple offers to buy me a milkshake, to which Pippa responded by reassuring me that not everyone can be skinny like Kate Moss and it was okay to be 'a little bit fat.' So, my first impression of my new-found friends was that Cat was insecure and feels she needs to buy people's affection (or attention), and Pippa was a bitch.

Months later, I still haven't really told them anything personal about myself and they don't ask. I don't tell them that my second year of high school was my first year without my brother. I don't tell them that I could never make friends until I met Ebony, but I don't think she actually likes me and I don't know if I necessarily like her. We sit together, but does that make us *friends?* We both like books, but does that mean we have to like *each other?* I don't tell them that tagging along with them fills some sort of void for me, like I'm back to being the third wheel in Eric and Liam's friendship.

The lake is eerily quiet; I can't even hear the water sway. It is close to 12:30am now. The buzz of the New Year's celebrations is non-existent already. The lingering smell of coal rides on the warm breeze. A few small Webbers on the reserve suggest that the big communal gas barbecue didn't even get used this year.

Mum and Dad used to love the New Year's countdown. Evidently, they just sleep through it now.

My eyes scan the shore. Liam will be out here somewhere, I just know it.

The leaves of the trees all rustle in unison, sending shivers through my body. I tighten the wrap of my army green cotton shirt and move closer to the water, attempting to create distance between me and the trees but they are everywhere here, even in the lake. They surround me with every step, like they are stalking me. It's haunting. I used to think they were peaceful.

Liam is sitting up ahead; distracted by the enchanting darkness of the water. He doesn't notice me coming until I am standing right over him, arms folded, my stance purposefully intending to unnerve him. I am ready to unleash an entire year's worth of my thoughts. On him.

His hair is darker and his legs are longer and hairier. He is wearing his glasses. His gaze has yet to leave the lake and acknowledge my presence, which fuels my hatred for him even more.

"Beatrice."

His smirk intensifies my anger. "It's Bea. You know it's Bea."

"We don't need to talk to each other."

I don't know what I was expecting him to say, but it wasn't that. My confidence dwindles. I mentally remind myself why I came looking for him. I need to be in charge. "I want my brother's notebook."

He looks at me for the first time since Eric's funeral. "No."

His attitude stumps me as I desperately try to regain control of the situation. I wanted him to be nervous, intimidated by me. This is my moment to put him and his pompous family in their place. I won't let him take that away from me. "I said I want Eric's notebook."

He stands, robbing me of my physical superiority. He is so much taller now, so much taller than me. He doesn't lower his head; he just looks down on me. Literally. Figuratively. I wonder if Eric would have been just as tall as him.

"I heard you. And like I said, no."

I narrow my eyes, confused by his new-found assertiveness. "Why?"

"Because you won't find what you're looking for."

My lips part, releasing a slight gasp. I can't get my words out, so I attempt to give my sternest frown instead.

Liam reciprocates in exaggeration, mocking my face.

"I didn't come here to fight with you," I resign, intending to show-off my maturity. "I just want to talk."

"Because you want to blame me, just like your

parents."

"No. I don't. They don't either. Nobody does. He did it to himself."

"Keep telling yourself that."

I'm enraged at his insensitivity. "If you've got something to say, just say it!"

"Like I said, we don't need to talk to each other."

His blasé attitude exasperates me. "You mean you don't *want* to talk to each other, right?"

Liam narrows his eyes and I instinctively back down. "I just want to talk."

"Listen," he demands, "stay away from Cat. She's trouble."

"What?" I ask, bewildered. "How do you know Cat? How do you even know I hang out with her?"

"She'll want you to go to the clubs with her soon. You're too young. If you insist on being friends with her, stick to the car park at Hungry Jacks."

"You're like a year older than me, I'm not that young.

And don't tell me what to do. I don't need you looking out for me. You're not my brother." I hate myself the second I say the words. They sting my tongue. They hurt him.

He turns away, deliberately knocking his arm against my chest.

"Happy New Year, *Beatrice*," he calls out as he coolly slithers up to the cabins. He doesn't look back at me. It's a familiar sight.

"Happy New Year, *prick*." I have never sworn out loud before. Now I know why Dad does: it sure does make me feel better.

New Year's Eve 1995

Cat can legally buy alcohol now and she has plenty of money (she tells us all the time), but her penchant for smuggling Sambuca from her parent's (unlocked) liquor cabinet seems to be more for kicks than out of necessity. I only ever take a few sips from the bottle we share between the three of us, because I don't like it, and because my parents would die if they knew that I was hanging around a couple of older girls most Saturday nights who shoplift Vodka Cruisers for the sheer thrill of it. Mum and Dad don't even know that I leave the house without them.

Our neighbour, Mr Randall died right at the beginning of the year. When we got back from the lake, Mum baked an apple pie for him but he didn't answer her knocks at his door. She cautiously let herself in and found him on his recliner, peacefully, permanently, asleep.

His son didn't even bother to come back from London to say goodbye. He rang us one evening, or one morning on his side of the world, asking us to box up 'anything of value' and post it to him. Mum agreed to help clear the house out for sale, but it really pissed her off. She doesn't swear a lot, maybe ever, but she called Mr Randall's son a word I've never even heard *Dad* say. After she'd hung up the phone, of course.

It took us all weekend. I carried the cardboard boxes full of his belongings to the car; Mum planned to take them to the charity shop. Lots of stuff needed to be thrown away too, and I was in charge of the trips back and forth to the bins. Years worth of receipts stapled to bills, half-completed word search books and opened bottles of shampoo and Lomani Eau de Toilette: evidence of a life in progress, now rendered useless, destined for the bin.

One particular box doomed to be landfill made a slight detour: to my bedroom. Turns out Mr Randall didn't just like that dark red liquid; he liked drinks with fancy looking labels and cute mini bottles that fit in the palm of my hand. Cat and Pippa were pretty impressed with me when I showed up with a new drink for us to try every week. I scored big points and felt like I truly fit in for the first time in my life. There was a part of dear old Mr Randall that got to live on too, for just a little while longer. I kept him alive. Cheers, Mr Randall.

The days of hanging out in the car park at Hungry Jacks are slowly coming to an end, even though I've only just recently discovered my own drink du jour, courtesy of Pippa's swift hands at the bottle-O: Red Bear. It's like creaming soda for grown-ups. Cat got me a fake ID from some bouncer she hooked up with, so I could join her and Pippa when they frequent the clubs. I haven't been yet, but I want to. Cat even gifted me a silk camisole to wear and eagerly encouraged me to pair it with fitted jeans and high heels. Pippa however didn't think it would be a flattering outfit on me. *It's nice, but maybe for someone a bit thinner. Silk is clingy, not the best material for everyone.* Plus, it would show my arms, which apparently look better *covered up*.

I wonder if Pippa isn't Mrs Sanderson's long-lost daughter.

Cat brushed off Pippa's remarks and promised that she would name her first song after me if I wore it. I asked her if that meant she was working on being a songwriter or knew how to play an instrument, but Pippa freaked out that the conversation wasn't all about her and brought it back around to talk of the clubs. It's weird, but I was actually interested to hear Cat's reply, had she been given the chance to give me one.

I've hid the camisole in my wardrobe, behind the shoe box that contains my old painted rock collection. Maybe I'll wear it when I finally bring myself to throw the rocks out into the garden.

I sussed out whether or not Ebony would go to the clubs with me but she was thankfully disinterested. I don't really want to socialise with her outside of school. Plus, she is a stickler for rules. She likes order and routine. It's no wonder she wants to join the police force when high school is over.

I missed out on going on the Year 10 camp. Three days in Port Vincent. Dad had been getting plenty of work since his new Yellow Pages ad came out and Mum had started doing two days a week at the dry cleaner's, so I don't think it was about the money. I'm sure they would have been okay with me going had the school put a callout for parent chaperones. I say this like I actually wanted to go on the camp, but I didn't. Not being able to go home for three days straight might have made me feel even more lost than I do every other day of my life.

"We're just not quite ready yet, Bea," Mum reasoned. "You will understand that more when you are older."

At the year level assembly to go through the rules and expectations of the camp, the principal read out the list of names of everyone who couldn't go, advising that they would need to go to Mr Van's Homeroom for those three days instead. By list, I mean me. I was literally the only student in the whole year that couldn't go. Pretty sure the stupid principal could have informed me privately which classroom I'd need to go to.

Absolutely no part of my life so-far has shaped me into someone who would enjoy being the centre of attention in assembly. Consequently, in the middle of that hall filled with green plastic chairs, I had suddenly found it necessary to hold back the tears reminiscent of eleven year old me.

Don't cry in front of everyone, I inwardly coached myself.

Simone's soft snigger when the principal then issued an assignment for me to complete during those three days truly resurrected that young girl riding around on her purple scooter. Silent tears shamed me just as Mindy glanced back, perhaps innocently, but in the row right behind her, my shit frame of mind compelled me to flick her the finger, abruptly ending the most interaction we have had in years. She quickly turned back around, I got myself together, and the principal moved on to packing requirements.

At home, my parents and I play a lot of board games and watch a lot of movies and I do love it because it makes them happy and that's what I live for: to make my parents happy. But sometimes I find myself mentally counting down the hours until Mum and

Dad go to sleep so I can sneak out my bedroom window and go for a walk, or meet up with Cat and Pippa on Saturday nights. Sometimes I just need a break from being the one who makes up for everything else. I'm the one who stayed, so I never get to go away.

If I don't sneak out for my walks to nowhere, I'll suffocate. When Mum needs to get groceries, she won't let me stay home alone, even if it's just for half an hour. I have to go with her. I can't wait in the car, either. I have to go everywhere with my parents, or stay home with them. I'm a prisoner in my own adolescence.

We pull up to the lake later than ever before. Making the trip seemed more like an obligation, even a chore, so we didn't leave home until after lunch.

The resort appears full once again this year. The cabins are booked out, caravans and tents occupy every lot. The barbecue has already started and everyone has gathered on the reserve.

Pat and Joanie are setting up deck chairs by the side of their caravan, which looks to be freshly painted, or maybe just thoroughly cleaned. It must be nice having a sibling who doesn't want to leave you. Or a best friend who plans a trip away with you every year, if that's what they are instead. I guess I've just always envisioned that they're sisters as opposed to friends because they dress the same, like Eric and I did. Once upon a whole other lifetime.

We settle into Cabin 2. My bedroom window looks out over the camping zone. I can't even see the lake. I don't mind: the camping zone is relatively clear of trees.

Dad pours some Cheezels into a bowl, opens three cans of coke and sets up one of our board games on the table outside on the deck. I really don't know why they bother to make the time and effort to drive up here if we just do exactly the same things as we do at home. I'm amused by the irony; coming to the place of my brother's death, to play the Game of Life.

We haven't come across the Sandersons yet, although Mum and Dad periodically cast their eyes over to the other cabins, so they suspect that they are here just as much as I do. Their distracted attention works in my favour and I win the game before we drive into the main street of the town for a quick pizza. We don't even watch a movie when we come back; Mum and Dad are tired and say good night at 9.15pm.

I lie on the couch and read my hard-cover book in its entirety. I borrowed it from the school library at the start of the year but after my fourth time returning it and then attempting to check it out again straight away, the warden of a library teacher sternly advised that other students might like to read it too and she forbade me from borrowing it again until next year. As soon as her back was turned, I tucked the book inside my dark green school blazer. My name will forever be the last four entries on the check-out card. It is mine forever. I will never have to borrow it again. Stuff that library teacher for trying to take something I love away from me.

Outside, the countdown to midnight is loud and celebratory but by 1am, tranquil silence ensues. I make certain that Mum and Dad are still asleep, put my pillows under my blanket where my body would ordinarily lay and climb out my bedroom window.

Liam is skipping stones on the lake and hears me approaching. I wish I could unzip my fat and step out of it, as if I was just climbing out of a sleeping bag. My steps wouldn't have given me away if I was thinner.

He doesn't turn around.

"Mum wasn't sure you were here this year," he says coolly. "We didn't notice your car."

I stand level with him and stare out onto the lake. Liam doesn't look at me so I don't look at him either. I'm simultaneously overcome with dread and excitement just by being near him. "We had to get a new one. Well, a second-hand new one. The Datsun got too old and wouldn't start anymore."

"Harold will be disappointed. He could have got you a good deal on a new one."

I smile to myself. I bet Mr Sanderson would have loved lording that over Dad but he doesn't own the only car yard in the state. Since when does Liam refer to his step-dad by name? He sure is overdosing on testosterone these days.

"Too bad our families aren't friends anymore," I remind him.

Liam's face and shoulders are chiselled like stone. I wonder if I would even notice how much he is changing if we still saw each other all the time, as opposed to just on New Year's, here at the lake. I haven't caught up to him in height; it seems he will forever be a head taller than me. He looks more like a man than I do a woman.

It is just a matter of time before we each get our own lives and stop coming up here with our parents. There will come a day when it is the last time that I ever see him, and I likely won't even realise it in that instance. I know what that feels like: it's empty and desperate and there is absolutely nothing you can do to get time back. Memories can never be experienced for the first time again. For some reason I don't understand, it scares me how much I don't want to lose Liam. I don't want there to be a last time that I ever see him.

Our heads turn simultaneously and suddenly we are

looking at each other, both visibly ready to argue, but over what I just don't seem to know in this moment. He is wearing his glasses. He seems so much older than me, so much older than Eric. *I* seem so much older than Eric. That's when I realise: I *am* older than Eric. I am older than my older brother.

"You're still not getting the notebook," he firmly reminds me.

"Yeah, I know." I don't try to match his tone. I want to cry and run away. I physically crave his presence. He can't stand mine. "Can I at least read it though?"

"I'll think about it. Maybe one day."

I frown, perplexed by him, this encounter and the way both are making me feel. "Why can't you just let me read it now? I know you would have brought it up here with you."

He sits down, relaxing his arms over his raised knees. His knee-length shorts emphasise the unexpected sight of his calf muscles. I guess he started playing sport. Or maybe he works out. Both would please Mr Sanderson.

I sit down next to him, apprehensively. "Please?"

"You didn't listen to what I said about Cat."

His deliberate change of subject infuriates me. "You don't need to be my big brother. And she's harmless."

"No, she's not. She drinks and steals. And maybe I do."

"How do you even know who I hang out with?" I ark up.

"The guys at footy know her. She gets around a bit with some of them. A lot of them."

"Football?" He's not the only one who can change the subject. "Didn't expect that."

He nods, to himself. "Me either."

I always knew Mr Sanderson didn't accept Liam the way he was. It saddens me to think that maybe Liam didn't like himself the way he was either. Or even sadder still, maybe he did, but he felt pressured to change so that Mr Sanderson would like him. Imagine feeling disliked by someone who was meant to be your father.

I can't miss my brother without inadvertently missing Liam, too. I'm engulfed by a sense of panic; after we go home, I won't see him again until next New Year's. He will disappear from my life again, just like when I lost Eric.

I want to keep talking.

I am desperate to keep talking. To him.

I want to know everything. I want to know who his friends are now. I want to know if Mr Sanderson goes to his football games, because clearly that's the only reason Liam would play. I want to know if he gets good grades, which of his teachers are okay, which ones he hates. Why don't I ever see him walking home from school or getting on the bus when I drive past with Mum? Is it hard being there without Eric? I want to know if he still draws. Did he keep that old ALF t-shirt he used to wear all the time? Does he ever read The Monster in the Lake and yearn for those days so much it's like he's living on pause until someone can figure out how to rewind life like an old VHS tape? Does he ever wonder the same sort of things about me? Does he ever *wonder* about me, *at all?*

He doesn't know it, but every time I'm with him, things stop hurting just a little bit.

"You're too young to be going to those clubs," he scolds me.

"What?" I laugh uncomfortably. "How do you even know that?"

"Guys talk. That Cat girl you hang out with is trouble. I told you that, you didn't listen. Just be careful. You don't need her or that Pippa girl either while we're at it."

I guess he *does* wonder about me after all. I mentally rejoice at the thought that he has been asking around about me. Under the light of the moon, the ripples in the lake shimmer like crystals.

"I haven't gone to any clubs."

"Not yet, but Cat got you a fake ID."

"You don't need to check up on me," I lie. I want him to check up on me.

He smiles at the lake, as if he is expecting it to smile back, like they share a private joke. He is bare foot and digs his toes into the grass, seeming to relish the sensation of burying himself. He removes his glasses, folds them and tucks them away in the side pocket of his shorts. He stands as I watch him, confused.

"See you next year, *Beatrice*," he says, gazing down at me.

He doesn't smile as he turns to walk away and he doesn't look back, not that he ever does.

"See you next year," I whisper into the night.

Guys talk, and they talk about Cat, which means that she knows them. And they know Liam.

Cat is the inside source I need to help me figure out Liam once and for all. Once he sees how well I understand him, he won't walk away from me, not ever again. He will never want to leave me.

New Year's Eve 1996

We are next in line in the kiosk, behind Mindy. Her polka dot bathers look and smell damp, so she must be grabbing some snacks in between dips at the pool.

Her body is much more developed than mine. She has perky C cup breasts and her waist is cinched in exactly like it's supposed to be, like the 'greater than' and 'less than' symbols in math. I don't really have breasts; they just blend into my torso like one big blob. I was a size 12 when I was 12 and a size 14 when I was 14. I'll be 17 soon and I have no intention of weighing myself. I'd rather not see if the pattern continued.

The elderly lady behind the counter fills a small white paper bag with Milkas and Redskins. She has blue-rinse hair and glasses shaped like love-hearts. Her name badge says Edna.

"Fifty-five cents, love."

Mindy passes over the exact change and graciously thanks Edna. Always the prototype of the perfect young lady.

She steps aside and Mum places our order of three hotdogs with cheese and sauce. Edna picks up the first roll and slices it down the middle, ready to butter it up before adding the sausage.

Mindy is still standing off to the side, like she is waiting for me to look at her. But I don't. She gets everything she wants in life already. She doesn't need my personal interest on top of that.

I roll my eyes when Mum gives in to her ploy for attention.

"Oh, Mindy! Is that you?"

Mindy smiles coyly, as if she is suddenly surprised to see Mum too. "I wondered if it was you guys. It's so great that you still come up here."

Mum tucks her lips in together and scratches her neck. "Of course, it's a beautiful spot. Bea's father and I have been coming up here since before she was even born. And how are you going? Still snacking on marshmallows? You used to eat all the pink ones when you and Bea had your little play dates. I'd go to have some at night and there'd be nothing but white ones left in the bag!"

I cringe inside. That must have been ten years ago now, Mum. Mindy and I don't even talk to each other anymore.

Mindy chuckles. "I forgot about that! I'll have to get Mum to get some marshmallows again! You should come to the barbecue tonight. Dad always says how much you're all missed."

Mum smiles shyly. "Thank you, dear. We might."

Liar, I think to myself.

Mindy is oblivious to Mum's discomfort. "Okay, great, I'll let Dad know you might come!"

Mum panics. "We'll just see how we go. Maybe don't mention it in case we can't get there."

"Oh," Mindy sighs before perking up, "well, I'll tell him anyway! Just in case!" She hurries out the door before Mum can even reply.

"Shit," Mum utters under her breath, really emphasising the *sh*.

The passing of someone you love is undeniably heartbreaking. The passing of someone you love before their natural time is due, I believe is the worst pain the human heart is capable of withstanding. And yet somehow, it keeps beating.

Our hearts were shattered in front of a live audience.

Now we are forever on display.

I guess that's why Mum and Dad hide us away from the world. And maybe why I'm so desperate to sneak some time in it.

Hot dogs in hand, we join Dad down at the lake and sit in a line, knees bent; the water glistening in the sun as we eat. A nearby pelican stalks an elderly couple, harassing them for a sample of their picnic.

Mum releases an exaggerated breath. "Fancy making

an appearance at the barbecue tonight?"

Dad almost chokes. "Fuck no."

Mum whacks his knee. "Jesus, Mitch. Language! Bea doesn't need to hear that kind of talk."

Mum still thinks I don't know what any of those swear words are but I know them all, and I learnt them from *both* of my parents. Despite what Mum thinks, she says them too, like when she's fighting with Dad about the *bloody council rates* being *bloody due again* when she thinks I'm asleep. But I've only ever heard her say the bad ones once or twice before.

Liam was deserving of my first cuss word. I even said it out loud.

"Sure, let's make an appearance so everyone can gawk at us and tell us how *good* we're doing!" Dad huffs at his hot dog. "Fuck that shit."

Mum extends her disapproval to his shoulder this time, gently punching him.

"I love you too, dear," Dad chuckles.

Mum doesn't press the subject further. From the

look on her face, I'm assuming it's just for now though.

Back at the cabin that evening, after Dad reigns victorious at Scrabble, Mum brings up the New Year's Eve party again. It seems Mindy planted a seed for something that Mum wasn't aware she was ready to grow.

"Sounds like everyone is having a good time out there."

Dad looks to the glass sliding door separating us from the rest of the resort and merely nods. "I hate this song though. I've heard nothing but Leo Sayer all night. Barry must be in charge of the music. He never could get the mix just right."

Mum's enthusiasm swells. "Barry, gosh! I haven't thought about him for a while. Years. I wonder how he and Lisa are doing? Last I heard, she made partner at the firm and they were trying for another baby."

"They have four already, what are they going for, a whole basketball team?" Dad scoffs.

Mum's face is awash with disappointment. Tonight marks three years since she lost her son, but in the weeks that initially ensued, she lost friend after friend after friend. The realisation renders me selfish. I have my escape: out through my bedroom window. I can walk for hours while the sun sleeps and recharge myself from the constant pressure of being two children rolled into one. I guess Mum doesn't have any kind of escape at all.

When Mr Sanderson forbade Mrs Sanderson from seeing Mum again, Mum lost all her friends by association. Marge stopped calling to organise their monthly catch ups, because who would she invite, Mum or Mrs Sanderson? All the mutual friends must have felt the need to choose a side. I don't know if we lost, or everyone just thought we needed space, but no one came around to visit Mum and Dad any more. Mum lost her son, as well as her entire social life and support network all at once.

Our annual New Year's neighbours are a mix of regular guests and first-timers. It's uncomfortably awkward with the ones who do know us, or of us.

They smile, occasionally wave, but they keep their distance. They were first-hand witnesses to our pain. Mum and Dad were the life of the party, now they are the elephant in the room. Ever since Eric died, none of the so-called adults have known how to approach us, or whether to at all. It took a teenage girl with a historical affection for pink marshmallows to break the ice.

Maybe Mum is craving a bit of her old life back. Maybe she misses her old self.

Maybe she just wants to have some fun.

She wants to go tonight but she will never be able to convince Dad without my help.

"I'm actually kind of hungry. It's past six, are we going to the pub for tea? I'm pretty tired, I'd prefer to just pop over to the barbecue. I can smell the baked potatoes from here!"

Dad rolls his eyes. "Has anyone seen the Sandersons yet?"

Mum sits up excitedly. "No, no sign of them, and even if they do come, we will just do our own thing.

We don't have to have anything to do with them."

"I'm outnumbered." I'm sure he simply means about his vote to avoid the New Year's barbecue, but the unmistakable sorrow behind his eyes suggests that maybe he feels outnumbered in another way. Maybe in the family dynamic, without Eric. "I don't want to stay long. We'll grab some grub and then come back here, okay?"

Mum smiles, somewhat shyly. "Thank you, Mitch." She leans across the table and kisses him softly, prolonging the comforting touch of his lips. She kisses him like he is her man. "I'll just go freshen up quickly."

Dad returns her sweet smile. They are so in love sometimes, and it's not even grocery shopping day.

Mum brushes her wavy chestnut hair and colours her lips with the only shade of lipstick I've ever known her to wear: frosted pink. She looks really pretty. Dad loosely takes hold of her hand as the three of us commence the short walk down to the barbecue, past a few cabins that already have their blinds closed, in preparation of its occupants' impending late night.

Pat and Joanie are drinking a can of beer each, on the small patch of grass next to their caravan. Legs outstretched on sun lounges, they laugh back and forth in conversation and raise their beers in the air when they notice me staring at them, as if in a toast. I quickly smile and tuck my hands in my pockets, realising that we could run into the Sandersons, and hence Liam, any moment. I need to be alert.

As we approach the crowd, the aroma of steak and mushroom intensifies. My tummy rumbles in anticipation.

A stocky man I remember having to call *Uncle* Martin taps his wife gently on her shoulder as she stands chatting to a woman I once knew as *Aunty* Jane. "Meryl, they came," he announces in shock.

Dad chuckles. "Typical Martin, always trying to make a scene!"

Martin warmly accepts Dad's outstretched hand, shaking his head in disbelief. "Gosh, it's good to see you come out tonight, old mate." He pulls Dad's grip, bringing him into an embrace, and repeatedly pats him on the back. "Just so glad you finally came out."

Jane and Meryl seem to be fighting back tears as they wrap their arms around Mum. "We just thought we should wait until you were ready."

"Alright, alright," Dad abruptly declares, "that's enough of that nonsense. Who do I speak to about the music around here? What is this? Elton John?" He theatrically covers his ears as Yellow Brick Road coos out of the ghetto blaster resting on the railing of the closest cabin. "I'm taking charge of the music!"

A crowd of their old acquaintances swarm on Mum and Dad. I stand back, protectively looking around to see if the Sandersons are anywhere to be seen. It's imperative that tonight's yearly reunion with Liam goes as planned. I've got stuff to say.

After Eric died, Mr Sanderson threw out Liam's art supplies. He ripped up his comic books. He sent him off to an elite private college where he boarded during school terms.

The same elite private college that took Cat's mum about forty-five minutes to drive to.

Mindy is sitting in a circle with Simone, one of her bitchy friends from school, and two boys I don't instantly recognise. She smiles excitedly and waves me over. I'm confused and look around but she laughs and nods simultaneously, then waves me over again, more animated this time.

I catch Mum's attention and point over to Mindy. I'm stunned: Mum nods in approval. She knowingly lets me wander off without her for the first time since Eric died. I apprehensively take a few steps towards Mindy before looking back at Mum, expecting to see her following me. But she stays with her friends as they all chatter away, and smiles encouragingly.

"Bea, come join us!" Mindy calls. She is wearing a fresh, navy one-piece bathing suit underneath denim shorts that look a size too big for her at the waist.

Her friends all space out, making room for me in their circle. I sit cross-legged like the rest of them, tugging my brown corduroy button-up shirt to make sure it is stretched down as far as it can go. We are close to the edge of the lake, and that settles my nerves. The gentle sound of the water is familiar. Nostalgia is comforting.

Mindy puts her hand on my knee. "Guys, this is my old friend, Bea. We used to be besties when we were annoying little brats back in what, like Year 2 or something?"

"Something like that. Long time ago." *And overnight, I ceased to exist for you.*

"Remember me? Ant," the guy sitting to my left reminds me.

Of course I remember him. He used to play table tennis in the games room with Eric and all the other kids, but I was never allowed in there, thanks to Liam. Ant has a mop of chocolate-coloured hair that flops just above his eyes and his Nike t-shirt looks older than he is.

"Well, Anthony, actually. But everyone calls me Ant. Mindy said you might come tonight. She was bugging her parents to ask your Mum and Dad to come back out."

Mindy rolls her eyes. "Ant thinks he knows everything."

I smile with my lips pressed together. "Are you from Adelaide?"

"Ballarat, remember? Eric used to call me Rat instead of Ant."

I look down at my lap to avoid the awkward tension that suddenly settles over the group. "Yeah, I remember."

Ant clears his throat. He is visibly uncomfortable in the aftermath of saying Eric's name. "We should head to the pool later. They close the water slides at ten."

Mindy claps her hands together. "Psyched!"

The water slides. Ladybugs. I haven't been back there. I can't go back there.

The guy sitting directly opposite me introduces himself next, shifting my rising panic about potentially returning to the pool, to what this gorgeous eighteen-year-old boy must think of someone like me. He is hot and tanned. I am fat and pale.

"I'm Wesley, but everyone calls me Wes."

"I'm Beatrice, but everyone calls me Bea." I shift my eyes to the lake because I can't bring myself to look at him but I am very aware that he is looking right at me. I fiddle with the hem of my shirt, subtly making certain that my tummy is covered. I am so aware of my weight right now. I wish I was skinny like Mindy.

Wes is intimidatingly attractive yet lacks the smug confidence that most good-looking guys his age possess. The sun-kissed blonde waves in his hair curl under his ear lobes, drawing my attention to a small silver hoop pierced through his helix.

"We've never met before," he continues. "Not now, or when we were annoying little brats. This is my first time here, I'm from Perth."

He looks right at you when he talks to you, like *at* you. It's as if he has nowhere else to be and nothing else to do but to be right here, present in this moment. And this moment completely absorbs him.

My god, I like his voice so much, and the way he *uses* it. He draws out his words, as if his mouth is lazy. I could say the same sentence in half the time. He is the epitome of chilled. I bet he's never owned a watch. I bet he surfs. I bet all of his mum's friends have a secret crush on him.

I nod, trying hard to look interested. "I haven't been there before."

"It's pretty similar to Adelaide really. We visited my nanna for Christmas then got here this morning. We're here for a few days."

I wonder if the gossip has been passed on to him. I wonder if he knows about me. I hope he doesn't. I instantly shut myself off when I sense that someone feels sorry for me.

Simone looks to Mindy, slightly annoyed. "You never told me you and Bea used to hang out."

I had assumed that Mindy relished in telling her friends all about me. She could have been famous by association: it was in all the papers, even one of the news programs did a segment about teenage suicide, featuring the *boy at the lake*. A camera crew showed up at our house, relentless in their pursuit to get an interview with Mum and Dad. Dad firmly commented through the closed door that our family had been through enough and to please leave us alone, so the reporter went up and down the street door-knocking on all our neighbours' houses instead. We never watched the program, so I don't know whether any of them gave an interview about us.

Mum wouldn't let me take one step outside of the house until the buzz of the story died down a couple of weeks later. I wasn't even allowed to check the letterbox or take Gilbert for a walk. What a potential claim to fame for Mindy: childhood friends with the girl whose brother hung himself from a tree. But evidently, she doesn't gossip about me. I like her so much more now.

"Didn't I tell you that? My bad. I used to go over to her house and eat all the pink marshmallows."

We both smile. Surprisingly, at each other.

"You're friends with that girl with the wild hair," Simone ponders, "Ebony, is it? She seems nice, pretty tough."

"She is nice, we're good friends." I hear myself say the words so casually, as if the fact that I have been able to make a friend isn't the most unexpected accomplishment of my life so far. If only she actually liked me for me, not for who I just pretend to be around her.

"Cool," Simone replies, just as casually.

"So, how about it then, are we going to the pool?" Ant clearly hasn't forgotten his suggestion like I was hoping he would.

Wes is looking at me. I could get addicted to that.

"Let's go," Mindy gushes. "Bea, do you have to check with your mum?"

"Um..." I glance over at Mum. She is surrounded by a group of excited women, some I recognise, some I don't. She looks occupied, and happy. "No, it should be fine."

I'll be back here before she even notices, just like at home.

I follow behind Mindy and Ant as we commence the short stroll to the pool. Simone had to run back to her family's cabin to change into her bathers. I squeal internally: Wes walks next to me.

I sneak a sideways perve. His skin is clear, like it has never been tainted by a single pimple. His bottom lip is fuller than his top lip. He radiates contentment. He's the most relaxed person I've ever met. Stress and drama must be alien concepts to him.

But it's his voice that drugs me.

"Do you need to go grab your swimmers, too?" he asks.

Mindy and Ant are chatting away just ahead of us. The illusion of privacy, paired with that velvet voice of his, nurtures my confidence to say what I actually want to say. "I don't really like the pool."

My honesty seems to activate Wes' unexpected lust for heroism. "Guys, Bea and I are going to make a detour to the lake. We'll catch up with you."

Mindy raises her eyebrows as if she is impressed. "I'll talk to you later, Bea."

I raise my eyebrows too, but more so out of shock. I don't know whether because a boy wants to be alone with me, or because Mindy said she will talk to me later. "Okay."

Wes and I turn off the gravel path and head down the hill through the tall blades of dry grass, leading to the lake.

"Wonder if there's snakes here?" Wes casually ponders.

"Probably. I wouldn't dawdle if I were you."

He grabs hold of my hand and bolts, playfully pulling my arm to keep up with him. My laughter prances with the chirps of the crickets. Who knew boys could be so much fun. I don't know if I've ever actually had fun before. Certainly not like this. Certainly not with someone like him.

He is weightless; floating through life. I am weighed down by trauma and heartbreak. Bad memories. Regret.

Uncertainty.

Guilt.

He is as light as a feather.

The lake is eerily tranquil tonight. The glass-like water perfectly mirrors the sky, as if the wispy clouds have delicately dropped into it. A leafless tree protrudes from below the surface. It's almost haunting. But maybe it just feels that way if you're already haunted. Maybe what we've seen determines what we see.

Wes tucks both his hands into his pockets. "Can I tell you something?"

I shift my focus from the hypnotising aura of the lake to Wes' equally hypnotising deep blue eyes. "Sure."

"I've never kissed a girl before," he admits without visible fear of judgement. He is completely at ease with himself. "I'm about to start uni, but I've never kissed a girl before."

"Why?"

Wes laughs. "Interesting reaction. Do you think it's a

bit weird for a guy?"

"Sorry, I didn't mean it like that. No, I don't think it's weird. I've never kissed a girl before either." We both smile. "Or," I hesitate, "or anyone, really."

"Yeah, but it's different for girls. Plus, aren't you like fifteen or something?"

"I'm sixteen actually, turning seventeen in a couple of months. I'm starting Year 12 when school goes back."

His eager eyes gaze into mine as he inches his face closer, painfully building the anticipation. His attention solely belongs to me. There's no sense of urgency or panic that he is going to leave me. In this moment, I am all that he wants. I am enough for him. He wants to be with me. He wants to stay with me.

I think I've already fallen in love with him.

"It's a romantic setting for a first kiss, don't you think?" he breathes.

"Uh huh." I am so ready. I don't know what to

expect, what to feel. But he doesn't either. I am his first kiss, too. I'm not alone in my feelings.

I close my eyes and tilt my face upwards, gently meeting his silky lips with mine. He grips his hands onto my ample hips, digging his fingers into my curves. Sensing his desire for me to hold onto him in return, I reach my arms over his shoulders and clasp my hands together behind his neck. I hope he likes that.

"What the fuck is this?" a voice booms across the evening air, robbing me of the most perfect moment my life has ever gifted me.

It's a voice I listen out for everywhere I go. I listen for it when I'm at the shops with Mum. I listen for it in crowds. I listen for it when I'm walking to nowhere in the middle of the night. I listen for it when I'm back in my bed, in my dreams. In my memories.

Liam.

He storms towards us and thumps both his hands onto Wes' chest. "Back off!"

"What are you doing?" I gasp, mortified.

Wes holds his hands up like he's negotiating with an armed robber. "Nothing's wrong here. I wasn't making her do anything she didn't want to do." He retains his mellow composure. His easy-going cadence could calm a wild beast. He has no intention of getting into a fight tonight, if ever in his life.

Liam lunges at Wes. "Are you calling her a slut?"

Maybe Wes' voice only works on me.

I jump in front of Liam. "Stop it! What's the matter with you?"

"I didn't mean it like that," Wes promises. "Chill, bro."

"Liam, go away," I demand sternly, burning my eyes into his.

He smirks, looking down at his chest, at my hands, firmly holding him back. I hopelessly try to suppress an urge I've never felt before. Pretty sure it's called lust. My fingers involuntarily hold their pressure, drawn to the athletic physique barely disguised by his black linen shirt.

He pushes his torso harder against my hands, as if wanting to show me that his body *feels* just as good as it *looks*. And it does. I'm not sure I hide that realisation adequately enough; it's written all over my face.

Liam slowly drags his attention back to my eyes, his guise as smug as ever. His ego is having a great time with this. I can't look away: my eyes are magnetically locked to his. I wish his lips had been the first I'd tasted. His stupid, arrogant, beautiful face has tainted the momentous event of my first kiss with regret.

I bet that's exactly what he wanted.

"Happy New Year, *Beatrice*," he says after a sobering pause, gently removing my hold on him and guiding my hands back to myself.

He narrows his eyes at Wes, no doubt attempting to intimidate him even more. It works: Wes takes a giant step backwards, further away from me. Satisfied, Liam turns from the lake and slinks off towards the New Year's celebrations. He doesn't look back.

I know things about Liam.

Cat told me.

Mr Sanderson has another son, Daniel. A biological son.

When Daniel was three years old, Mr Sanderson abandoned him and his mother to be with Liam's mum, whose husband (Liam's real dad) had just been killed in a workplace accident at the same car yard Mr Sanderson worked. The hefty insurance payout and additional compensation meant that Mrs Sanderson was suddenly in possession of more money than she could spend in four lifetimes. While she grieved the loss of her husband and faced a life raising a child alone, her vulnerability was like a beacon for Mr Sanderson. He saw his opportunity to be on easy street, and left his family to get there. Daniel never heard from his father again and a new Mrs Sanderson was born when Liam was five years old.

Daniel and his mum moved interstate and eventually

she remarried and added a daughter to their family. They are happy. They have a nice home, a nice life. Daniel is heavily into sports and is rumoured to be training for the Olympic swimming team. His mum, sister, and his new dad, all cheer him on. He's apparently a really good person too, like the kind everyone wants to be friends with. He got his good looks from his mum, who was even approached by a local skin care company to be the spokeswoman for their forty plus range.

That's what Mr Sanderson gave up: an outgoing child who loved sports, a beautiful, caring wife and a family built from love, for an introverted child who would rather pick up a pencil than throw a ball, a woman he didn't even like, a family used for gain. Liam had to become someone he was not, to win the love of someone who didn't deserve his own in return. Liam was the replacement child, and in Mr Sanderson's eyes, he was the inferior model.

Liam and his mother were never good enough for Mr Sanderson because they were not the family that he truly loved. And they both knew that damn well.

The family that Mr Sanderson did love were so much better off without him. And *he* knew that damn well.

Cat knows a lot of things about a lot of people but she had to do some digging around when I first asked her about Liam, particularly because she had already graduated. But she knew of him, and she still kept in contact with the footy guys. Liam had boarded at the school and kept to himself bar a few close friends on the team. He ended up in detention a few times for doodling in class. Cat once dated a guy on Liam's team so she went to all the games, but she never noticed if anyone was there to watch Liam. She didn't seem to think there was.

"One day, I'm going to have a number one song about why girls shouldn't date guys on the footy team," she'd told me.

I had big plans for my highly anticipated New Year's run-in with Liam. I wanted to tell him that he has always been good enough, just the way he is. That he isn't less than anyone. I wanted to tell him this because he needs to hear it. He's needed to hear it his whole life. I found out the thing he needs, the thing that could make him happy, that could make him feel good. If ever he felt that he needed fixing, or saving, I could be the one to do it. That healed something in me.

I figured him out. I understood him.

I had big plans. I had the upper hand. And I wanted that with Liam. I wanted to prove something to him.

Instead, I'm just confused. He's confused me. He's confused everything.

My senses have heightened. I look to Wes, wanting to initiate another kiss, because I've got a taste for something now. I don't know if it's a taste for him specifically, but whatever I'm feeling, I want more of it. I want him to look at me the way he did just a few moments ago. Wes wasn't distracted by anything. I had his full attention. It was real. In that moment, he *only* wanted to be with me. Just for once, why can't I have that, why can't I have something wonderful? I bet he's lost interest in me now. He must think I'm bad news. His life is relaxed and peaceful. No conflict. Whereas my mum and dad's mad frantic voices are currently bellowing my name across the lake.

BEA! BEA! WHERE ARE YOU?

I sigh, embarrassed.

Wes's previous desire for heroics was evidently short-lived. "Maybe you should answer them?"

I roll my eyes, disappointed in his lack of rebellion. Liam would get us to hide.

"I'm over here!" I shout in reply.

Mum and Dad rush to me from different directions. Panicked phrases like *where the bloody hell have you been* and *how could you just wander off like that* render me completely humiliated in front of the cutest guy I've ever seen, just moments after I got my first kiss, that got ruined by my dead brother's best friend who hates me and has a chip on his shoulder so big it's amazing he can even stand up straight. But gosh he felt good. He finished school this year. I wonder if he did okay. Has he applied for uni? I wonder if Cat heard any more whispers about his past, or knows anything about his future. I bow my head while my parents fuss over me, too deflated to look at Wes, partly because all I can think about now is Liam.

"Go home, young man," Mum firmly instructs Wes. "Your mother probably wonders where you are, too."

Dad checks my arms, seeming to be looking for any sign of injury, while Mum strokes my hair and literally starts to cry. Over what, I don't really know.

"Don't ever do that to us again."

Wes backs away, his breezy preliminary existence now exposed to more drama than one of those daytime soap operas my nanna watches.

I won't expect to hear from him again. I don't even know if I want to.

He is choosing to leave.

People tend to do that.

But he's not the one I wanted to stay.

New Year's Eve 1997

Mum and Dad are fighting. Dad and I are fighting. Mum and I are fighting about Dad and I fighting. And yet they still insist on driving up to the lake.

I roll down my window, subconsciously hoping the breeze will blow away the tension.

As is tradition, we arrive at our first stop about an hour after leaving home; the petrol station next to the rusted old windmill at the bottom of the hill. The diner is packed with long-haul truck drivers grabbing greasy take-away food to sustain them for the next leg of their trip. I order bacon and eggs and leave the crispy bits on the side of the plate.

Whenever I have had a bad day, or a bad year, I don't feel that I can declare it. Because surely, I've already endured the worst day imaginable, the day I lost Eric. So, comparatively, it's really a bit overdramatic to complain about anything else.

But I'm going to anyway, because it has: it's been a *bad* year.

We had to put Gilbert to sleep. He reached an impressive twelve years of age but arthritis had begun to rob him of his quality of life. Mum didn't cope well. Dad basically had to carry her out of the vet. She started dinner preparations as soon as we got home but broke down while the oven was preheating. Dad was reading in the lounge and naturally came rushing in when he heard her crying. He protectively wrapped his whole body around hers as they huddled on the kitchen floor, shielding her from the world so that she could let go and surrender completely to her grief. She sobbed into a well-used tea-towel embroidered with an image of the Outback while Dad hummed Always on My Mind. I recognised it from the Willy Nelson cassette I'm forced to listen to every year on the drive to the lake. I thought it was an odd song choice when trying to comfort someone but maybe he didn't think too much about it and just already had it stuck in his head.

I used to think that Mum and Dad didn't love each other as much when they couldn't afford to get the good groceries. Things had been pretty hard at home. Dad had been rolling his own cigarettes and Mum was having the Home Brand coffee that she pretends to like, but there was so much love in the way that Dad held her that night. It made me realise how wrong I'd been: when life is hard, they love each other the most. Sometimes, maybe love is about more than just groceries.

Gilbert was sleeping a lot towards the end but the house still feels extra quiet now he's gone. He was Eric's dog. Home's permanent feel of *there's something missing* suddenly became much more apparent. Much more unbearable.

I couldn't find my favourite necklace a few days later. I was bordering on hysterical as I searched the whole house for it with Mum. I yelled at her, like *at* her, as if it was somehow her fault. I ripped through the pile of washing that Mum had only just finished folding, clinging to the hope that it perhaps might have come off with my uniform. I aggressively hurled freshly paired socks across the room; not intentionally at Mum, but admittedly my panic blinded me to the closeness of her proximity.

We eventually found my necklace, slid underneath the toaster. I must have put it on the bench when I was getting my breakfast before school. The relief sucked away my breath, and then I just couldn't get it back again. Mum held onto me tightly, just like Dad had held onto her, reassuring me that the air would find its way back soon. My ribcage had been lassoed together: the tightness was suffocating. But the air did find its way back, just like Mum promised me that it would. The gratitude of being able to breathe again burst out of me in the form of heavy, uncontrollable tears. I was merely releasing the stress of nearly losing my favourite necklace and not passing out from lack of oxygen, but Mum said she was glad that I was finally letting myself cry for Gilbert.

I hadn't given him much love or attention since Eric died. I didn't pat him when I walked past or return his enthusiasm to see me when I got home from school. When I fulfilled my obligation to take him for a walk, I didn't jingle his lead enthusiastically and exclaim *walkies* like Eric did.

Of course, Gilbert never understood why Eric didn't come home with us. For the rest of his days, Gilbert's preferred napping location was right in front of Eric's permanently closed bedroom door. Maybe he was waiting for Eric to come out, or to go in. Or maybe he eventually pieced together that Eric wasn't ever going to go in or come out that door again, so he just basked in the fading remnants of his owner's scent before it dissipated forever. I wanted to scream at him, *stupid dog! He's never coming home! Stop reminding me all the time!* What kind of horrible person dislikes an animal? Me. I disliked him, just because he was close to Eric and now Eric was gone. And Gilbert constantly reminded me of that.

After the dog died, Dad found a slide of Eric when he was about 7 or 8, hugging Gilbert as a puppy. He got it developed and now the framed photo sits on the mantelpiece in the lounge room, right in the centre of the family gallery. Mum looks over at it a lot, almost quizzically, especially when she's watching telly on the couch. I can almost hear her brain trying to work something out, like she's trying to calculate an absurdly complicated algebra equation or something. Every now and again when she does the dusting, she forgets the order that the photo frames were in and accidentally puts that one back behind all the others. Dad notices eventually and returns it to the front row for her.

Year 12 sucked. It was my final year of high school and I craved to hear a story about a green monster who lurked beneath the surface and ate someone's bathers. I never liked the story about the luckless goblin who fell in love with the bitchy fairy, but I even wished I could hear that one again too. I needed my brother more than ever and he wasn't there.

Up until I got a boyfriend, I made out with a few random guys at the clubs, using my fake ID to get in, secretly hoping that word would reach Liam. I subconsciously wanted to recreate the rush I felt when Wes kissed me; the kiss that suddenly made Liam appear, angry that I was with someone else. I feel like I will forever be chasing that feeling when I held Liam back, and he pushed against me, hard. I want more of it. I have never felt so awake. Every day I feel like I'm just *enduring* life but, in that moment, with him, I *experienced* it. I felt it.

I've made out with precisely three guys since Wes, but Liam didn't show up, not even once. I pashed complete strangers on the dance floor and in the club's darkened corner booth; one eye open, scanning the crowd. But Liam never came storming towards me, insisting the guy get off of me.

I wanted Liam to worry about me, to scold me for hanging out in the wrong clique again. But during the year, it's like he doesn't even exist, which for some ridiculous reason makes me feel like *I* don't exist. I look for him everywhere I go. I double-check the face of every man in every crowd in every place, just in case it's him.

It never is.

Never knowing where Liam was cultivated an insatiable need for him to know where *I* was. But he never came looking for me. Cat graduated high school two years ago, Liam one year ago, so that fleeting connection had expired. He had no means of finding out about me and I had no means of finding out about him. A permanent, subtle state of irritability relentlessly reminded me of this. But what really tortured me was the realisation that he likely didn't give a second thought as to where I was or what I was doing, or how I was going. Or who I was with.

Ebony and I quizzed each other during our lunch breaks, in constant preparation for the absurd number of tests and exams school threw at us. She thrives under pressure. I just counted down the hours until I could sneak out my bedroom window to go for my midnight walk, or frequent Hindley Street's hotspots on Saturday nights, to reward myself for all the study. The night clubs were my regular remuneration.

Being housebound with my parents most evenings perhaps helped ensure I got a high enough score to be able to put a Bachelor of Podiatry as my first preference, but they haven't put the offers out yet. Feet gross me out. I can barely touch my own, let alone someone else's. I have no idea what I was thinking.

The whole concept of knowing what you want to do when you grow up always eluded me. When I was ten, I genuinely thought that I could just trail along behind Eric and Liam on my purple scooter forever; *that* would be my job. Whatever Eric would do, I would just be a part of it somehow. He was going to be a famous writer. It didn't matter what I wanted to do, only that I could make Eric excited about his future. I never gave any thought to my own, without him.

I should have.

Because I always knew that he would leave me.

We drive through the gates of the resort and Dad collects our keys; cabin 9 this time. The underlying panic that I feel all year suddenly subsides now that we are here, replaced with the most terrifying yet promising and perhaps even most essential of all human emotions: hope. Liam will be here. My soul just needs to be where he is.

In my room, a lone wrought iron single bed with cream coloured bedding, straight out of a Country Style Living magazine, beckons me over. I lay down and stare blankly at the ceiling; a moment of rejuvenating nothingness imperative to my state of mind, short-lived thanks to my mother's apparent desperation to restore peace in the family.

"Monopoly!" she loudly summons, as if she isn't necessarily speaking to anyone in particular.

This will be interesting: none of us are talking to each other. I bet Dad will relish sending me to jail.

We drove about five hours to get here and now we're going to play Monopoly. Just like we do at our own kitchen table back home. How exciting.

As much as I hate to admit, it actually is. Traditions are a comfort in an otherwise uncertain and overwhelming life.

They found a pregnancy test in the bin. I thought I had buried it well enough but evidently not. So that's why Dad isn't speaking to me. Then Mum got mad at him for reacting without listening to what I had to say first, so that's why she isn't speaking to him. I thought she was on my side; women stick together and all that, and thanked her for standing by me, but then she got mad at me for putting her in a position to doubt me in the first place. And yet they still packed up the car and drove us to the lake, even though we're all mad at each other.

I'm not pregnant.

I mean I could have been, but the test was negative.

I'm pretty sure it would have been Damian's if I was, but there was an overlap between him and another guy I hooked up with one night; the night that Damian ditched me.

Damian lived in the house next-door, with his parents and two younger siblings. The very first week that they moved in, they hired a gardener to dig up all the rosebushes. Mr Randall's rosebushes. They bought his house, and then eradicated the physical

155

pieces of him left behind. After the rosebushes, they got a new letterbox. They painted the front door. They took away the tangible evidence that a man named Mr Randall once lived next door to me.

The batteries to my Discman died the same day they dug up the rosebushes. Despite my manic search, I couldn't find any new ones in the kitchen drawer. I begged Mum to go to the shops but she didn't want to use the car until she could get some more petrol when she got paid in a few days. I cried all night. I loved my Discman and I hated that I couldn't use it.

Although I begrudged his heartless and insensitive parents for what they did, I loved Damian. I fell for him hard and fast. I included myself in every aspect of his life and he embraced my odd family dynamic as if he genuinely didn't think it was weird that my mum and dad accompanied me when I came to watch his soccer games on Saturday mornings. He'd come back to our house after and we'd watch boring, mindless action movies on the couch. He seemed to enjoy them at least. He loved Mum's spaghetti bolognaise but it secretly upset me when Mum gave him extra meatballs like she used to do for Mr Randall. Sometimes we'd lay in the backyard under the clothesline, shaded by cotton bed sheets and Dad's hi-vis work vests hung out to dry. Damian would play his Gameboy and I would read my book, until he would predictably want me to watch him get to the next level instead.

Damian and I were allowed to hang out in my bedroom with the door closed, as long as it was before six o'clock. I guess it never occurred to my parents that people can still have sex in the middle of the day. It took me months to figure out what I was supposed to do other than just lay there, but I wanted to get it right. I concentrated so hard. I studied the way his skin prickled and hyper-fixated on his breathing so I knew when to moan. I even counted the seconds between his heavy breaths, allowing me to accurately predict the timing of his orgasm so I knew when to pretend that I had one too. He would tense his shoulders and fold his lips in together, so I just mirrored that. Giving him pleasure, even with the complete lack of my own, was oddly satisfying. It's a powerful thing, being able to give someone what they need. It's a *power*, being able to give someone what they need.

I wasn't really ready the first time. But Damian was. He told me all his friends had already done it, and I was holding him back. I never want to be the cause of someone's unhappiness. That can kill you inside. So, I went along with it. We didn't kiss very much, and my body didn't really respond. He cupped my breasts with the tiniest amount of pressure so it more tickled than anything else. The waistband of my jeans had left red marks on my tummy and all I could think about was how fat he must think I am. At least with my clothes on, he might have thought I was skinny underneath. I couldn't relax. I hated being so exposed. But Damian came prepared with a tube of lubricant and said that was all that I needed.

Damian loved the clubs, just like Pippa and Cat. We had a lot of fun, sneaking out together. He would meet me at the top of the driveway after I snuck out my window and we'd bus it into town. Cat waited for us outside the club, with whomever she'd attached herself to for the night. He liked Cat; always commented how pretty she was and how I could be really pretty like her if I lost a little bit of weight. He assured me that I was pretty enough just as I was though, but I could be even prettier if I ever wanted to be.

"You know how much I love you, right?" he shouted one night over the *doofdoofdoof* pulsating from the DJ's speakers.

I nodded, as if it was part of my dance routine and concentrated hard on keeping to the beat. I braced myself, fully aware that he was about to shatter me. No one says they love you like it's a reminder unless they're about to break your heart.

He applied to study at Melbourne University. He told me right in the middle of the dance floor, as if it was no big deal. *I'm so easy to walk away from.*

Apparently, our state universities weren't good enough for him. He had his hopes set on some obscure degree that wasn't on offer here. He was optimistic about us making a long-distance relationship work, but *let's just see how we go and leave ourselves open to new opportunities.* He kept on dancing while my heart broke into a million pieces beneath the multi-coloured strobe lights. No matter how he presented it, the bottom line was clear: he was leaving me. And he wanted to be available just in case he met someone new in Melbourne. I ran off the dance floor right in the middle of a Severed Heads song.

Cat comforted me in the girl's bathroom, adamant that I was better off without him and didn't need to put on a brave face. She kept telling me that it was okay to cry, almost as if she actually wanted me to, but I had no intention of crying over him, even when she offered to buy me a new outfit if I let myself *get it all out*. It's pointless crying over something that can't be changed. Or someone.

I had devoted myself to doing whatever, and being whoever, Damian wanted. And it still wasn't enough. I could feel the tears coming, but they just couldn't break through. I've cried over so many trivial things in my life; papier-mâché volcanoes, scolding seat belt buckles, lost necklaces and broken windows. All things that I guess can be fixed or replaced. I can't ever bring myself to cry over people. They can't be fixed. Or replaced.

Ordinarily, girls flush and wash their hands and out they go but that night taught me something about women: they never let another woman hurt alone. My private heartbreak in a public bathroom was a beacon to every other girl in the club who needed a hug or a compliment, or validation or perhaps even therapy. Chynna cheated on her boyfriend and can't forgive herself. Lexi's boyfriend cheated on her and she can't forgive him but he wants to make it work. Hannah is scared to take the next step and move in with her partner. Joanne has the hots for a guy she works with but thinks she's not pretty enough for *someone like him*. Lexi hugged Chynna and told her that she was allowed to make mistakes. Hannah hugged Joanne and told her that she is *secy as fuck*, and if a man can't see that then he is the one who isn't good enough *for her*. And me? I was told that I was beautiful, and loved, and worthy, and enough. Women are a special kind of magic like that.

Back out in the club, there was no sign of Damian. I

threw myself at the first guy I saw. His name turned out to be Brett and he was exactly what I needed in that moment: horny and the rightful owner of a car. I was desperate to hold on to the self-esteem that my bathroom cheerleaders had gifted me, and under the impression that I was much more attractive than usual thanks to the Ruski Lemons filling my confidence with blatant lies.

"I'm Bea. And I'm depressed. You could cheer me up though!" Subtlety eludes broken-hearted inebriates. But for the first time, I wanted to hook up because I felt like it, not just because I was someone's girlfriend and thought that's what you have to do, regardless of whether you are even in the mood. I wasn't trying to please anyone, or make anyone else happy, other than *myself*. Cat was okay with me leaving with Brett, as long as I promised to give three rings to let her know when I got home safe.

I liked the way Brett wrapped his arm around my waist as he escorted me out of the club, holding me close to him. It was as if he wanted everyone to see that I was with him, like I was someone to boast about, not feel embarrassed by because I'm not skinny. I didn't even feel self-conscious about the excess padding I would ordinarily try to suck in when Damian touched me. Sometimes a girl really needs to be held, no matter how fat she feels.

I got in his car with him. Not my smartest decision in hindsight, but also not my dumbest. That would be reserved for the fact that I went back to his place.

Brett lived in a share-house with four other guys; potheads disguised as uni students, he told me. From the scent of the lounge, I believed him. But we didn't hang out there. Brett took me straight to his bedroom.

He asked me what I wanted. What I liked. I wanted to cry and tell him that I didn't know what I was supposed to want. Or like. "I just like the normal stuff."

Brett pushed me back onto his bed with a slight force that caught me pleasantly off-guard, and crawled on top of me painfully slowly. Curious eyes trailed up my body; his captivating gaze boldly daring to make me feel worthy of desire. His knees almost clamped me in place, rendering me powerless in the most empowering way. Lying beneath a man was a position that had traditionally made me loathe my body, and feel overwhelmed with a sense of inadequacy. Lying beneath Brett made me feel sexy as fuck, as the bathroom cheerleaders would say.

"The normal stuff," he quotes sceptically. "Let me show you my normal."

That was the night I had my first orgasm. Right after my boyfriend broke up with me.

Up until Brett, I had no idea that there are things you can do before sex that make your body feel ready, and responsive.

Brett probably doesn't even own lubricant.

I reassured my parents that Ebony had taken the pregnancy test, not me and I'm almost certain that they believed me. They still think I'm tucked up in my bed at night, not tracing around town. Mum blamed herself for not being *more of a mother figure for the poor girl* and wants me to make sure that Ebony knows she is welcome to come over any time she likes. I have no intention of telling her that.

Mum and Dad sit waiting for me at the table on the deck of our cabin, Monopoly all set up ready to play. The silence is deafening as I join them, taking my seat facing the lake.

Things just seem to resolve themselves in my family, without intentional effort from anyone. We seldom talk about our problems, or the cause of a fight or a drama, let alone say we're sorry if needs be. We endure the hard times and the difficult moments, give or take some space, and then we just move on, as if everything is just the same. Maybe that's just the reliability of family. Unconditional security.

"I'll start," Dad declares as he rolls the dice; the familiar comfort of the game instantly lifting the tension. "Seems only fair considering I'm the one who has to put up with the pair of you."

Mum and I look at each other knowingly, both trying to suppress a smile. Dad rolls a double six and makes sure we know *that was God, commending my strength for living with two women.*

Mum takes her turn next, leisurely shaking the dice in her cupped hands while she and Dad playfully banter back and forth about who is really putting up with whom.

I glance over the railing to Pat and Joanie's caravan, subconsciously wanting to give my parents some privacy to enjoy their flirtation; restorative after the tension of recent days. Pat and Joanie are relaxing with their legs stretched out on their faded blue and white sun lounges, next to their beloved silver caravan with the chocolate-brown stripe and orange curtains.

Pat is reading the latest New Idea and Joanie is circling her pen in a word search book. They are always so content in their own space, a concept that makes me realise that I never actually see them venture away from their caravan. They don't technically come to the New Year's Eve gathering; they are just there in the background. I don't see them walk along the lake or take a dip in the pool. They don't even go down to the kiosk. They are a part of the community, from afar. They keep to themselves in their own little world, adjacent to ours.

I went to the movies with Mum and Dad last week, our Christmas Eve tradition. Joanie was there, with a man who was obviously her husband and their three young children. It was the first time I had ever seen her outside of the holiday park. At the time I felt somehow perverted; seeing someone in a habitat I wasn't normally privy to, like when someone accidentally leaves their curtains open at night and the whole neighbourhood can see inside their house. I had only ever known Pat and Joanie as sisters, or friends, who caravanned together at the lake every New Year's, maybe as some sort of escape from their demanding lives. I pictured them going straight back to their jobs after their short getaway; Pat worked at the library and Joanie was a florist who lived interstate. They stressed about overdue bills and fought with their husbands when their kids were asleep, just like all grown-ups do. They talked to each other on the phone every Sunday evening, counting down the days to their next break from reality at the lake. And now that I had actually seen one of them at the movies with their family, it looked like the everyday life I had conjured up for them was pretty spot on.

It's sobering how quickly everything you thought you knew about the world can change.

Pat puts her hand on Joanie's thigh and leans over, sensually caressing Joanie's plump lips with her own. I swallow a gasp and abruptly switch my focus to the lake ahead: the only thing it seems that is always exactly what it appears to be. Life changes, usually independent of our control, but the lake stays the same.

There is a slight breeze today and the water ripples in response. My cheeks burn and my vision blurs. I have no idea what I want to do now I've finished school. Everyone else did. Ebony has always known that she would join the police force. I heard Mindy is going to study nursing. All I know is that I am on the cusp of entering a stage of my life that Eric never reached, and now I have left my secondary education behind and he is stuck in his forever. I am older than my older brother. I have graduated high school. Everything feels new and scary and uncertain, and unfair and wrong.

I've had a boyfriend. I've gone through my first break up.

Eric never had a girlfriend. No one ever broke up with him.

I am experiencing things that he never got to experience.

I grew up. I'm still growing up. That makes me feel like I'm betraying him.

I am realising things about the world that he never got to realise.

That kiss wasn't between sisters. It wasn't between friends. Maybe everything I had imagined about their lives was true, but their annual weekend away is just a little bit more than anyone is supposed to know.

Pat and Joanie are secret lovers.

All these years, I assumed I knew them. But I don't even know their real names.

I get things so wrong sometimes.

Eric used to tell me that he was going to kill himself. All the time, ever since we were really little. He would say it light-heartedly, but sometimes, on his dark days, he would clearly mean it. I thought if I could just be with him all the time, he wouldn't do what he had always joked about doing. He would just make up his stories and get the release he needed from that. I shut my world out, so I could devote myself to making sure that he stayed in his.

But I got it wrong.

He left. He left, even though I spent every recess and lunch with him. He left, even though I snuck into his room late at night, pretending I needed to hear a story because Mum and Dad were fighting. I didn't. Their fighting didn't bother me. I knew they would sort it out. But their fighting meant that Eric wouldn't be asleep either and it scared me to think he was on his own in the middle of the night, with no one to stop him from killing himself if he tried to. I let him think that his stories saved me, but I was hoping that they were really going to save him.

I got that wrong, too.

He crept out of the cabin in the middle of the night and I couldn't stop him.

I wanted him to feel that he was a master at saving everyone, so that he felt needed and wouldn't be able to go.

I got that wrong, too.

He could save everyone but himself.

His gruesome stories were his outlet. He fantasised about death; for other people but mainly for himself. Maybe Liam and I enabled him by listening to the stories, illustrating them, turning them into graphic-novels. Maybe we shared the same hope that Eric would be satisfied to live out his morbid desires through horror stories alone. Maybe we wanted to believe it was only a fantasy, not the reality he was so adamant on creating for himself. We got it wrong. We didn't save him.

The goblin slaughtered the fairy.

Bogart had been truly enamoured with her. He hand-picked her daisies and ordered the hummingbirds to sing her a song every morning upon waking. But no matter how much he persisted and pursued her, the fairy just wasn't interested. Bogart declared his love for her despite her adamant rejection and asked for her hand in marriage. The little fairy scrunched up her face in disgust, her wicked laughter tormenting his soul. The stares from the other fairies burned through him. She said that his nose was too big, his skin too green, his feet covered in bumps. Why on earth would someone like her, she reasoned, ever be interested in someone like him?

Bogart was heartbroken.

Humiliated.

He sought his revenge. He crept up to the sunflower where the fairy slept and hacked at her delicate wings with a knife he had carved from stone. Bogart left her to die in a pool of her own blood. Eric's eyes lit up when he told me the part about the petals of the sunflower turning red from the stain of her death, as he called it. I had nightmares for weeks, envisioning the fairy laying there, fading away in agony. But I could catch up on sleep. It helped Eric. I was helping him. I thought.

My parents were told drastically different versions of Eric's stories. Mum and Dad think the goblin and the fairy got married and had little green winged babies. I convinced Eric that the story was much better that way, and Liam even started coming up with some designs for it. But there were no happy endings in Eric's disturbed stories.

It was my job to make sure everyone thought Eric was okay. I tried so hard to cover it all up. I was responsible for him. I had to make sure they thought he was perfect, so they would treat him like he was and he would want to stay.

I looked for Eric's notebook when I came back to the cabin that morning, after they couldn't get any air down into his lungs and breathe him back to life. I expected it to be where he had left it: right on top of his bedside cupboard. But it was gone. I guess Liam made a detour on the way back to his family's cabin.

I tug at the collar of my baggy olive linen shirt; suddenly somehow too tight against my neck. The lake seems to move like a see-saw, as if I am looking at it through a wobbly telescope. My head throbs and my eyes squint, hopelessly trying to contain the tears forcefully attempting to break free.

Mum grabs hold of my arm. "Bea, what's going on?"

I yank my shirt away from my skin and hold it there. "I can't breathe!"

"It's okay," Mum consoles me, "it's just a panic attack. It's been a big year. Everyone gets anxious waiting for their results. Breathe with me."

She inhales theatrically whilst gliding her hands softly through the air like a musical conductor, then holds her breath and nods her head in count before slowly exhaling. Dad copies her, like the parent in the background trying to distract their baby so the doctor can administer an injection. I glance back and forth between their puffy cheeks and encouraging eyes.

They look ridiculous.

"That's it, Buzzy, deep breaths," Mum says soothingly.

She has never called me that before. Nobody ever

did apart from Eric. I don't react when she uses his nickname for me, because I'm not even sure she really said it. But it's what I heard.

I simulate their breathing until my clothes no longer feel like they're cutting off my circulation and the lake is no longer swaying side to side like those drunk girls on Hindley Street trying to load into a cab. I grin affectionately at my parents' absurd faces. "I'm alright now."

Mum pats the back of my hand and passes the dice. "It's your turn, Bea."

Dad wins the game of Monopoly just as everyone starts to gather close to the lake. A man about my father's age runs an extension cord through the window of his caravan and props his CD player under the most central tree. The crowd gathers until it seems that we are the only ones left in our own residence, other than Pat and Joanie of course.

During the day, the holiday park buzzes with activity but everyone is in their own space, doing their own thing, divided up into families. As dusk settles and the chill of the evening air creeps in, the atmosphere undergoes an almost instant shift. The men fishing in the lake move their chairs closer together so they can chat. One family's softball game becomes everyone's game. There is one radio, one barbecue, one celebration.

Mum tilts her head, asking without asking if we can join the festivities again this year.

Dad smiles, replying without replying that we can.

We pack up the board game and head back in to freshen up.

Mum stands at the bathroom mirror, applying her timeless frosted pink lipstick. "No wandering off this year please, Bea. My nerves can't handle any more drama."

I smooth my hand through the length of my long hair, twirling the split ends. "I promise, Mum. I don't think I know anyone here this year anyway."

Dad puts on his brown leather jacket and shakes his packet of cigarettes before tucking them into his pocket. "I've gone through them quick," he says to himself. "You do know someone here this year. The

Sandersons."

Mum jerks her hand in surprise, nearly running the lipstick up her cheek. "What? How do you know? Have you seen them? Why do you say it so calmly?"

"I only saw Liam. He was fishing on the far side of the lake when we got here. Arrogant shit he's turned into."

I light up a little inside. "Did you talk to him?" I ask eagerly.

"No, I don't want anything to do with the fucking prick."

"Language, Mitch," Mum scolds him.

"Well, I don't. Last I heard, he was about ready to move in with his girlfriend. I think he's doing his plumbing apprenticeship."

Girlfriend: I die a little inside.

Last he heard: I didn't realise Dad asked around about him.

Our appearance at the New Year's festivities is only a brief one; I suspect because the Sandersons are here,

177

too. Mum and Dad make us stay together and don't even let me go up to collect a plate without them. The Sandersons, however mingle with everyone who isn't within our near proximity, as if we are surrounded by an electric fence and they dare not get too close for fear of getting shocked. I sit with my parents and a small group of their old friends who talk passionately about the Prime Minister and what a mess he is making of the country.

Mrs Sanderson dutifully accompanies Mr Sanderson while he goes on a social rampage; determined to establish himself as the life of the party and claim everyone as *his* friend. His hair line has receded and he has grown a moustache, as if trying to compensate for the lack of hair on his head these days. His voice projects over the crowd, perhaps a deliberate move to announce his presence to us, though he knows full well that we can see him anyway. He was always such an unlikeable person.

Mrs Sanderson is still skinny but the magnitude of her husband's obnoxiousness and overpowering stature makes her appear downright emaciated. I feel obese in comparison, and I'm sure that's exactly what she would think I am. She looks older than she should. She's the same age as Mum, but if I didn't know that I'd say she was at least ten years older than her. She tries to disguise her obvious embarrassment about her husband, but it's still clear that she can't stand him. I guess it would be even harder to be married to a life-sucking parasite when you don't have a best friend anymore to complain to about him.

Mum and Dad exchange a few anxious glances while I field the barrage of predictable questions about how I found Year 12 and what I'm going to do now school is over. They eventually excuse us from the evening, despite their old and new friends insisting that we stay for the countdown, and we return to our cabin with full bellies and renewed mingling skills.

They are tucked up in bed by 11pm.

I climb out my window half an hour later.

No one notices me as I slip past on my way down to the darkened lake. An atmosphere of drunken merriment and wearied interactions co-exist: singing and unenergetic dancing amidst laboured chats and checks of the time. The barbecue is cooling down, depleted after catering to the ravenous appetite of the community. Little kids are falling asleep in their parents' laps. Older kids play chasey under the glow of the fairy lights strung between the low branches.

The music from the party seems to soften when it reaches the lake, as if overpowered by the inherent ambience of peace. I stop next to a tree with a trunk so wide I wouldn't be able to wrap my arms around it. I wait in the night, surprised to notice the back of a boy I once knew, only just last year. He is sitting with a girl with hair just as blonde and wavy as his, only longer. The moon highlights their faces as they turn towards each other.

Wes looks so good I'm pretty sure I gasp. I remember his lips. They were the first lips to ever connect with mine. Their touch is imprinted on my brain.

"Can I tell you something?" he asks the girl, coming over shy.

She is pretty. Thin. She puts her hand on top of his,

resting in between them on the patchy grass. "You can tell me anything."

"I've never kissed a girl before," he says coyly.

My tummy jolts and I shake my head in disbelief. *You've got to be kidding me.*

"I'm at uni but I've never kissed a girl before. This is a nice setting for a first kiss, don't you think?" he intimately recites, as if it's something he tends to say quite a lot.

The naïve girl leans in and they kiss under the romantic moonlight; softly and for much longer than he and I did.

I'm such an idiot. And guys are dicks.

Disheartened, I follow the shoreline of the lake until I'm safely isolated from boys who play with girls' hearts. A wistful smile forces its way through my melancholy mood. The ripples glisten like shards of glass and I am grateful for their commanding beauty in this moment. The lake must have seen a lot in its time and yet it so effortlessly retains a sense of simplicity and innocence: untainted by the ugliness of the human lives it witnesses. I bet the lake would have rolled its eyes at Wes, if it physically had them.

I sense Liam is approaching before I hear his footsteps. He plonks down next to me, takes his glasses out of his pocket and slowly puts them on.

"At least they didn't get into a punch up like they did at the funeral," he says, seeming to be equally entranced by the shimmering patterns on the lake's surface.

"True. Your parents gave us a wide birth."

"Did you go alright with your exams?" he casually enquires.

I inhale deeply. I want to scream at him. *That's* what he wants to talk about? "Spare me. Don't pretend that you care. Can I read the notebook yet? I know you took it."

He shakes his head. "Just let it go, Beatrice. It's done; there's nothing in the notebook that will change anything for you."

"That's a decision that I'm entitled to make for

myself!" I snap.

He hangs his head low. "What did you apply for?" he mumbles into his chest.

"What?" I ask, forever infuriated by his unwillingness to resolve anything.

"At uni."

"Oh." I answer merely to appease him and to finish at least one conversation for once. "Podiatry."

"Podiatry?" He tilts his head back, looking up at the stars. Even his neck has a mesmerising beauty that seems to cast a spell over me and I can't help but stare. "Why?" he laughs.

I reluctantly chuckle along with him. "I have no idea. *That's* why: because I have no idea!"

He smiles to himself, awash with a sense of nostalgia. "That makes two of us."

It's possible that I wasn't the only one who devoted themselves to making sure Eric was excited about his future, so that he would *want* one, at the cost of even contemplating their own.

Liam's gaze affectionately drifts over the lake. I know he would prefer to sit in silence, but I need to talk. He will leave any minute. He will leave me any minute.

I don't recall the last thing I ever said to Eric. I neglected to commit it to memory because I didn't know that they would be the last words that he would ever hear me say. It didn't occur to me that when I said *Happy New Year,* or *good night,* or maybe *see you in the morning,* or *thanks for reading me your new story,* that that would be *it.*

But I do remember the last thing that Eric said to me.

Time for you to sleep. Get some sleep now.

When I went to bed on New Year's Eve, Eric sat at the end of my bed, gleefully telling me about his new story idea. I'd heard so many lately, and they were scaring me. I hadn't been getting more than a couple of hours sleep each night before waking up in a panic. I had even fallen asleep on my dad's lap, right in the middle of the party; rampant with relief that I could finally rest with my dad there to keep me safe from the scary stories.

The fairy didn't die.

The day after the attack, Bogart returned to the sunflower to bask in what he had done, only to find her still breathing, recovering. All her fairy friends were gathered around, tending to her wounds with fairy dust, mending her wings with daisy chains. She couldn't recall what had happened to her: the trauma had blocked her memory. Everyone assumed that a roaming baby crocodile had mistaken her for an insect or a small frog. Enraged, Bogart planned to kill the fairy that night, this time for certain. Leaving the scene before she was well and truly dead was not a blunder that he planned on making twice.

Get some sleep now.

Ironic. Sleep became the one thing I can't get.

Eric had been writing a lot in his notebook in the lead up to his final night as my brother. He had been getting all his bad thoughts out and turned them into tales of mere fantasy. I thought I had managed to delay it, for just a little while longer.

Delay the inevitable.

Desperate to keep talking, words I don't even plan spill out of my mouth. Still, I ready myself for the foreseeable sight of him sauntering off. I don't know how I can get him to stay. "What are you doing now?"

"Podiatry."

We laugh at the exact same instant, together. It might be the best feeling I've ever had.

"Nah, I don't really know either, Beatrice. I want to go somewhere. Somewhere else. Sometimes I think I don't want to *do* anything. I just want to *go*. One day, I think I need to just go. Imagine being somewhere nobody knows you. We can't. You and me, we can't even imagine that."

I don't want to imagine that. I can't think of anything worse.

I hated Liam when we were little kids. Part of me still does. Maybe there's a part of me that always will.

I hated him because I felt like he was trying to take Eric away from me, and deep down I knew that life with my brother was on a time limit. Liam stole some of that precious, invaluable, painfully, unfairly short time. I don't know to forgive that. But I also don't know how I would have coped without him.

In the background, the muffled countdown to New Year's is nearly over.

5! 4! 3! 2! 1! HAPPY NEW YEAR!

Liam's voice is shaky. "Happy New Year, Beatrice."

"Happy New Year, Liam."

He shifts to face me and apprehensively offers me his hand, palm down. My lips release a heavy breath, as if my body is aware that I am about to forget to breathe all together.

I place my trembling hand on top of his and wait in uncertain anticipation. My eyes plead with him to go through with it. He swallows loudly, mentally psyching himself up. The cheers and applause in the distant celebration die down. The world is still and suddenly quiet, for us anyway.

And then he does it: he closes his eyes, pressing out a

defiant tear and delicately turns his palm over to face mine. He opens his eyes and we stare at each other for just a moment, mystified; as if Liam now sees the girl who rode around on a purple scooter and painted rocks, and I see the boy who wore an ALF t-shirt and taught me how to skim stones. The sister and the best friend: two people who could no longer exist after Eric was gone.

But now they are here.

We calmly slide our joined hands apart, click our fingers, slap our knees, click our fingers again, high-five, fist-bump and make an exploding sound as we open our fists like fireworks.

The special handshake.

I have been waiting my whole life.

My eyebrows tense in the middle and I will myself not to cry in front of him. He stands to leave and for once I am grateful. He walks off into the darkness and doesn't look back.

I reach into my pocket and pull out one of Dad's smokes, routinely stolen from his packet. I hold the cigarette loosely between my lips and light it up, mentally willing the tears building up to push through, but they don't.

The thing about life is, it kind of ends every year.

And then it begins again, the very next second. No matter how awful it was.

But only if you're really lucky. We're all so aware of just how lucky we are, because we literally count down the seconds at the end of the year, so grateful that we get more time in this wonderful and horrible life. Because we know that one day, it will end, but not right now. For now, we get to count down.

The years end and then they begin again. It won't always be like that.

The good years, the bad years; they all end.

The years all end.

I guess that's how you know you're *alive*.

New Year's Eve 1998

Well, this will be interesting (and by that, I mean potentially catastrophic): we are next-door neighbours with the Sandersons. It was bound to happen eventually.

Two log cabins, each with its own ambience of peace and tranquillity, housing two families, each with their own complex hatred for the other, separated only by the brand-new Toyota Land Cruiser parked in between them. I guess Mr Sanderson is still enjoying the perks of taking ownership of the car yard. Mrs Sanderson gave him such a good life. I wonder if she enjoys her own at all.

We arrive early in the evening, long after all the other guests have settled in. The lake is already abuzz with the celebration of New Year's Eve. The aroma of the barbecue wafts through the air. Mum and Dad seem self-conscious as we drive up to our cabin, as if they are sneaking in somewhere we are not allowed. Men relaxing behind their fishing rods all look our way. Siblings racing go-karts begrudgingly move over to the gravel, having expected the road to be theirs at this time of the day. An elderly couple reading discreetly peer over the worn pages of their favourite books. Everyone wants to know who is only just arriving *now*. Someone has already put a ghetto blaster under a tree and the vacations of twenty-odd families have already morphed into one.

Mum and Dad have yet to realise who our immediate neighbours are and I'm not going to point it out to them. I haven't technically seen the Sandersons but my bedroom is directly opposite Liam's. His glasses are hooked over the bottom of the open window, as if purposefully left there like some sort of signal. He must be out with his family. If he was out on his own, he would have packed them in his pocket, or even worn them.

He wants me to know what cabin he is staying in: he has left the window open, wide open, so that I can see right into his room. So that I can see his bedside cupboard, and Eric's notebook on top of it.

I have to get in there. And now seems like the perfect time because the Sandersons are out, most likely at the barbecue. Frustratingly, both our bedrooms have crank windows and there's no way I could squeeze my body through the opening. I could easily use the front sliding door, assuming it's unlocked, but there are too many people around. Getting into their empty cabin *now* seems depressingly impossible.

Liam just wants to taunt me.

We left much later in the day this year because Dad was waiting for someone to collect his guitar. He advertised his Gibson 500 in the Trading Post, even though the story of how he came to acquire it is the stuff of legend in my family. Just before Eric and I were born, Dad met the band members of Cold Chisel backstage after one of their concerts. The guitarist let him have a hold of his Gibson 500, and

Dad astonished him with his own jamming skills, so much so that the band member signed the guitar and gifted it to him right there and then. Dad has told us the story so many times. But Mum and Dad couldn't afford the cabin fees this year, and even though I voted to skip the lake for just one New Year's, he sold the guitar instead.

"I'm perfectly fine if we just stay home," I reassured him.

My uni books were so expensive. Dad had an operation on his knee. Mum had to give up her job at the dry cleaner's so she could go down to my grandparent's house every day because they were getting old and needed help. A few times, I'd spied a ripped up letter in the bin, but I was able to figure out it was a final notice for something. No matter how hard Mum and Dad try, and they do try, so hard, life never lets them win.

"It's tradition, Bea," Dad insisted. "Traditions remember who you were, enable who you are, and shape who you'll become."

After a drawn-out wait, the buyer finally got to our

house around 11.30am, to take away a prized possession that my father truly loved. Dad handed over the guitar in exchange for a thick wad of notes, and then excused himself and sat in his shed for a little while.

When we packed up the car and drove to the lake shortly after, Dad played the Willy Nelson tape for the first time in five years and cranked On the Road Again as loud as the dial would allow. Mum sobbed in the front seat; no doubt overcome with grief for another time. She rested her hand on Dad's thigh and he drove with one hand on the steering wheel, just so that he could hold onto her as well. Mum cried herself dry while Dad bellowed the lyrics and radiated with pride that he had made it happen: he was taking his family to the lake. I don't really understand how that must have felt for him, but when I started singing along too, something in his voice changed.

He loved that guitar. He loves our family more.

I hope he and Mum can go grocery shopping with the leftover money and buy all the things they always want for themselves, but never get. Mum doesn't even get the home brand coffee now. She doesn't buy coffee at all these days.

Willy Nelson's raspy voice was a painful comfort; a heartbreaking reassurance that somehow life really does just go on, remembering who you are when you've forgotten yourself. I didn't realise how much I had missed those songs; songs I wasn't even aware that I actually liked, and the sound of his voice. I felt them both in my veins. An inherent knowledge of every beat and every lyric somehow made everything seem okay again. Made *me* feel okay again. A gentle smile settled on my lips as I kept an eye out for koalas. The country melodies captured in the ribbon of a cassette tape had brought me back to myself.

A knock on the cabin's front door lures me out of my room.

Dad slides the glass panel open and Mindy steps inside without being asked.

Her whole face beams. "I knew it was you guys!"

Mum puts down the cup of coffee that she was *really*

enjoying and greets Mindy with a strangely heartfelt embrace. "Good to see you, darling. It's been a while!"

"What are you up to now?" Dad actually sounds interested.

"I'm just being a sticky beak, really. I was wondering where you guys were. We don't come up every year like you do, so it felt kind of weird when I couldn't see any sign of you. I got a bit excited when I saw a late arrival!"

Dad nods to himself and smiles warmly. "We just had some business to take care of before we could leave, that's all. I meant what have you been up to since school finished?"

Mindy chuckles sheepishly. "Oh! I'm just at uni, fumbling my way through medicine. I had planned on doing nursing but somehow managed to get enough points to get into medicine. I'm mainly at the city campus. It's, um, different to school, that's for sure."

"In high school you're the big fish in the little pond,

but then all of a sudden you're the little fish in the big pond," Dad articulates in true fatherly fashion.

"Yeah, that's it, exactly!" Mindy sighs.

I find it hard to believe that Mindy didn't flourish with perfect ease in her transition from high school to university. I bet she's Vice President of the Young Liberals on campus, or co-ordinated the protests against inadequate funding for community radio. I bet she hangs out on the lawns with the philosophy students playing hacky sack and goes to the Uni Bar on Friday nights with her boyfriend, who's naturally in his third year of Law, and thanks to the generational wealth behind him, is minus the HECs debt that burdens every one of his peers. *Different to school*, yeah right. Everything always works out for her.

Mindy did a good job of growing up: her prettiness has smoothly ripened into sheer beauty. She is petite and aesthetically, well, perfect. Her iconic childhood plats have matured into a slick, darker blonde ponytail. She has nice clothes; a floral red dress that swings above her knees, as featured in the most current Myer catalogue. I subtly run my hand over my baggy black jeans and loose-fitting t-shirt, feeling unbecoming and masculine in comparison.

Mindy must have heard my thoughts.

"I'll find my feet, I always do! Anyway, um, I was just wondering if you guys are coming out to join everyone? My boyfriend came up with us this year and we're hanging out with some new friends. I'd love for Bea to meet Felix."

"Felix?" Mum and Dad repeat simultaneously.

"My boyfriend, Felix. Can Bea hang out with us tonight?"

Thank God my parents will say no.

"Sure, Bea would love that," Dad answers. "We'll be out in a few minutes."

"Awesome! We'll be down by the jetty when she's ready!"

I hide my annoyance with a tight-lipped smile and wave half-heartedly as Mindy excitedly rushes out the door.

"You've got to be kidding me!" I grumble. "Thanks a lot! Do I make plans for you on your behalf?"

Mum wraps her arms around me. "Don't wander off too far."

"I don't want to hang out with Mindy and *Felix!* Seriously? Is he named after the family cat?"

Dad chuckles and Mum scolds him with her eyes.

"He could be a very nice young man," she reasons, "and it's important that you put yourself out there a little bit more."

If only they knew how much I have put myself out there. "What, now that *you're* okay with it?"

Mum shakes her head sadly. "I'll never be okay with anything, Bea but I need you to be."

Guilt saturates my conscience. "I didn't mean it like that, Mum. I'll hang out with Mindy, okay?"

The tables turned once I started uni. Mum and Dad made a concentrated effort to give me more freedom. They drove me to my lectures and seminars but encouraged me to soak up the culture of campus life, as if everything was okay now that I had reached adulthood. Apparently only in the throes of puberty could someone possibly make that catastrophic decision to end their life.

Whatever Mum and Dad were afraid would happen to me, substantially subsided after I finished school. They encouraged me to meet new people and even said I could go out at night with a curfew of 11pm. I haven't yet, as far as they are concerned. I prefer to sneak out of my bedroom window and come and go as I please. I like to be in control of that.

"We're trying, honey," Mum says softly. "We just want to protect you. It's been a process, letting go of the constant worry that something could happen."

Ebony's life became pretty busy after she was accepted into the police force. She moved into a share house with a couple of other recruits and seems to be doing really well. We call each other up every now and again but she's on a rotating roster and really keen on her new friends. Every time she calls, which isn't often, it's that little bit more strained, as if we are becoming strangers. We've only managed to catch up in person once this year and even though our lives have both been overwhelmed with new experiences to report, we had nothing to say to each other. I guess our convenient friendship wore out its convenience.

I see Pippa around sometimes; she went to Uni SA too but she must be about ready to graduate soon, depending on what degree she is doing of course. For the most part, our lectures are in different buildings but every now and again we'll walk past each other and just kind of nod out of obligation, but I can see that look of recognition petering out too eventually. If we were to see each other at the shops in five years, I doubt we would even bother to exchange smiles. I've noticed her out at the clubs a couple of times but it's just like when we were in school; we act as if we have never seen each other before.

I wonder if she's moved out of home yet. She was never happy after her Mum remarried. She wouldn't wonder anything about me. She wouldn't know what to wonder about. She never even knew me.

Cat works at the front desk at her mother's highly in-demand, upmarket interior design company. She makes a contractual appearance for a few hours and then goes home to her rent-free three-bedroom apartment in the East End, thanks to Mummy and Daddy's perpetually generous financial aid. As far as I'm aware, she never auditioned to be in a band or wrote any songs, but she has hooked up with a few musicians.

Cat picks me up on Saturday nights, around the corner from my house. She always pays for my ticket into the club and shouts rounds for us and random friends we make on the night. Cat gets her purse out a lot and I shouldn't let her really, but I know it's just what she wants, or needs, to do. She bought the Hungry Jacks and these days she buys my ticket, as if my friendship requires weekly payment. She doesn't need to; I like her without the perks. It's like she's paranoid about *me* leaving *her*. It feels wrong to say, but that makes me feel good. Maybe that's why out of everyone else in my life, Cat's friendship is the one I value. She needs me, and I need her to need me.

Cat wants me to move in with her. I wonder how my parents would feel about that, if I ever asked them. I do like it at her apartment. We sometimes hang out there, just the two of us. Jewel plays on repeat whilst we sit outside on the third storey of the fire escape, sharing a smoke before we hit the club to dance until our blistered heels insist that we call it a night.

Next to me, Cat is skeletal. She lives on carrot and celery sticks and 'treats' herself to a proper meal once or twice a week. She drinks too much when we go out, but I always make sure she is okay. At the end of the night, I smooth a cleansing wipe over her sleepy face and help her into her king-sized bed, with those slippery, pink satin sheets that I hate. The bottom one bunches up when I swing her legs up onto the mattress.

"They're salmon, actually," she'll drowsily correct me. "And Mummy assures me that they're on trend. And that makes her happy, if even my goddamn sheets are a fashion statement."

"They're pink," I always insist, stroking her forehead as a timely snore omits from her grotesquely ungraceful widened mouth, "and they're awful. They belong on the set of a 1970's porno, much like your whole look. Which I love by the way. I love everything about you."

I sometimes sit on the edge of her bed for a brief moment, envious of her ability to slumber so peacefully. I check twice that all her doors are locked and taxi home before my parents wake up for the day.

I like being Cat's friend. I like the way it makes me feel. I like saving her from herself.

I judged Cat before I knew who she really was. I dismissed her as a spoiled, entitled rich girl whose biggest dilemma would be choosing from the entourage of loaded bachelors who would inevitably call for her, honoured to keep her in the opulent lifestyle she was accustomed to. I scoffed that she had nothing to rebel against, completely overlooking the reason behind her insatiable need to buy people's attention, and love: because that was the only way they were ever given to her. She got every*thing* that she wanted, but what she needed and wanted weren't *things.* Now she looks everywhere for something she can't find; in random hook-ups and with a Louis Vuitton purse that's open to everyone, with an obvious eating disorder feeding the emptiness she feels inside.

Cat's apartment is awash with eclectic décor. Hand-painted portraits of Frida Kohl adorn the lounge room walls. Floor lamps with white, fluffy shades, coffee table books about Dior and circular rugs with beaded tassels create a strategic illusion of cultured personal style, yet she chose none of it for herself.

I barely lasted one semester of Podiatry. I changed over to a Bachelor of Science but then switched to a Bachelor of Arts, which basically just feels like an amalgamation of high school subjects disguised as a uni degree. I've endured subjects called things like Film, Feminism and Psychoanalysis, and Justice, Law and the State, and I wouldn't be able to say what any of them were actually about. I sit in the lectures bored out of my mind, incapable of retaining any of the knowledge I am acquiring a lifelong debt to learn. I recite Eric's stories in my head to keep myself from falling asleep, or mentally pick what board game to play with Mum and Dad that night. Then I envision the darkened neighbourhood streets, comforted in the fact that I can aimlessly wander them for as long as I need that night.

I have no direction, no plans, no interest and no idea.

And what scares me the most, is the possibility that this is exactly what Eric felt like.

Mum and Dad kept me in a bubble for the duration of my high school years, almost as if they were just waiting it out, wishing that stage of my life to go by quickly. Maybe so that whatever snapped in Eric's mind, wouldn't snap in mine too. Maybe they just attributed it to his age and now that my teenage years are basically over, they think it's finally safe to pop the bubble.

But I don't.

I'm scared for myself.

I walk the streets in the middle of the night, lost, wondering what the difference between my brother and I really is. It can't just be our age. I get up in the middle of the night to go for a walk, maybe just the same as he did that one time, but I always go home. It terrifies me to think that one night, I won't. Just like Eric.

I think Mum and Dad feel secure now, as if I've proven to them that I'm okay. I'm further from okay than I've ever been, yet they think they can let me go now. I'm not ready for them to let me go.

I need to go for my walks, and then I need to go home. Because Eric never got to. And he should have. He would have, if it weren't for me.

I freshen up in my room in preparation for my evening of forced socialising with Mindy and her darling new boyfriend, *Felix*. Mum and Dad are chatting in the kitchen. I change into a flowy maxi skirt and a cream-coloured turtle-neck jumper, even though the heat from the day has yet to subside. I apply a tan lipstick and brush my long straight hair forward over my shoulders. No matter how nice I try to make her look, the fat and frumpy girl in the mirror always stares back at me with deflated confidence.

Mindy is a perfectly nice person, but I hate her. I hated her when we were 17 and the school voted her Head Prefect. I hated her when we were 16 and she invited me to sit with her and her friends on New Year's, and I met Wes. I hated her when we were 15 and she got the trophy for Most Valuable Player in netball, even though I wasn't on the team, so it didn't actually have anything to do with me. I especially hated her when we were 7 and she ate all the pink marshmallows and played with Gilbert. We were the same, her and I. But I was trying to keep my brother from killing himself and she had the luxury of being just like everyone else. She had the luxury of being a child, a teenager and now whoever the hell she wants to be, not who her fucked up past made her become.

I look over to the wardrobe in the corner of the room. It doesn't go all the way up to the ceiling. I'm warmed by the sentimental memory of being ensconced atop a wardrobe in a cabin just like this, many years ago now, when my young mind was so completely consumed by thoughts of Eric; was he acting weird, was he saying bad things, was today going to be the day that those bad things became bad actions, that mere stories became reality. Truly, only in the pages of books, was I ever able to escape the terror I suppressed every single day and let my mind be still. I could live in fictional worlds, instead of the real world where the life of my brother rested solely on my shoulders.

Solace.

The onerous duty of keeping Eric from harming himself trapped me in a relentless cycle of exhaustion. Even when Liam took him away to hang out just the two of them, or when Mum took him to piano practice or Dad took him to tutoring, I just lived on pause, waiting for Eric to come back. Trying to help someone you love outrun death while they secretly taunt and egg it on, depletes you. Mentally, physically. I ran the marathon for so long and now I am incapable of catching my breath.

I might climb to the top of the wardrobe when I get back later and read my book up there. That's the magic of this place; here, life feels simple again, unburdened. The lake strips everything else away, all the stress, trauma, big decisions, small dramas, and all that's left is who you are. I guess sometimes though, that's not necessarily a good thing.

Out in the kitchen, Dad drapes his arm around my shoulders. "You look beautiful, Bea."

I tuck myself under his chin. "Thanks for getting us here this year, Dad. I'm glad we came."

Mum tilts her head, seeming to be proud; I'm not sure if of me or of her husband.

Dad squeezes me harder. "Let's have some fun tonight. It's been a bit of a shit year."

Mum's embrace engulfs us both. "We're so proud of you, Bea. We should tell you that more. University is a whole new world. And we want you to see that it's okay to enjoy it."

"I know, Mum. I don't make friends easily."

Dad laughs softly. "You never did. You only ever wanted to follow your brother around."

Because he was my responsibility. Because I knew he wanted to kill himself. Because I knew that one day he would. I had to make sure that everyone thought he was amazing and would achieve so much, so that he would believe it too and not give up. Because I had to make sure that you both thought he was okay. Because I needed to be with him all the time, so he couldn't shatter our family into a million pieces by leaving us and then we would never be whole again. It wasn't a spur of the moment decision, Mum and Dad. He had been planning it for years, for my whole life. I thought if I had a real friend, maybe he would think I was fine on my own, without him. And I wasn't. I'm not.

"Yeah," I merely agree, "I know. He was worth following around."

Mum swiftly directs the conversation away from Eric. "You don't seem to hear from Ebony much these days. Everything okay there? I know you said you thought you were growing apart."

"She's just really busy with the police force now, and really in with that crowd."

"Some people are seasonal, not everyone stays in your life when the weather changes." Dad loves his little pearls of wisdom.

I hope Ebony has the best life, exactly the way she

plans it. I'm grateful that she was a part of mine. Dad is probably right; not everyone stays in your life forever. But maybe a little imprint of them does. *Books let you have a different life.*

A look of worry flashes over Mum's face. I know she liked Ebony. Well, maybe not her personally, but just the fact that I had a friend. It was a reassurance for her, maybe even a validation of sorts that I was normal. I can't tell my parents the specifics of my friendship with Cat but I think it might please them to know that I'm not regressing back to the socially-stunted child who could never make any friends. Little do they know, I actually could have, if I wanted to.

"I have some of my seminars with this girl, Cat. She's really nice, you'd like her. We hang out a bit sometimes."

Mum perks up. "Cat? I like the sound of her! Is it Cat for Catherine? Kathleen? Catarina?"

"Natalie, actually. She calls herself Cat because her Mum wouldn't let her get a cat when she was younger, something about not wanting it to put scratches on the furniture." I decide to test the waters. "She lives in an apartment near the East End markets, on her own."

Mum and Dad exchange anxious glances. I knew they weren't ready for that.

"That's nice, dear, for *her*."

It's okay, Mum; I'm not ready for that, either. We're all emotionally screwed.

"We'll have to have her over for your ma's famous spaghetti bolognaise!" Dad enthuses.

"I'd like that, I'd like you to know her," I return his enthusiasm. I'll have to remember to tell Cat that she goes to uni with me.

Stepping out of our cabin, the festive atmosphere of the lake sweeps up my parents. Dad twirls Mum under his arm and they groove their way over to a few familiar faces by the barbecue. I fill my plate with a sausage and salad and remind them that I'll be near the jetty with Mindy and *Felix*.

Mum kisses my cheek. "I'll try not to watch you like

a hawk but I'll likely fail."

I roll my eyes, pretending to be annoyed.

It is already quite dark as I cradle my full paper plate in both hands and head down to the lake, but Mindy's blonde hair is luminescent under the jetty lights and it guides me over.

I sit myself down on the edge of the pier, next to Mindy, who is dangling her lithe legs over the side. A group of her new and old friends sit shoulder to shoulder, all enjoying their barbecue meal from the plates resting on their knees.

Mindy leans forward so everyone can see her. "Guys, this is Bea." She turns to me and points to everyone in time. "And that's Felix, Lily, Mel, Rosie and Nathan."

They all wave and say *hi* in unison.

I smile *hi* in return.

We clear our plates as we exchange mundane information about where we're all from and what we're going to do with the rest of our lives. Felix literally *is* a law student; I clasp my tongue between my teeth to stop myself from sniggering. Lily is from Queensland; she's about to start Year 12 and wants to be a teacher. Mel is from Adelaide too and is taking a gap year to travel Europe with the money she saved up from working at KFC. Rosie is only fifteen and apparently has the worst parents in the world because they won't let her start dating yet. She wants to be a model. Nathan is cute; nineteen, studying journalism. But I'm wary of cute boys at the lake.

Why is it so easy for them? We're all kind of in the same stage of life; how can they have everything figured out already? My eleven-year-old self was a stranger to the girl I was when I turned sixteen, and I'm sure that eighteen-year-old me will be a stranger to thirty-year-old me. So how is *she* meant to decide the life of *her*? I feel like everyone else just gets it, understands the way it all works. I don't understand anything. I think I really missed the point somewhere along the line.

I listen without interest, adding the occasional *wow,*

okay and gentle nod of my head to make it seem like I care. But I don't, at all. How many people are we expected to remember throughout the whole of our life? The more people I meet, the less memory I'll have left to remember the only person I care about forgetting.

The level of indifference I feel about what these people's names are and what they want to do with the rest of their lives could categorise me as a psychopath. All I care about is sneaking into the Sanderson's cabin while I've got the chance, to get my brother's stories once and for all.

I excuse myself from their little get-together before I've even swallowed the last mouthful of my dinner.

"It was nice meeting everyone. I promised my parents I'd catch up with some of their old friends, so I'll see you guys around."

Mindy looks disappointed. I don't get why.

I chuck my plate in the bin by the barbecue and tell Mum that I'm going to go back to the cabin to read.

"Okay, darling, we won't be long behind you." She is

holding a glass of champagne. I don't think I've seen her or Dad drink alcohol since Eric. They seem really relaxed tonight. Dare I say, happy.

On the other side of the festive gathering, Mr and Mrs Sanderson sit on deck chairs facing another couple whom I've never seen before. Mrs Sanderson looks as skinny as ever, and tired. I suspect her hair started to grey against her wishes because it is dyed now, but noticeably a few shades darker than her natural colour which merely highlights how gaunt her face is. Mr Sanderson glances over to Dad while bragging intentionally loudly about the new shares he bought on the stock market. Dad has yet to give him the attention he is so obviously hoping to grab.

As I approach our cabin, I look to see if anyone is around before letting myself in to the Sanderson's instead. No one locks their doors here. They even left the kitchen light on for me.

The layout is a mirror image of our own cabin. I step into the conjoined lounge and dining area, walk through the kitchen and warily push open the bedroom door on the right, the one that my bedroom looks into. Liam's lamp is switched on. Eric's notebook is directly beneath it, as if purposefully left out for me. *Why is it suddenly so easy?*

I enter Liam's room, leaving the door ajar behind me and cautiously walk up to the cupboard on which my beloved brother's well-worn notebook rests. His dreams and nightmares: immortalised.

I am about to be reunited with the fairy and the murderous goblin who haunted my dreams.

But it's the stories Eric never got a chance to tell me that I really want.

I urge myself to quickly grab the notebook and run, but I can't shake the feeling that I'm being set up. I've been lured here.

He wanted me to come.

He wants to see me.

I turn around swiftly, realising that Liam is behind me. I want to scream at him for startling me, but I'm the one who kind of broke into his family's cabin so I guess my accusation wouldn't really be valid. He is wearing his glasses; the same ones that told me this was his room when they were left hanging over the bottom of the window frame.

"I knew you'd come," he says smugly.

"Are you giving me Eric's notebook?"

"No. But I'm offering to read it with you, if you want. You shouldn't read it on your own."

I tsk loudly. "I'm not a baby. I'm aware of what was going on, just as much as you were."

"Maybe. Maybe not. We were both kids, trying to make sense of things kids shouldn't have to. We're not little kids anymore," Liam hesitates, uncharacteristically uncertain, "so I thought maybe we could try to make sense of it all together."

I sit down on the edge of his bed, resentful that he so arrogantly feels that he has some sort of power over me. Or responsibility for me. "I can just pick it up and leave right now. You wouldn't be able to stop me."

He sits down right next to me, his bare knee resting

against my skirt. We've never been on a bed together before. My stomach knots.

"I could tackle you, actually. You wouldn't get very far."

I laugh, in spite in myself. "I weigh more than you."

Liam must still be playing footy. His black short sleeved shirt emphasises his defined arms and his linen tan shorts tighten against his hard thighs. He smells different, like he wears cologne nowadays. His hair is more styled, trimmed close to his ears with a floppy quiff. He looks properly grown-up. A man.

He responds to my self-critical remark with a pensive glance around the room, as if searching for the safest words to say. "I wanted to see you. That's why I showed you where we were, not that I realised you would be right next door, of course. I thought maybe you'd just see my glasses on your walk past to the lake. It's just, I wanted to tell you something."

"I'm listening," I reply, full of ostentatious confidence.

"I was always jealous of you. I mean, that's not the

thing that I want to tell you. But I was."

I'm completely stumped. "Jealous of me? He chose you. He was just stuck with me. I was always jealous of you, because you were his best friend."

Liam absorbs my words. "I was always jealous of you, because you were his sister. You were the one who really mattered to him, when sometimes nothing seemed to matter much to him at all. It's important that you know that. When we read his notebook together, remember that he really did love you. I was so jealous of your relationship. I mean, not that I would want you as my sister, you're pretty annoying. And then I'd never be able to kiss you."

Shock renders me linguistically simple. "Huh?"

Liam takes off his glasses and puts them in his pocket. "I'm not going to be here next year, like here, at the lake, I mean. That's why I wanted to see you. That's what I wanted to tell you."

If I could bottle our brief moment together every New Year's, I would drink from it during the year like it was a medicine, prescribed to keep me from losing myself completely. "Why?"

"I'm moving to Melbourne with my girlfriend. She's studying psychology and wants to transfer, that's where she's from. I can finish my apprenticeship there. I just wanted you to know, I don't know, in case like you looked for me or something, like I always look for you."

"Oh." My heart beats rapidly, starving my body of oxygen and inducing an instant headache. *Don't leave me.*

"I made you something, it's stupid, really." He opens his palm to reveal a small rock, painted like a ladybug. "I picked the rock from here, right by the lake. I painted it for you. Just a nice memory we share, I guess. Look, I even did nine little spots. Remember?"

My eyes dart back and forth to my trembling hand, now holding the gift that Liam made for me, and my knees. I can't slow things down. I can't make him stay with me. We saved so many ladybugs. We didn't save Eric.

"That's actually one of my most favourite memories, Beatrice. And it's not just mine. We share it. We share that exact same memory. That's pretty special. Did you know that a group of ladybugs is called a loveliness? That's pretty lovely, hey?"

His smile kills me.

I wish he'd stop talking.

"I feel bad that Mum will have to deal with Harold on her own, but she's the one who married him because she was scared to raise me alone. She doesn't even like him." His voice is so far away now, muffled in the distance. "That's why I thought maybe tonight we could read through everything together. The stories aren't what you think they are, Beatrice. It's not the way you remember it, the way you forced yourself to remember it. We need to see that together. Get some closure before we move on to a new stage in our lives."

I concentrate on the cream-painted wall opposite me, mentally reassuring myself that I really can breathe, despite the building pressure in my chest. I need Liam to know that I understand him, that I figured him out. I need to get him to stay. With me. That's when I realise: I can.

"No one is better than you." I blurt the words out so fast they barely even sound like an actual sentence. "Mr Sanderson made the choice to leave his wife and son. You don't need to compare yourself to Daniel, or to make up for something or someone your step-father lost because of his own decision."

Liam shifts his whole body to face me. He seems amused. "What on earth are you on about?"

"Your dad's ex-wife, and their son, Daniel."

"My dad died when I was five."

My lack of sensitivity shames me. "Sorry. I meant your step-dad, Mr Sanderson."

"Harold's an asshole. Everyone knows that. I've never thought of him as my step-dad, let alone my dad, and he's never thought of me as his son. He's just my mum's husband. Why are you going on about his ex-wife and child? They're absolutely no relation to me."

"I know, but it must have hurt. All those little comments and digs. Mr Sanderson wanted you to be tough and athletic, like his real son."

Liam looks to the ceiling, exasperated. "What the fuck, Beatrice," he mumbles to himself before settling his eyes back on me. "So what? Everyone has things in their life that shape who they are. Harold said it a lot to me over the years. Daniel would have kicked the winning goal. Daniel wouldn't waste his time on those silly drawings. I don't give a shit what he thinks of me. I bet you a million dollars Daniel doesn't either. I determine who I turn out to be. Nobody else."

Every capillary in my face ruptures. "I just thought I could help you understand what was wrong is all."

"Beatrice, there's nothing wrong with me. I don't need you to fix me. Or help me. Or save me. Fuck's sake," he laughs, "what did you hire a private investigator or something?"

I bury my chin deeper into my turtle neck, wishing it would creep up over my face and swallow me whole. I feel like a child, scolded by a sensible adult for being so ridiculous. "I just wanted to make sense of someone, I guess. I didn't do so good at that in the past. I just wanted to understand you. Maybe then you would be okay."

Liam rubs his temples with his thumbs, releasing a contemplative sigh that's almost a groan. "Everything *is* okay. Every*one* is okay, okay? Sometimes people leave because they love you, not because they don't."

I can merely whimper. "I don't understand. I don't understand anything."

"Look," he says softly, "have you got a mobile phone yet? We can swap numbers. There's a lot we can figure out together. I'm moving at the end of next week but we can stay in touch."

My mouth is so dry and the room is so cramped. I can't blink because that will push out the tears welling behind my eyes. I feel like I'm about to pass out, possibly even die. I've got just enough oxygen left to speak one final time, and I squander it so foolishly.

"Don't go! Don't move. Stay here. Please. With me. Stay with me, Liam. Choose me. We can make a life together. I think I'm in love with you. No, I am. I know it. I'm in love with you."

Fuck.

I hastily tuck the ladybug rock in my pocket and stand abruptly.

I have to get out of here. My nine years aren't up yet.

I scoop Eric's notebook and bolt for the door.

"Jesus, Beatrice!" Liam calls after me.

Darting out of the cabin, I frenziedly gulp the fresh night air, swallowing it deep down into my lungs. That, and the confrontational sight of my father and Mr Sanderson throwing punches at each other on the grass below, snap me alive.

Dad's voice booms across the trees. "Don't you dare speak about our boy! You have no fucking idea what we did to keep him here!"

Mr Sanderson lunges at him, wrapping his arms around Dad's wide waist and bowling him to the ground. His bulky build is much stronger than Dad's relaxed physique and he pins him down with ease.

"Why would you want to? That kid was seriously messed up!" Mr Sanderson sniggers in his face, staring down at him. "He did the world a favour. And you never accepted me. You hated me from day one. You never even gave me a chance because you lost your precious little friend and then I came on the scene. He and Eric were both weak!"

Dad pries an arm free and pushes up on Mr Sanderson's shoulder, before a raised fist comes slamming down onto my father's cheek.

"Dad!" I scream, dropping the notebook. I rush to the quarrel and leap onto Mr Sanderson, smacking him repeatedly on the back of his head. He jolts to the side and I tumble onto the ground next to my father.

Mum frantically runs up from the lake, two steps ahead of the whole party who have been alerted to the ruckus.

For the first time in her whole life, Mum is truly

angry.

She stops directly in front of Mr Sanderson and glares into his enraged eyes. "Back off, Harold!" Her tone is intimidating even to him.

Mr Sanderson smirks. "Put your head back in the fucking sand like you always do."

Her feminine hands land roughly on his chest. "I said back the fuck off!"

Mr Sanderson sneers, taking a generous step back from Mum. "You're all psychotic! Fucking psychos, the whole lot of ya!"

Mrs Sanderson smooths her hand over his shoulder, gently brushing off the dirt. "It's okay, honey, let's go."

Mr Sanderson pushes her hand away as if swatting a fly and storms off to their cabin. She self-consciously tucks her vibrantly tinted hair behind her ear, a fleeting look of apology crossing her face, then dutifully follows after him. Mum watches her leave, somewhat reflectively, before addressing the crowd behind us.

"Happy New Year, folks!"

Laughter, applause and cheer emit from the intrigued, slightly inebriated group of campers. Mum offers her hands, pulling Dad and I up from the ground.

"Bed time," she sternly advises.

Mum hates making a scene. She hates our family being considered entertainment. She will want to leave first thing in the morning.

Tucked up in bed (because Mum literally tucked me in tonight), I listen to hear the atmosphere of the party die down after the countdown and then get dressed again, unable to shift my stare from the ladybug rock sitting on my bedside cupboard. Liam made a tactile representation of one of my most vivid memories of my brother, and of the three of us together. I simultaneously love it and hate it. It's painful to look at, but it's a pain that feels almost comforting.

It's also a physical reminder that maybe it's not such a bad thing that I'll never see Liam again, since I completely humiliated myself in front of him.

Mum and Dad are sound asleep. I don't even try to be quiet when I let myself out the sliding door at the front of the cabin.

The lake is aglow with moonlit ripples. I sit myself under a tree and watch them intently, bewitched. I bring my knees to my chest to keep my body warmth close, necessary now that the midnight air has turned to cool. I take out a cigarette, tucked into the waistband of my skirt and inhale deeply, releasing the smoke especially slowly. It registers in my brain that I have unknowingly put myself right next to the tree that claimed my brother. *Nature's Ladder.*

Dad sits down next to me, strangely ignoring the fact that I am puffing on one of his cigarettes, and lights his own. Thank God he put his dressing gown on; I'm pretty sure he sleeps in his boxers.

"What did you mean by that, Dad? What did you do to keep him here?"

"Your brother wasn't well, Bea. We tried to help him, and to keep you safe. But we just couldn't save him."

All this time, I genuinely thought they didn't know what really went on in Eric's mind. I was the one who was responsible for him, *wasn't I?*

"How did you try to help, like I mean, how could anyone help?"

"Eric never played the piano. Mum took him to see his psychologist then. I never took him to tutoring. That was the psychiatrist day. There were so many appointments, so many drug trials, so many professionals, so many diagnoses. Your mother and I were mentally, physically and financially depleted. We lived on payment plans. Arrangements. IOUs. We're still climbing out of that hole but by God we would go right down to the bottom again if it meant he was still here with us. Maybe we needed just one more professional in the mix. Just one different medication. We will never know. It didn't work and I will never understand why and always wish I had done more. Even though I feel like I did everything I possibly could, to the point of getting him a damn dog, *everything* will never feel like *enough*. There is nothing more important in this life than your family,

Bea. And no matter what anyone else thinks of us, we are perfect."

"My brother wasn't. I wanted you to think your son was."

Dad nods, sorrowfully. "He was perfect too, Bea. His mind just didn't know to cope, so it made up a way. We didn't want you to be aware of it."

I mirror his contemplative nod. "I didn't want you to be either. I thought I was keeping everything together."

Dad drapes his arm over the back of my shoulders. "That was our job."

It was mine. And I found him, hanging. I couldn't scream. I had failed him. I was meant to make him stay. But I found him. Did I see his toes move? I froze. I don't know how long for. Too long? Long enough to make a difference? And then Mum screamed.

He squeezes his embrace tighter and I let my head fall onto his chest; that special place where I am protected, loved, secure. Safe. I inhale his scent, awash with gratitude that I get to call this incredible human being my father.

We watch the lake in silence, taunted by the leaves rustling in the tree next to us. But maybe they rustle to comfort me, not to scare me. Dad doesn't even realise why this particular tree is evil. I guess we would all remember different details about that day. I guess we would all remember different details about Eric, and how we managed what was going on.

When we read his notebook together, remember that he really did love you. The stories aren't what you think they are. I'm beginning to think that I don't remember my own life correctly.

I take another drag of my cigarette and butt it on the dirt next to me. Dad does the same and then kisses me goodnight.

"Don't tell your mother."

Part Three

New Year's Eve 1999

Don't tell your mother, he'd told me.

All year, that's played on my mind. At the time, Dad's revelations about Eric induced a cathartic sense of closure; a shaky voice had finally been given to the words everyone around me had always been so reticent to speak. When Dad casually wrapped up our life-altering conversation with a neat, seemingly trivial sentence and trotted back to bed, I had assumed that my dressing gown-clad father was simply urging me not to rat on him for letting me smoke.

Oh, how a moment can change the more you analyse it. There's only so much analysing you can do before it morphs into sheer distortion.

He didn't even ask why I was sitting by the lake in the middle of the night.

Don't tell your mother…that I know all about your mindless midnight walks. Don't tell your mother…that we sat underneath the tree that Eric hung himself from. Don't tell your mother…that we talked about him, about things you're not meant to know, and about things you thought we didn't know.

Don't tell your mother…that we know you twisted the stories that Eric came up with. Made everyone around him think that he was a writer and not a monster who just enjoyed thinking about people getting hurt. I created the illusion that Eric was okay. Normal. If there were doctors involved, if Mum and Dad were trying to help him, did the stories that Liam and I developed from Eric's disturbed ideas instead make something worse? *His mind just didn't know how to cope.* With what?

Every single possible answer merely breeds a new question.

I wanted to ask Dad as soon as we woke up that morning, but it already felt too late. Now here I am a whole year later, packing the car to go back to the lake, still fixating on an ostensibly meaningless sentence, that I've turned into a triple entendre laced with philosophical undertones. As if four words could ever change anything, let alone everything. It feels like I'm always looking, searching, hoping for that one thing that will eradicate the guilt and responsibility I feel over Eric's death, and everything that lead him to the point of finally surrendering to it. But mostly, I'm just looking for an answer as to why. Living with why tortures your soul. *Why why why.* I walk through life desperate to know why. I walk through the night desperate to know why.

I've mentally replayed Dad's conversation so many times but it just grows in vagueness. He spoke about psychologists and professionals, drug trials and diagnoses. Diagnoses of what? Psychologists to treat what? How did Mum and Dad even know something was wrong? I covered up his sadistic stories, I created happy endings. On the surface, as far as anyone should have been able to tell, Eric was fine. I made sure of that.

Once on the drive down to my grandparent's house, we passed a cat lying on the side of the road; the life knocked out of it by one of the many cars that sped along the main road. I begged Mum to stop so we could see if it was wearing a name tag, but the traffic was too heavy for her to pull over. I tried not to, but I cried quietly the rest of the way there.

While Mum helped Nanna with some chores, Eric jumped into big brother mode and tried to cheer me up with a new story he'd just thought of, called *Vengeance Purrs*.

"Bea, the ghost of the cat haunted the driver of the car that killed him. He scratched the man's eyes out and watched with smug pride while the blind, defenceless man desperately crawled around, screaming out for help. Blood and mucus wept from his eye sockets. Anyone could do that to someone for real. It would be so easy."

I thanked Eric for making me feel better with his story, which made him feel good but in reality, I was too scared to sleep that night. By the end of the week, my teacher had sent home yet another note to my parents about my inability to control my emotions, considering my latest outburst to be "disproportionate to the incident" after I scraped my knee in P.E.

I knew I had to fix Eric again, so I came up with a new story about a cat who got hit by a car but he didn't die because he had nine lives, and he devoted the rest of his eight lives to ensuring that all the other cats in the world knew not to get too close to the traffic. Liam loved illustrating that one, and Eric loved coming up with the names of the characters and arguing with Liam about what colour the cat should be.

Mindy didn't like Eric, not that she ever said so. Mindy loved everyone and everyone loved her but there was a mutual aversion between her and Eric and a definite wariness on her part whenever he was around. I remember teasing her that she must have a crush on my amazing big brother. I couldn't think of any other reason why she would quickly look at her feet when he came into the room, or why she was so reluctant to cross the courtyard with me at recess to go say hello.

Mindy used to come play at my house a lot when we were little, until one day, she didn't anymore. There was no weaning off; she just stopped coming around altogether, like something had scared her away. All of a sudden, there were still pink marshmallows left in the bag.

"I forgot how much better the pink ones are!" Mum commented one evening, enjoying her cup of coffee. "Say, it's been a while since Mindy came over, how come we don't see her anymore?"

I didn't know how to answer. I didn't know why she didn't want to play with me anymore. She avoided me at school too, but I didn't exactly try to find out why. I just wanted to hurry through class so I could go sit with Eric at recess and lunch. So, when Mum asked me what had happened, I shrugged like I didn't care and it was genuine: I didn't. It was better if I didn't have friends anyway. It just somehow felt safer that way.

The very last time Mindy came over was a Sunday. Gilbert's barks of joy bounced around the backyard, as if cheering for Mindy and I while we leapt through the light sprays of the sprinkler in our matching Minnie Mouse bathers. The leaves on Mum's plants were almost cowering, the inescapable heat from the cloudless sky stripping them of their usual will to stand proud and tall.

Mum had changed all the bed sheets that morning and they were hanging out to dry, a safe distance from the sprinkler on the other side of the yard. Eric sat cross-legged in amongst them, his back resting against the pole of the clothesline.

He was mostly concealed by the sheets but his bottom half was visible from where we played. His notebook rested on his lap and his hand was writing so madly he almost seemed to be in fast motion. But I don't think Mindy realised he was around. She excitedly decided that the clothes line could be our fortress and spontaneously ran into the drying sheets to stake claim on our territory. I couldn't hear what was said over Gilbert's barks, but Mindy wanted to go home when she ran back to the sprinkler moments later. She never came over again after that day and started playing with Bess and Anna at school. Maybe she finally told Eric that she had a crush on him, and he didn't like her back.

Mindy is a piece of the puzzle that I've spent my whole life trying to put together. I just can't figure out where she fits.

Liam isn't coming to the lake this year. My obsession with figuring him out and getting my hands on Eric's notebook kept me alive, at a time when I didn't know how to live without trying to save someone else. Liam and the notebook gave me new purpose, after the sole meaning of my life became suddenly, painfully, redundant. Maybe trying to decipher the probable non-existent meaning behind *don't tell your mother* just filled the void somehow. For the first time since I lost Eric, his notebook and the man who keep it from me won't be at the lake tonight. I have nothing, no one, left to obsess over.

I aspire to survive uni as inconspicuously as possible, despite my parent's constant encouragement to 'get out there more' and 'soak up the experience.' I don't contribute to the discussions in my tutorials, I barely pay attention in my lectures and I certainly would never reciprocate an offer of friendship. I have met enough people in my life already and once I finish my degree and get a job, I'll no doubt meet more. Cat's apartment is only a ten-minute walk from campus and I have a key, so I head there if I've got a couple of hours to kill in my schedule. If I hang around at uni, someone could try to talk to me. The older I get, the more my youngest memories will fade. New people and new experiences aren't good for me. I can't over flood my memory bank.

I've mastered the art of forced composure, but underneath I feel almost frantic, manic. It's as if I am bleeding somewhere *in* my body. I can feel the wound, but it's buried deep inside beneath my skin, behind my organs, tangled up in my veins. There is no way to reach it, and it can't heal unaided.

So, it just keeps bleeding.

The mere thought of being at the same place as Liam when one year ends and another begins has been the bandage. And now that I will likely never see him again, I'm bleeding to death. The years all end and then they begin again. I wanted, needed for them to end and begin with him. It seems I would rather have half an hour with him just one night a year than all the hours in all the days with someone else.

If I never see Liam again, I will never get to read the stories that Eric wrote. The ones that we tried to keep safely hidden in the pages of his notebook, like the supposedly haunted dolls that are kept locked behind glass in a museum, so they can't hurt anyone. Eric would tell me stories, but I never got to read what he actually wrote down in his notebook. The stories he recited were bloody and violent, vicious and cruel. I can only imagine the content that flowed when he put pen to paper.

I wrote the stories that he and Liam worked on together, the ones he read aloud to Mum and Dad; the ones that were going to make him bigger than May Gibbs. The ones that Liam illustrated. The ones that were meant to give him purpose, and a reason to stay. The stories that Eric wrote stayed in his notebook, where they couldn't hurt anybody.

"Are you sure we've left out enough food for her?"

I pack the last of Cat's bags in the boot of her car. "How much stuff are you bringing? We're literally going for two nights! And Cleo will be fine; you've put out enough food for a whole week."

"But what about her litter tray?" she panics. "What if it fills up too quickly? You know she hates standing in her own mess."

I push down hard on the boot, amazed it can actually close with Cat's four suitcases cramped inside, and give her the reassuring hug she is seeking. "She'll be fine, promise. You're such a good mum. Don't stress."

Cleo is Cat's cat. She finally got a cat. It was my birthday present to her.

Birthdays are a big deal to me. It's not a celebration of the day you were born; it's a celebration of the victory that you're still alive.

The gift Cat's mum got for her was quite different to mine. She 'updated' Cat's apartment. Eclectic boho apparently wasn't on trend anymore, so Cat was forcibly introduced to what the interior decorators called 'Hamptons' style. It didn't seem to bother Cat much; she wasn't emotionally attached to any of the décor, but I miss the tasselled rugs and floral curtains every time I come over now. Bare floors, white walls and coral couch cushions achieved the look her mum desired, and now Cat looks odd in her own home, but evidently in my eyes only. Cat was unaffected, completely indifferent to the whole process and outcome, whereas I was anxious and unsettled for days and I don't even live there. It's strange to me that the things that were a part of Cat's everyday life held such little, if any, sentimental value to her. A person's belongings represent who they are and enable part of them to live on after they've gone. Literal pieces left behind. Frida Kohl and the Dior coffee table book were replaced with the latest issue of Home Beautiful magazine and canvas prints of marine life. If everything in a person's life is so temporary and replaceable, how can anything have the power to prompt the memory of them after they've gone? Surely the longer someone spends with something, the more meaning it will retain to the people left behind.

People die, sometimes without warning or expectation, but their *things*, whatever was unique to them, ensure we don't forget them. So maybe for selfish reasons, I wanted Cat to have something that wouldn't be able to be upgraded, something that was unmistakably *her*, whether it was on trend or not. I drove us down to the shelter in her car and made Cat's lifelong dream to have a cat come true.

Cleo is a black cat with fierce yellow eyes. She had been in the shelter for exactly 106 days before we adopted her. She was found in a sewer drain when she was just a few weeks old, along with four other kittens who all found homes within the month but for some reason no one ever chose Cleo. She does look pretty scary, I guess. If she were a human, she would still hiss at people.

Cat shimmies her bony shoulders to reposition her white fluffy shawl, worn with a pastel pink satin camisole and tight-fitting jeans. We're going to the lake. She's dressed like a 1976 movie star on her day off. Cat always looks out of place and yet she ironically fits in wherever she goes.

"Do I look okay?" she worries.

You look ridiculous, as always. "You look gorgeous, as always."

"Thanks for coming over to help me pack. Are you sure your parents are cool with me coming? This is like the longest-standing family tradition in the history of family traditions and I don't want to screw it up!"

"1999 is a pretty special New Year's Eve." Self-consciousness takes me hostage. "And, it's just, well, you're, um, you're like my best friend, so if it's a special one, I would like to spend it with you." I stare at my worn sneakers, thoroughly embarrassed by myself. She must think I'm so needy.

"You're my best friend, too." Stunned, my head shoots up, greeted by Cat's satisfied expression. "You're how I've always imagined a sister would be."

She wouldn't think that if she knew what a terrible sister I had been to my brother. "Anyway, Mum and Dad love you. They wanted me to invite you."

They do. They did. Cat comes over every Sunday for spaghetti bolognaise and we all watch the 8.30pm Movie of the Week together. Mum insists Cat give three rings to let her know when she gets home safe. She counts the rings out-loud, announcing "Cat's home!" to the whole house after the third and final ring.

Tomorrow is not just a new year; it's the start of a brand-new millennium. There has to be something symbolic in that. If ever you wanted to start over, head into a new chapter, surely this would be it.

I click in my seatbelt as Cat starts the car, then picks up her own by the metal buckle.

"Ouch ouch ouch," she whinges, quickly plugging herself in and blowing on her fingertips.

"You should always pick it up by the strap in summer." I'm sure I'm smiling so I'm surprised to see my lips appear straight in the side-view mirror.

Cat and I set off on the short drive to Mum and Dad's house, in the very car that picks me up when I sneak out in the middle of the night to go clubbing. I smoked my first cigarette in this car, while I was the designated driver and Cat made out with some guy named Isaiah in the back seat. Cat's pulled over so I could vomit in the gutter after too many Kahluas. We've sung along loudly and badly to Alisha Attic's I am I feel; our song for a long while, it seemed. We've talked about things that maybe we otherwise wouldn't have, were it not for the implied full disclosure of this blue Volkswagen. I've spoken about Eric. Not the fact that he died, but just about him as a person. I think I've lived out every adolescent rite of passage right in this car, with her. This car. It's a special one.

When one of us drinks, the other doesn't. At all. We can depend on each other like that. It's not just me looking out for Cat; she looks out for me too. Some nights I drink and dance until I'm dizzy, but I can fall because she's there to catch me. And when it's my turn to do the same for her, she knows without a doubt that she can rely on me too.

My parents stand waiting in the drive way, a shared duffle bag at their feet. Dad excitedly waves his arms in the air in animated greeting and Mum dances joyfully on the spot. The same car that chariots us through the streets of town while we're on the prowl for hot guys to flirt with will now chaperone my parents on a wholesome family holiday to the lake. I don't know if that makes me feel old, or blessed.

Dad wraps Cat and I in the same embrace; characteristically warm and protective.

Mum steals Cat from Dad's hold. "Natalie! You're looking too thin, darling! Let's get you some decent food!"

Cat's laugh is laced with affection. "I've heard that it's tradition to stop at a petrol station along the way. So, who's this Willy Nelson guy Bea keeps telling me about?"

Dad reaches for the back door handle. "You'll soon find out! You've got a tape deck in this thing, right?"

Cat quickly steps in-between him and the door. "My baby is a vintage classic, of course she does. And I believe it's tradition that you drive." She looks mighty pleased with herself.

Dad nods his head, obviously impressed. "Bea's told you all our secrets. Hope you've got insurance. The fucking koalas have it in for me."

By the time we reach the end of the street, On the Road Again is dispensing its annual dose of nostalgic comfort. It doesn't take Cat long to pick up the tune. She is singing along by the second chorus.

To my surprise, Dad turns down the volume before the song is over. "The first time I ever laid eyes on Bea's mother, Always On My Mind was playing on the jukebox."

Mum stretches her arm across the handbrake, resting it on Dad's bare skin below his shorts. She gently strokes the hairs on his knee. I have never heard this story before. I keep my breaths shallow so I don't miss one word.

"I was getting a milkshake after school with my best mate, god I miss him, and in walked this girl, and I knew right away that she would always be on *my* mind from that moment on. I went up to her and told her that one day we would take road trips with our kids and make them listen to Willie Nelson. She said she admired my confidence, but didn't like country music. I told her I didn't either, and I didn't, I don't. But here we are."

"Here we are," Mum lovingly echoes.

It's strange to think of my parents as teenagers. They met when they were younger than I am now. Mum was 16, Dad was 17. I'll be 20 in a few months. When they were my age, they were about to get married. I've never really considered the magnitude of that before. They were my age when they had it all figured out. They could have never predicted the catastrophic heartbreak a blue rope would ultimately bring them.

Yet through the everyday stresses and stressors of life; the constant worry about money, their parents' creeping onset of old age, lost friendships and irreversible, unbearable trauma, they keep going. Living. Together.

I just exist.

Dad said he was getting a milkshake after school with his best mate. I've pieced together that back then, his best friend was Liam's biological father, the man who was killed in a workplace accident. Mum introduced him and Mrs Sanderson at Dad's eighteenth birthday party and they fell in love so fast they got married even before my parents did. I've overheard Mum reminisce with Dad about how different Mrs Sanderson was back then, before she lost the love of her life. Fun. Silly. Excited. The successive marriage of mutual convenience to Mr Sanderson must have chewed up her likeable personality and spat out a shallow, heartless bitch.

Mum hadn't liked Mrs Sanderson as a person for a long time. I don't know why she held on to their friendship for so long. Maybe Mrs Sanderson was the tangible thing that Mum associated with Liam's biological father. Maybe their friendship kept him alive for everyone.

It must have been agonising for Mrs Sanderson to see Mum and Dad together, while she was mourning her husband and bracing herself for a life raising a child alone. Maybe she just wanted what they had, what she had lost. Family. Maybe she's just human after all.

Maybe I should stop myself before I become obsessed with trying to figure out some woman who's not even in my life anymore. My humiliation in front of Liam clearly taught me nothing.

We stop for breakfast at the usual petrol station at the bottom of the hill. Dad struggles to find a park amongst all the trucks, so we park over by the windmill. Cat says it looks old and worries it will collapse right on top of her beloved car.

Although the diner is full, we manage to score a table by the window. The conversation is minimal but it's not uncomfortable; we would need to shout to be heard properly over the clatter of dishes and conversations of every other table, each it seems competing with the volume of the table next to theirs.

When our breakfast arrives, I cut off the crispy bits of bacon and push them to the side of the plate. Cat says I'm crazy and scoops them up to eat. I cringe inside but don't say anything because I'm so happy to see her eating a full meal.

Close to the holiday park, Dad swerves past a kangaroo hopping across the road.

"Jesus, Mitch," Mum utters under her breath, firmly clutching the grab handle.

"Fucking kangaroos!"

We're in cabin 7 this year, right in front of the barbecue area. Cat opens every single cupboard door and every single drawer in the kitchen and bathroom, full of excitement and wonder. Even if you're used to getting everything you want in life, these tiny rustic cabins somehow feel like the epitome of luxury.

There are two single beds in the room Cat and I share. I take the one by the window, looking out to the lake. It is the sole window in the room and it is mine. My mind slips back to another time, and I am empowered by a familiar yet illogical sense of ownership. The lake belongs to me. The jetty looks older than my nanna. But I guess it probably is. I'm amazed the wooden planks haven't collapsed into the water yet. I gift myself the luxury of staring out the window in quiet reflection while Cat unpacks her suitcases and lays out her expensive skin care products on the dresser. She seems to be ruminating about something herself.

At the kiosk, Edna takes our order for two hotdogs with cheese and sauce. Edna and the jetty have something in common: they are both still standing, even though they look like they should have retired years ago. Edna must surely be in her seventies these days. I guess she's content to keep working forever.

We gobble up our lunch while I show Cat around the holiday park. I'm overwhelmed with a sense of pride, as if giving her a tour of my own private resort that I built myself. Cat ogles a hot guy in board shorts and jokes that she wants to follow him to find out where he's staying.

It's packed this year. Every single cabin looks to be occupied and the camping section is completely full. Pat and Joanie wave in neighbourly fashion, playing a game of Uno by their beloved caravan. Joanie is wearing a beanie even though it's the middle of a scorching hot summer day. I don't tell Cat their secret. I have to keep that safe.

We rest on the grass down by the lake and mindfully gaze across the surface, glistening like diamonds in the sun. Cat looks to the sky, seeming to marvel at the impressive height of the gum trees, and breathes in deeply, as if consciously allowing the fresh country air to cleanse her lungs. "I like it here."

"Me too."

"Do you know, as soon as I turned thirteen, my mother weighed me every Sunday morning to make sure I wasn't getting *puffy*." She looks to the clouds and laughs. "I think if I ever did put on weight, she might disown me. Pretty fucked up."

Cat has had breakfast today, plus the crispy bits of my bacon. She ate all of the hot dog, and Edna really piles on the cheese. My heart aches at the realisation that she'll most likely make herself throw it all up later tonight.

"When I was thirteen, my brother hung himself from that tree, right over there."

"Eric?" Cat's eyes widen and she gasps involuntarily. "I didn't know that he had died. You never mentioned that. I just assumed he had grown up and moved interstate or something. Shit, that's fucked up too."

This conversation suddenly feels like a game. The winner finds out everything there is to know about the other person. What makes them tick. What makes them who they are. I get addicted to that. I'm desperate to win. "What else have you got?"

"Hmm," Cat contemplates, "ooh I've got a good one! I got an A for my tenth-grade history essay on the Industrial Revolution and my father told me *not to worry about all that nonsense* because we were rich and all I needed to do in life was *keep that pretty face and not get fat.*"

"Ouch!" I self-consciously tug the bottom of my t-shirt to make sure it's covering as much of my torso as possible. Cat's parents thought that being fat was the worst thing a person could be; the worst failure she could make in life. Not being cruel, or selfish, or ungrateful. Just being fat. Gosh, what would they think of someone like me? "Guess it's my turn again. I got an A for my sixth-grade English assignment.

We had to write a journal as if we were a passenger on the Titanic. When I got mine back, Miss Blunt had put a gold sticker on it and wrote, 'You should be a writer one day. This is really good.' I was so scared that someone else would see what she said, especially my family, so I ripped up the whole assignment and chucked it in the bin at school. Writing was Eric's thing, and I couldn't take that away from him. It gave him a reason to stay. He loved making up stories."

"I like writing, too. Well, I did. I used to write a lot of songs. I wanted to be a songwriter, but every song I wrote just felt like a waste of time really, considering all I was expected to do in life was look pretty and stay thin."

For the first time ever, I am unafraid that the more I learn about someone, the more I might not be able to remember every single moment that I shared with my brother. There's room in my memory for other people. There's room to make more memories for myself. The moments I have tried so desperately hard to not forget are becoming clearer anyway. Less distorted by my own sugar-coated idealisation. Not everything happened the way I remember it. I don't remember my own life accurately. I don't remember my own brother accurately.

The magnitude of what I am about to say, what I am about to admit out-loud to myself, threatens to steal my breath, but it's my turn to play. "My mum doesn't like talking about Eric. Sometimes I think she didn't love him. And sometimes when she looks at me, it's like she's, I don't know, kind of grateful things happened the way they did. Like if only one of us could be here, she's glad that it's me, not him. As if she is okay that he's gone."

"Fuck. Okay. You win."

We spend the rest of the afternoon playing Scattergories with my parents on the front deck, while the set up for the big barbecue begins around us. Soon eskies are brimming with ice and a large trellis table has received bountiful contributions of salad, coleslaw and buttered bread rolls. The smell of chicken shashliks and chevapchichis wafts across the evening air directly to our senses. Mum takes the meat plate that she put together out of the fridge and tells Cat and I to freshen up so we can head out to join everyone.

It's going to be a huge party tonight. Cat has her hopes set on finding that hot guy in board shorts.

All week, every single radio station has been playing Prince's 1999, multiple times a day. Yesterday when it came on, I was so sick of hearing it so I immediately flicked over to the next station and it was playing on there too, only a few seconds behind where it was up to on the other station. It's been inescapable. I guess there'll never be any other time when that song will be so perfectly apt.

There's been talk on the news that the world will end when the clock ticks over midnight. Banks, nuclear power stations and basically anything driven by a computer are possibly going to collapse or fail, bringing about the end of civilisation. I don't know how I feel about that. It doesn't scare me like I suspect it's supposed to. I don't have a mobile phone yet. If the world doesn't end, maybe I should get one. Maybe I should start keeping up with the world

I live in now, instead of trying to figure out the world I lived in when I was a child. In every sense, that world doesn't exist anymore.

Someone has wheeled a tv out to the grass, powered by an extension cord, and it plays in the background while everyone celebrates the end of the decade with new and old friends. A special program about all the major events from the past ten years airs until just before midnight, when the live footage of the Sydney Harbour Bridge comes on, in anticipation of the impending fireworks.

10! 9! 8!

I don't think anyone in this crowd is particularly worried about the Y2K bug.

7! 6! 5!

The Sandersons didn't come this year. I knew Liam wasn't going to, but I thought maybe Mr and Mrs Sanderson still would. I wonder how they're celebrating tonight. It must feel so isolating for Mrs Sanderson, now that she's stuck with that man on her own.

4! 3!

Cat found the hot guy in board shorts. His tongue is currently in her mouth.

2! 1! HAPPY NEW YEAR!

On the tv, the Sydney Harbour Bridge lights up with an impressive display of multi-coloured fireworks that explode across the sky.

The lake glows from the light of our own firecrackers, solely yellow; quite pathetic and measly in comparison to the ones on TV, but somehow so much more awe-inspiring. A lady in black trackies and a Led Zeppelin t-shirt cries softly. I guess she had a hard year. Or maybe she thought the world really was going to end.

"Fucking 2000!" a drunken man roars into his chest. "Holy shit! Aren't we meant to be driving cars in the sky now?"

Cat hugs me with her whole body. "Thank you for making me a part of your family." Our embrace evolves into a huddle when Mum, Dad and the hot guy in board shorts join.

Experiencing the start of a new millennium is a once-in-a-lifetime phenomenon, not even a possibility for most generations. But here I am. It's a pretty special thing. I'm not so sure I am worthy of it. I'm not so sure I deserve it.

My brother isn't here.

And in a different sense, Liam isn't either. I don't know where he is, but wherever it is, it feels so far away from me.

It's past one in the morning when everyone finally retires to bed. I wait a quick minute before sneaking down to the lake. I'm so tired and could fall asleep easily, but I need to check.

I know Liam isn't here.

But I sit by the lake in the middle of the night, waiting for him anyway.

New Year's Eve 2000

"Look Bea, I'm really sorry. I just think we kind of want different things." Jake shakes his head sorrowfully, trying overtly hard for his heartache to come across as genuine. I can see through it, yet I'm still desperate for him to think I'm worth fighting for. "Come on Bea, surely you must have seen the signs."

I swallow to create moisture in my suddenly-dry mouth. Of course I saw the signs. I just thought if I did everything he liked and wanted, it would be enough for him. He is breaking up with me after only five (relatively nice) months together. On New Year's Eve. We're meant to be heading to the lake with Mum and Dad in less than an hour. Not that they particularly like him.

Just last week, Jake told me that he wants us to have three kids when we get married one day. But when I asked him whether he thought we would have boys or girls, he was too preoccupied with the hot blonde girl in the even hotter gym pants to hear me. He always looks at other girls, even if he has to look straight past me to see them. I suck in my tummy as much as I can when we are together, to the point of feeling giddy, and I make sure my head is titled upwards so I don't have a double chin. I waste so much mental energy trying to present myself in the most flattering light possible, for nothing. He barely even looks at me most of the time. He'd rather look at every other girl around.

I met Jake on a Thursday night. I had woken up in a frantic state after only an hour's sleep. The glowing red numbers on my digital clock told me it was 11:47pm. I willed myself to keep my eyes closed and go back to sleep. I had a seminar at nine and I was too close to graduating to start slacking off now. I needed to stop *thinking* so I could sleep, but I couldn't. My mind was fixated on a goblin named Bogart.

Bogart had planned to return to the fairy's sunflower and kill her, this time for certain. I knew that. But what I didn't know was whether he had succeeded. Eric never read the next part of the story to me, but he would have written it in his notebook. I needed to know if the fairy survived. She had been through so much. I needed to know if Bogart really did try to hurt her again. Maybe something stopped him.

I checked the red numbers again, perspiration rendering me thirsty. 12:02am. Sleep grew more and more impossible and I desperately needed a drink. Fed up, I wrapped myself in my cosy dressing gown, skulled a glass of water and then quietly pushed up the window behind the couch and climbed out onto the fire escape. I had stayed the night at Cat's. I did that sometimes now.

Cat's apartment is on the third floor of a four-storey building, right next to a boutique hair salon where women pay two hundred dollars to get their hair cut. Cat gets her hair done there, of course. In the dead of the brisk cold night in mid-July, I began my descent to the bottom of the stairwell. I didn't feel safe walking around town in the middle of the night alone. The city streets are scary in the dark, even though there's noticeably less trees around in comparison to my childhood suburban home. I had become almost emotionally reliant on my mindless midnight walks over the years and needed to be able to walk somewhere, so when I stayed at Cat's, I just went up and down the emergency exit stairs instead.

I was on my second trip back up when Cat joined me, draped in a dressing gown that rivalled the cosiness of my own. The sound of the old metal steps must have given me away. Cat shivered, almost as if she was in pain, but I had stopped noticing the cold. All I could think about was what became of the goblin and the fairy.

Cat marvelled at the sight of her breath frozen in the air. "I'm going to freeze my tits off out here. Do you want to go somewhere? Let's go dancing."

"I've got uni in the morning," I laughed, "and you have to sit behind a desk and read magazines and get paid for it."

"Funny. Come on, it's only Friday! We can be tired

for one day. Or let's just skip the whole day! The club doesn't close til five. Stuff it, let's go! I want to, and you need to."

My mind had been going round and round in circles and I was certain that I was on the verge of slipping into a state of eternal insanity. I needed a distraction, Cat was right.

In a few short months, I would have been graduating with a degree that didn't really qualify me for a specific job, and I had absolutely no idea what I was meant to do with myself afterwards. I guess most people look forward to throwing their graduation cap in the air but I would have stayed at uni forever if I could. Not because I liked it, just because it gave me something to do. Considering I had never formulated an idea about what I actually *wanted* to do, uni was like a safety net. It was just an extension of my high school years and allowed me to delay that unavoidable step into the real world.

I had been missing Liam, which was absurd the more that I thought about it. He was just a boy from my childhood; I didn't even know him as a person beyond that. And yet for some illogical leap of reasoning that had led to the most humiliating moment of my life, I thought I was in love with him. I'd never gone this long without seeing him. It was officially *more* than a year.

So, between useless degrees, murderous goblins, traumatised fairies and my long-dead brother's best friend, life had officially overwhelmed me. Cat's idea to go out seemed like a good remedy.

Back inside the apartment, we glammed ourselves up whilst our usual soundtrack played softly. Jewel's Pieces of You never even got put back in its case; the disc just lived in the player. Although Cat only lived two blocks from Hindley Street, our four-inch heels deemed the distance too far to walk, so we hailed a taxi instead.

For a Thursday night, the club was unexpectedly packed. We squeezed our way through the dance floor and claimed the back corner. All eyes were on Cat but she was oblivious; determined to show off her sexiest moves for my amusement and praise only, bestowing me with the confidence to show her my

273

own in return. Only an hour before, we had been pacing up and down the fire escape in matching fluffy grey slippers. We danced until our Revlon-covered skin glistened in sweat and the heels of our feet were desperate to be flat.

"Drinkies time!" Cat eventually exclaimed over the thunderous *doofdoofdoof* pulsating through my ear drums. I thought I must be getting old; I didn't recall the music ever being that loud before.

"Yes please!" I yelled.

Cat shimmied her way over to the bar, gloriously glamorous in her cropped cashmere jumper and fitted leather pants. She would genuinely feel bad if she knew how fat and frumpy I felt next to her, as if it was somehow her fault that she was beautiful, and I wasn't.

The bartender looked to be a little older than us, maybe in his late twenties. He wore glasses similar to Liam's, only his frames were black. Liam's are gold, and more oval in shape. I guess they weren't really similar at all. I'm just forever wishing every single man I encounter is Liam.

But alas, he was Jake.

"What can I get you ladies?"

Cat seductively leaned onto the white marble bar. "Hey, sexy eyes! Two Cosmopolitans."

It was the first night out that Cat and I had let ourselves drink at the same time, so we made sure not to write ourselves off completely. Two Cosmopolitans each later, I slipped the bartender my number. I wasn't drunk, but just the taste of alcohol makes me way too brazen. I blamed his glasses. I liked them way too much, purely for the fact that they were glasses, and he was a man, wearing them.

I had caught up with the world and got a mobile phone. When I first brought it home from the shop, I expected it to magically contain the number of everyone I had ever known. I opened all the icons, hoping by some miracle to find Liam's number stored somewhere. The only thing of merit I found was a game called Snake. It seemed even the latest technology couldn't connect me to Liam.

Jake was a bartender by night and an aspiring theatre

actor by day. He was the understudy for Skimbleshanks the last time Cats was playing here two years ago but he had since been holding out for the perfect role.

Cat and I did end up staying in bed the next day, until I heard from Jake, asking if I wanted to hook up. Five months later, listening to him wanting to break up with me, I realise that that's perhaps all I've ever been to him. A hook up.

"I don't mind if you want to see other people." I shudder internally, disgusted at the words I let dribble out of my mouth. But it might change his mind about leaving me. "We can still be together, like around that. I don't really mind."

"You sure? I mean, I just think it's important that we're both on the same page. That's all I've been trying to say."

Women the world over must want to slap me over the head. I hear their collective sigh of exasperation. What would the public bathroom cheerleaders think of me now? "Of course. It's not a big deal. We can just keep things casual, no pressure."

He leans in and kisses me hard. "You're so awesome." He playfully grabs hold of my hand, tugging me towards the spare room I sleep in at Cat's when I stay over. She is holidaying in Bali with her boyfriend. I've tried to get Cleo to speak on the phone a few times to help with Cat's substantial separation anxiety, but Cleo wasn't exactly chatty.

Mum and Dad were okay with me staying here all week on my own. I've loved it, and still went home a couple of times after uni to play Scrabble and eat dinner with them. It's been a good test and I think we've all passed.

I don't feel like going into the bedroom with Jake right now. It's my first boyfriend all over again. Saying what you want for yourself shouldn't be harder than giving someone else what they want. I do one with vigour and ease, and one just not at all. I guess it's pretty obvious which is which.

I often wonder where that Brett guy is these days. I loved my one night with him, in his dingy share house that reeked of pot. I felt in control yet completely *controlled*. Desire for him and desired by him. He actually cared if I was into it. I've only enjoyed sex once in my whole life, and it was with a stranger. Sometimes, when Jake initiates it, I mentally visualise that night with Brett to help me feel more in the mood. Or I think about Liam, and the way he looked at me in that moment by the lake when I was sixteen, when he found me kissing that loser, Wes. Liam pushed his torso hard against my hands, wanting me to want him. A fervour of heat and dare, curiosity and a lifetime's worth of unspoken words swirled madly in the space between us. Liam wouldn't even remember that day, I bet. Years later, I still feed off of it.

"Let's save it for when we get to the lake. We'll have our own cabin."

Jake drops my hand, instantly disinterested in me. He scoffs like a bratty child who didn't win the big teddy at the fair. "Forget it, it's fine."

He flicks the kettle on, pulls his phone out his pocket and starts texting someone. I'm still here. I'm right here, right next to him, and I can't even hold his attention. *I'm never enough for anyone.*

Panic sets in and a sense of urgency takes over. "We can be quick!"

I rush to my bed, hearing the reassuring sound of Jake's eager laugh, chasing me into the bedroom.

My parents pick us up from Cat's apartment at eight thirty on the dot.

"Jake." Mum nods her head in greeting. "Nice to see you again." Her polite demeanour towards him is so forced it almost comes across as hostility. Mum tries to be nice to everyone, even if she very clearly doesn't like them. She just likes peace. I wish I could tell her that I don't really like him either.

We pack our bags in the boot and climb into the back seat. Turning out onto the main road, On the Road Again officially kicks off the annual road trip. Jake is texting someone, again, still. I don't know why he wanted to come. I didn't invite him. He didn't have any plans for New Year's and almost got annoyed when I told him that I did, as if he had lost a competition that I wasn't even aware I was competing in. Maybe he's still trying to find someone better to be with on New Year's. I sing along to

Willie Nelson with my parents, trying not to think about all that stuff.

After breakfast, we come across a kangaroo lying right in the middle of the road. We assume it has been hit by a car, though there isn't any sign of blood. It's safe to switch lanes because there is no oncoming traffic, but Dad puts on the hazard lights and parks right in front of the poor creature. There are no cars behind us.

"There could be a Joey in the pouch," Dad explains as he cautiously walks up to the body, "or someone could come tearing round that corner and then there actually would be blood everywhere, and not just from the kangaroo." Dad psyches himself up as he reaches for the animal's pouch. "Hope you didn't suffer, darling. Let's see if you've got a little one in there."

The kangaroo unexpectedly snaps alive, jolting its whole body and kicking about madly.

Dad jumps back in surprise. "Fuck me!"

Mum pushes open her door and shouts from her

seat. "Jesus, Mitch! Get back in the car, you bloody fool!"

The kangaroo jerks itself upright and stares at Dad. It must have only been knocked lightly and went into shock. It rocks back and forth and then hops off into the bushland next to the road while Dad hastily returns to the car.

Mum's hand claims its traditional spot on Dad's knee. "Ready to go now, dear?"

"Fucking kangaroos," he laughs as he accelerates away.

When we arrive at the resort, Dad and I both go into Reception to collect the keys. He wraps his arm around my shoulders while we wait, second in line. "I'm not sure how I feel about this, you picking up the keys for your own cabin for you and your boyfriend. Making me feel old, my girl."

I lean into his side, titling my head back to rest on his chest. "Can I still come over to play a game later? Jake won't want to spend all day with me."

"What does that tell you? You should be with

someone who wants everything with you. Adventure, boredom, excitement, calm. Games. Love. Fights. You should be with someone who does want to spend all day with you. Someone who wants to be your partner in life."

I sigh. "Let's not go there, hey?"

"Where we should go is back to the car, if these guys can bloody hurry up. Do you really think it's a good idea leaving your mother and Jake alone?"

"Mum has the best poker face of all time and Jake's got his phone. I doubt he even noticed we left. I'm pretty sure they're fine."

"It's not a poker face, Bea. It's a brave face. Don't confuse the two."

Great. I already know that I'll analyse and obsess over that sentence for the next few years now.

After check-in, we park in the gravel driveway between cabins 11 and 12. Jake heads straight over to ours, but my automatic inclination is to go with my parents into theirs. I am not intentionally avoiding Jake; it just feels more natural to go with them. I tell

Jake that I'll be over in just a minute.

Many minutes later, Dad puts on the kettle for us. "Planning on staying with us forever?"

I sit myself down at the table next to Mum, who is evidently amused by my presence. "Have you forgotten that you have your own cabin next door? With your boyfriend inside of it?"

My dramatic inner-child theatrically lays her head on the table in apparent agony. "What's wrong with me, Mum? Why do I only ever attract guys I don't like or who don't like me?"

She takes a long sip of her coffee. "I think the more applicable question is, why do you *stay with* guys you don't like or who don't like you?"

Before Jake, there was Oliver. He was only around for seven weeks and they were perhaps the longest seven weeks of my life, pretending to be someone I'm not. We met at one of Cat's infamous house parties, so I appeared cultured and sophisticated by association. Cat has a lot of society friends, and I try to blend in because I don't want to embarrass her, but it's abundantly clear that I come from, and live in, a very different world to them. But my act was thankfully enough to convince Oliver that I wasn't just a lost soul who walks around in the middle of the night for no reason or purpose, and with no apparent destination.

Oliver was so handsome and nice and smart that it was bizarrely almost off-putting. Intimidating. I felt inadequate around him because he had it all together, and I was just trying not to fall apart.

Oliver's father was handing over the reins of their family's mega successful real estate company. I wish I could say that he was puffed up with his own importance, but he was actually very humble and wanted to make a difference in the world. He spoke a lot of business jargon that I didn't understand, but I didn't say much anyway so it's not like he would have caught on to that.

I was enthusiastic about whatever movie he suggested we watch, even if I would have rather watched something else. I never said I wasn't in the mood when he wanted to have sex and I agreed with his political views even though I voted for the party he hated so passionately. I'd come home sometimes a stranger to myself. Mentally exhausted.

He broke up with me in the middle of a date on a Saturday night, at some absurdly expensive restaurant in the hills. Right before the waiter served our main meals.

"But anyway, just enjoy your steak," he encouraged, amazingly full of sincerity. He raised his glass, exactly half full with French champagne. "Cheers to what we had for a little while, and cheers to where life will take us from here. Thanks for being a part of my story these last few weeks. I hope everything works out for you. Now let's eat!" It was the most peculiar and kind of heart-warming breakup ever. He even insisted on paying the bill.

Oliver was a one-in-a-million type of guy. Everything I should want, but I didn't feel anything for him. I liked him, but I didn't *like* him. He didn't like me like that either, yet he knew how to move on and be okay with it. He thanked me for being part of his story. Maybe that's my problem: my own story is chapters behind everyone else's and I'm not even sure what the plot is. I don't even have a title yet.

Mum's reminder that I have my own cabin next door sits in the pit of my stomach like a brick. I roll my eyes at her wisdom. "You're lucky, you got Dad first try. You didn't have to sift through the dirt to find gold."

"Stop sifting then," she replies. "Stop looking for gold. Wait until someone buys it for you."

Dad and I laugh at Mum's attempt at being clever and funny. She laughs the most. It's a nice sound.

Reluctantly, I make my way next door to the first cabin I have ever stayed in without my parents. Jake is napping on the couch. His phone is on the coffee table right next to him. I watch for any sign of rousing and consider the high risk of getting caught, yet stupidly decide to go through it anyway.

The alphabetised list of names in his Contacts is predominately female. No real surprises there. But sitting at the top of the Recently Contacted is Ryan. I know him, he works at the club behind the bar with

Jake. I open up his message.

> **Jake:** Still no girls?
>
> **Ryan:** Nah mate. Everyone's already partnered up. Couldn't even get us a shift for the night. Stick with your girlfriend. We're too old now and it's too depressing to be single on New Year's.
>
> **Jake:** Let me know if you find any.

I delicately return the phone to the coffee table and take my bag to the bedroom. I'm missing my parents' cabin, very much.

I don't really have a right to be upset. I'm not exactly in love with Jake either, though I do still try to be a good girlfriend. Kind of. I did ditch him as soon as we got here to hang out with my parents instead. I know he looks at other girls, but the fact that he's actively looking for another girl to replace me with is what really hurts. No matter what I do, I just can't ever seem to give someone what they need. I'm never the one they want to stay with.

It's the middle of the day, and the front door isn't

broken. Yet I still find myself climbing out the bedroom window to go for the walk that my mind is desperately twitching for.

I haven't often done a full lap around the lake. Maybe ever. The trail takes just under two hours to complete but most people stay on the side of the resort. I text my parents to tell them I'm going on a long walk so they don't worry. I don't text Jake. I know he won't worry.

Pat and Joanie wave as I venture past their silver caravan with the chocolate-brown stripe and orange curtains. They are chatting away like an old married couple, relaxing on what looks to be brand new floral sun loungers. They look so happy to finally be together again after their year apart. Joanie is wearing a beanie despite the humidity. I recall she did last year too. She must feel the cold now that she's gotten a bit skinny, that's all. A sting forms in my throat. I consciously blink more than is natural, physically snapping myself out of entertaining the possibility that something could be wrong with her.

A group of little kids jump off the jetty, hand-in-hand with their older siblings. Their squeals of delight when they resurface serenade me as I continue on my way. I can't believe the jetty is still standing after all these years. Despite its waning structural integrity and visible need of urgent repairs, everyone has such blind faith in it, maybe because the lake and the jetty are so intrinsic: as long as the lake exists, the jetty does too, eternally branded as safe.

When I was little, I thought I only existed to keep my brother alive. But somehow, I'm still here, without him.

The trail soon becomes narrow, born from generations of footsteps. The holiday park seems far away now, though still visible off in the distance. It looks so small, like a model village on a train set. From this perspective, the lake appears bigger than ever. Stripping away the busy atmosphere of the resort emphasises just how glorious the lake really is. How magnificent. How simple. It clears your mind. The lake lets you lose yourself, confident that it will remember who you are on your behalf.

The colossal size of the gum trees makes my presence seem insignificant. I am an invisible speck in the landscape. Me and the bush. Alone.

Or so I thought.

"I didn't think many people came around this side."

I turn abruptly, expecting to see someone coming up behind me, but there's no one there. I could have sworn that was Liam's voice. Wonderful, now I'm imagining things. I'm imagining *him*. Disheartened, I turn back to the direction I was heading.

"If you didn't always look at the ground when you walk, you would have seen me coming."

A gasp falls from my mouth before I can catch it. I didn't imagine anything. I didn't imagine *him*.

The last time I saw Liam was two years ago, when I bragged about how much I understood him, just because I knew some random, superficial facts about his life. Oh, and when I blurted out that I was in love with him. Can't forget that part. As much as I try to.

"What, I mean…why…" I sigh, shaking off my

embarrassing stupor. His ego will be loving this. He's here. I can't believe he's actually here. I genuinely thought I would never see him again. My soul breathes a colossal sigh of relief. "You don't come here anymore."

"Nice to see you too."

He stands an arm's length from me. He hasn't changed, but I guess I haven't either. We're not really at an age of rapid change anymore. People just kind of look the same for a while.

Magpies yodel above us, somewhere high up in the trees. I instinctively look up to see where they are. When I return my sight to Liam, he is staring directly at me. His eyes smoulder behind his glasses, purposely trying to intimidate me. He holds my gaze before sending it down the length of my body. "Unusual for you to wear leggings."

I stretch out the side of my baggy t-shirt. "This is two sizes too big. Covers my bum." The surface temperature of my face soars. I can't believe I just said that. "I was planning on doing the hike around the lake this year, so just chucked them on this morning."

"You look good."

"My boyfriend doesn't think so." What is going on with my internal filter? "He always looks at girls wearing gym clothes. Just thought I'd try to fit the mould but I don't think he's even noticed that I've been wearing them all day."

Liam's fingers twitch. "Sounds like I'd really like to meet that guy."

"Sure, you can meet my boyfriend when I meet your girlfriend."

We both suppress a laugh, neither wanting to be the one to release it.

I step past him, crunching a large chunk of bark under my sneaker.

Liam steps on a piece himself, slowly uncurling his foot from toe to heel to maximise the crunch. "Mine was better. Can I walk with you?"

"If you want. I'm going all the way around the lake though."

"Avoiding someone?"

"Kind of."

We follow the trail side-by-side, trying to outdo each other with each strip of bark we trample. Liam keeps both hands in his pockets, so sure of himself even on the twiggy, uneven terrain. Most people would balance themselves with their arms by their sides.

"Well, I know you wouldn't be avoiding your parents. You're pretty attached to them."

I tread on a huge piece, dried out from the sun so it crunches extra loud. Liam looks impressed and I smile smugly. "What is your mum up to these days?"

He studies the ground with each step, hunting for a bit of bark to top my last one. "Mum? She's on a cruise at the moment. I keep telling her to ditch Harold and come live near me. She will one day. There's only so long you can convince yourself that you're happy when it's glaringly obvious to everyone else that you're completely miserable, even if you are cashed up."

I can't control myself any longer. I don't give a shit

about what Mrs Sanderson is up to. "Do you like living in Melbourne? Did you finish your apprenticeship? Are you still with the same girl?" I don't even take a breath. "Are you happy? Did you bring Eric's notebook? Why did you come back here?"

My manic interrogation doesn't even faze him. He slowly brings his foot down on top of an especially large chunk of bark. It sounds like someone biting into a carrot. He must find the noise satisfying because he steps on it a few more times, until it no longer makes a crunching noise at all. "I came here because I didn't know how to get through life without knowing that you were okay. So, I came. I came here for you."

I swallow hard. "I'm okay."

"Good. Yes, I like living there and I finished my apprenticeship and work for a big company. They won the contract to install all the plumbing on a new hospital, so that keeps me busy. I'm still with the same girl. You'd like her. I don't know if I'm happy. Yes, I brought Eric's notebook."

I don't know if I'm happy either. Are you meant to be able to feel if you are?

"I'd *like* her? As if I want to meet her. Yeah, no thanks."

"What if I wanted you to?"

"Why on earth would you want me to meet your girlfriend?" I scoff.

"I actually don't know," he admits. "Maybe because you and I have this kind of fucked up history that created an indefinable relationship where we're kind of absolutely nothing to each other yet something kind of incredibly special at the same time?" He lowers his foot onto a crisp piece of bark. "I just want to know if you like her."

All our interactions over the years would have ended with him sauntering off by now without looking back.

Something has changed.

I guess it straight away.

"You're getting married, aren't you?"

"She wants to, yeah."

"Do you want to?" I ask hesitantly, but I only want to hear the answer if it's *fuck no*.

"I don't know, Beatrice." I used to hate the way he called me that. Now I just want to hear him say it again and again. Forever. I wonder how his voice would pronounce my name after fifty years of practice. "No, I guess. But that's what you do, right? That's what's normal. You grow up, get a job and get married."

"As if we know anything about growing up normal."

He laughs quietly to himself. "Ah, so is that the problem? Abnormal children, clueless adults. I'm so busy trying to do what I'm meant to do, what we're supposed to do, I kind of really don't even think about what I want to do."

"Nah, I'm the clueless one. I think you've got it all figured out. I have to start my career now and I don't even know what my degree qualifies me to do."

"Shouldn't you be cutting people's toe nails and filing down their bunions?"

I dismiss his attempt to mock me. "You're hilarious."

"Sometimes. Maybe I do have it all figured out, but only what I'm *supposed* to have figured out. I've just tried too hard to be normal."

"I don't think you should get married."

He seems to like what I've said. "Enlighten me. Why shouldn't I get married?"

I frantically search my brain for a reason other than *because you should marry me* but my dad's words from earlier today block out every other thought. "You should be with someone who wants to be your partner in life." And then my own heart speaks, having obsessed over what the phrase *partner in life* means to *me* all day now. "You should be with someone who'd you want to go away with, just as much as you'd want to be home with."

The corners of his mouth curl upwards slightly. "Sounds like something your dad would say. She does, that's what she wants. I just don't know if she wants that with me personally. I think she just wants to get married for the sake of *being married*. Or maybe

I'm just sabotaging it because I'm sick of trying to tick all the right boxes. I don't really feel anything about it, like about getting married. I'm just indifferent. If you really want something, aren't you meant to *feel* it?"

I spend too long trying to figure out if he is asking that rhetorically, so it becomes awkward to say anything directly in response. I tread on a crunchy piece of bark at the exact same time as Liam treads on one himself. His smile smooths out the knot in my stomach and butterflies flutter in its place.

The trail starts to curve back around towards the resort.

"If I read Eric's notebook, do you think it will change anything for me?"

Liam runs his hand over the back of his head, brushing his hair upwards. "Fuck. Eric's notebook. Yes. I think it will shatter your whole world, Beatrice. It will change everything."

"I'll read it then."

"You can, I won't keep it from you. But just think

about it for a while, okay. I've got it, it's safe. The problem is, once you read it, there's no way to come back from that. Would you rather just not know something or spend the rest of your life wishing you could forget it?"

Bar the crunch of the bark, we walk the rest of the trail in complete silence. As soon as we reach the caravans, I rush past them to get to the safety of the cabins. I'm the one who doesn't look back this time.

"Beatrice!" Liam unexpectedly calls out. I was unaware he followed me. "It's not a notebook. Okay?"

"Huh?"

"Eric's notebook. It's not a notebook."

I'm so sick of everything being so cryptic and unresolved. I'm so sick of everyone tiptoeing around the truth, or more accurately, just not talking about things at all. Pretending none of it ever happened. I'm not a little kid anymore. I know my brother liked to make up disturbing stories. I understand that he had some sort of depression. I'm aware that he killed himself. I get it. I can clearly handle heavy stuff. There are no secrets in Eric's notebook. I remember the stories. I just didn't get to hear them all. "What do you mean it's not a notebook?"

Liam takes his hands out of his pockets and clasps them together in front of his chest like he's praying. His voice breaks. "It's a diary. The notebook was Eric's diary."

I take it back. I want to go back to everyone tiptoeing around the truth. Or not talking about things. I try to speak but my throat has closed over, trapping a million words. I've never been conscious of my vocal cords before, but I can feel them now, fused together.

Liam takes a step closer, so he is standing right in front of me. He puts a single finger under my chin, tilting my head up so I am forced to look at him. "Everything is going to be okay, Beatrice. Meet me at the lake tonight, after the countdown. Okay? We'll read the notebook together. We'll read Eric's diary together."

I can merely nod. And then he walks away, like he

does.

 "Okay," I whisper.

Inside the cabin, Jake welcomes me affectionately. He's in an amorous mood. "This is like having our own little house. Like how it will be when we get married one day and have three bratty kids running around."

I smile half-heartedly. "Sounds nice. I'm going to go freshen up for the barbecue."

Jake playfully slaps my bum as I turn towards the bedroom to change clothes. "I like your leggings."

I don't feel the same thrilling jolt that I did when Liam noticed I was wearing them. I really wish Jake wasn't here right now. "I went for a big walk while you had your nap."

"Ah, so you got changed! I didn't think you were wearing them this morning; I would have noticed!"

I can't be bothered arguing with him. I've had them on all day.

I smother myself in spray-on deodorant and get

dressed in the new boho blouse that Cat got me for Christmas and a long black skirt. Furious with Liam, I brush my hair vigorously at the mirror. Damn him. Now I don't even know whether I want to read Eric's stupid notebook. *Would you rather just not know something or spend the rest of your life wishing you could forget it?* Apparently, it wasn't even a notebook. It was a diary. And I don't really understand the implications of that.

The bristles feel like rusty nails against my pounding head. My blood is boiling and my skin is on fire. A frenzied desire to throw my brush across the room takes over and it lands with a vicious thud, snapping the handle off. I retrieve the brush and sit on the bed I will have to share with my boyfriend tonight, who doesn't like me and who I don't necessarily like either, plucking out the hairs caught in amongst the bristles. I consciously take exaggerated breaths with each strand I pull out. Inhale, pull out a hair, exhale, pull out a hair. Over and over until I can breathe again without having to remind myself how to.

Jake knocks to come in while he's already opening

the door.

"Ready? Worth coming after all, there's heaps of people out there! Looks sweet, let's go!"

My throat feels hoarse, as if I haven't had a sip of water in days. "Sure. I'm ready. We just have to go to my parents' and let them know it's time."

Jake releases an exasperated sigh. "Of course. Well hurry it up, it's beer o'clock!"

Mum and Dad are waiting for us next door. I greet them in relief while Mum feels my forehead with the back of her hand. "You okay, Bea? You look quite pale."

"I'm okay. Just tired and I need a drink."

Jake is clearly not as concerned. "Good, I wanna get smashed!"

Dad has never looked less impressed.

The reserve is packed. I can barely see the grass; it's completely covered in picnic rugs and deck chairs. And people, obviously. Music spanning five different decades booms from two tall speakers placed on either side of the salad table. I can feel Dad's brain trying to process the jump from The Beach Boys to Backstreet Boys. It must be hard for him not being in charge of the music now.

Mum lays our rug down, close to the slope that leads to the lake. Every year there seems to be less people here that we know, but Dad waves at a family I do recognise from when I was little. I remember calling the parents Uncle and Aunty, but their actual names elude me now.

Mum takes our seafood platter up to one of the shared tables of food. Scanning the crowd (mainly just to find out where Liam is sitting, and with whom), I wonder how everyone just seems to *know* about New Year's Eve at the lake. The gathering isn't advertised anywhere back at home and here there is no mention of it in the brochure. There aren't invitations. There's no banner up saying meet by the barbecue at 5pm. There are new people every year. And yet somehow, everyone knows the urban legend. New Year's Eve at the lake. There is always enough food and drink, even though not everyone contributes something. It's weird how that just seems to work out.

Dad brings me a can of Lemonade and I guzzle it gratefully before the bubbles even have the chance to die down. "I'll go get us some plates, you just sit and relax for a little while. Your mother's right, love. You look very pale."

Jake plops down next to me, having filled his plate with sausages and potato, and releases the two beers wedged under his arm. "One for me, one for you."

I really detest beer. I don't like the smell of it, let alone the taste of it. Jake would have never seen me drink a beer, because I don't. But I try to sound pleased anyway. "Thanks, I need that." I smile with tight lips, actively suppressing the urge to announce to the whole world how much I dislike my boyfriend. He doesn't even know what I like to drink.

Jake wants to be a theatre actor, but in the five months we've been together, I haven't heard about him going to one single audition. I showed him an ad in the paper, seeking supporting actors for a local production of Romeo and Juliet. He literally said "if they were looking for a Romeo, I would." He's so arrogant like that. Entitled. I don't even think he has an agent anymore. They probably dumped him when he turned down audition after audition because he thought the roles were beneath him.

Right now, sitting next to my boyfriend who I'm pretty sure I kind of hate, a strange, warped version of happiness washes over me. I don't like Jake. I don't like that he leaves for work ten minutes before his shift is about to start, knowing it's a fifteen-minute drive to get there. I don't like the way he only ever hugs me with one arm, never two. Does that even classify as a hug? And Jake doesn't like me. He likes hot girls in hot gym pants. He wants the best of everything; the most attractive girlfriend and the best part in the play. He's not for me, and I'm not for him. I've never been able to admit that to myself before, about any guy in my life. I've always felt that I had to do whatever I had to do to keep them, be whoever I had to be. Which was kind of okay at the time, because I've never known who I am. I still don't, but I'm starting to get a feel for who I might want to be.

Jake cuts up the three sausages soaking into his paper plate. I seem to have opened up some sort of portal and I don't know to close it again. I'm so in tune now with how much he annoys me and how freeing it is to be able to acknowledge it. He doesn't cut one piece and then eat it; he cuts up all three sausages, so his plate is soon full of bite-size pieces. It's the kind of plate a mother would prepare their kindergarten-aged child to minimise the risk of choking.

Mentally loathing my boyfriend, and bizarrely enjoying it, I greet Mum and Dad as they return to our rug with their own plates, plus one for me. Dad makes conversation with Jake while we eat and I keep a close eye on the crowd, trying to locate where Liam is sitting. But as soon as I spot him, I wish I hadn't.

On the other side of the reserve, Liam and his five friends sit facing each other on an Aztec blanket. They have a game of cards going but mainly just seem to be caught up in the atmosphere and genuinely entertained by each other's company. Liam looks so natural, like he is exactly where he is meant to be, and exactly who he is meant to be with.

The bubbly girl next to him is hard to look away from. The bubbly girl next to him is very clearly his girlfriend. I wonder what her name is. I bet it's something really pretty like Renee or Amanda. I'll just call her Bubbles.

Attractive is a subjective term, but every single person in the world would consider her to be pretty. She has shaggy, mahogany-coloured hair that skims her shoulders, highlighting her defined collarbone. She could be the lead actress in a romantic comedy. Her clothes look brand new. *She* looks brand new. She's thin enough and confident enough to wear a singlet much like the one Cat gave me, the one that has remained hidden in my wardrobe with my old painted rock collection for years.

She notices me staring and smiles sweetly. Most people would make an annoyed face, but she smiles. Of course she does. I bet she's the nicest person ever.

I stupidly pretend that I was looking straight past her and then casually commence picking at the plate in front of me as if I had been doing that all along, trying overtly hard to appear oblivious. But when I cautiously lift my eyes, Liam is on his way over, heading directly towards us. With Bubbles in tow, firmly clutching onto his brawny arm.

Had my body not gone into a sudden state of paralysis, I could literally wet myself.

"Mum, Dad," my voice croaks, "remember Liam?"

Mum drops her fork and Dad stands immediately, before he even sees him coming; arms tense by his side. Liam is half-way across the reserve now, and undoubtedly coming towards us, not the food table like I had originally hoped. Mum and I realise this at the same time, and stand up next to Dad.

Jake looks at us, confused. "Can I keep eating?"

Dad greets Liam in a voice that's equally welcoming and intimidating. "Liam. It's been a few years. Good to see you, lad." He extends his hand stiffly and Liam accepts it warmly.

"Thank you, sir. I hope you don't mind that I came to say hey."

I've swallowed a washing machine. My stomach is on spin cycle.

Mum glares at Liam, almost like a warning to be on his best behaviour and to not trigger Dad by bringing up Eric. She doesn't want to make a scene here. Ever, anywhere. Liam hasn't really interacted with my parents since the day of the funeral, when he tried to break up the fight between my dad and Mr Sanderson. Dad thought Liam was the last person Eric spoke to, and he was desperate to know if something had changed, or if Eric had said how he was feeling, anything at all about their final conversation that could bring some closure. But Liam wasn't the last person to speak to Eric.

I was.

And if Eric's notebook really was a diary, I'm petrified of what that conversation actually meant.

"Lovely to see you. This must be your lady?"

Ugh, Mum. Lady? Our family is already spoken about in whispers. I hardly think making us sound like we're from the 1800s is going to help people relate to us more.

Bubbles loves that Mum brought her into the conversation. She's been busting for someone to notice her. "I'm Laura," she says excitedly.

Liam and Laura. Sickly perfect.

"I already know who you guys are," she continues. "I've heard so much about you. I created your profiles in my mind but Liam really wanted me to meet you. I haven't even met his own parents yet, but he was desperate for me to meet you guys." She holds her hand against her heart. "Especially you, Bea. It's a real honour to meet you. You must be Liam's most favourite person ever."

"I wouldn't say that," Liam interrupts. "I just said we've known each other a long time is all."

We all seem to wear the same expression of sheer awkwardness. It masks the utter elation I feel inside knowing that Liam has been talking about me.

"I'm Jake," Jake announces, suddenly standing to join everyone. I had forgotten he was here. "I'm Bea's boyfriend."

Liam's smirk pisses me off. He's won this round and he knows it. His relationship is better than mine. "Well, it was good seeing you guys again. Take care."

Maybe that's why he came over, to gloat. To suss out who I ended up with and to rub it in my face that he found someone better than I did.

"You too, dear," Mum replies, already sitting herself down again.

Dad watches until Liam makes it over to the other side of the reserve, satisfied only when the physical distance between us is reinstated.

"Who was that guy?" Jake asks. "His girlfriend was pretty hot."

"Old family friend," Dad mumbles.

After we eat, my parents catch up with the few people here that they know and join their evidently thrilling round of Trivial Pursuit. Jake makes friends with a pair of tourists from New Zealand, Finn and Alison, and we spend the rest of the night drinking with them at one of the picnic tables. I look over to my parents a lot, wishing I was playing the game with them.

Finn and Alison met at the law firm where they both practice and have been married for ten months. They celebrated their marriage with a year-long honeymoon travelling around Australia in a campervan. Imagine enjoying someone's company that much. That's the kind of love my dad was talking about.

When they return home next month, they plan to buy a house and then start a family. They are both thirty-two years old.

Alison tops up my glass of wine. "Tell me more about you! How long have you guys been together? Any plans to get married? What do you do for a living?"

Jake and Finn are engrossed in their conversation but for the life of me I can't think what a driven, committed, inherently decent man like Finn could possibly have to talk about with someone like Jake. "Um, it's about five months now. No plans. I've just graduated uni, so I'll apply for some jobs now and just see, I guess."

"So exciting," Alison enthuses. "I remember those days. But it can be very overwhelming. There's so much pressure to plan the whole rest of your life, right now."

I like her. "I don't really have much idea about the rest of my life."

"That's okay. Some of the most interesting people I've met didn't know either. Who says you have to have everything figured out by a certain age anyway? We only think like that because we compare ourselves to everyone else and where they're up to. You can spend the whole rest of your life figuring it out, it doesn't matter."

I really like her.

The countdown begins, snapping me out of the hypnotising spell that Alison's enlightening outlook on life had cast on me. I frantically realise that I need to be with my parents before the new year starts. Liam is here, and I gather how gut wrenchingly hard it must have been for them to see him grown up, an adult, all set up in life. Eric never got to introduce a girlfriend to them. Would he have been just as tall as

Liam? Would he have worked out and had muscles too, or had padding like Dad and I, or stayed lean and petite like Mum? I forget sometimes: I lost my brother; they lost their son. Liam must have been a heartbreaking reminder of that.

I have to be with them.

8! 7! 6!

I promptly stand, visually locate my parents and hastily dart in their direction but one of my legs doesn't clear the bench, unexpectedly sending me on a thoroughly ungraceful nosedive to the ground instead. "Fucking hell!" I tug my leg, but my foot is wedged between the bench and the frame of the table, suddenly throbbing, obviously sprained.

5! 4! 3!

I probably should have declined that last glass of wine.

"Oh my god!" Alison cries, rushing to me.

"Far out, babe!" Jake laughs, still sitting. "Are you okay?"

At the same instant, Liam and my parents reach me from different directions.

2! 1! HAPPY NEW YEAR!

Mum cradles my head while Dad gently pushes my foot through. Liam crouches next to me, smoothing his fingers over my tear-soaked cheek. "I hate to point it out, but for someone who doesn't like to be noticed, you've started off the year with everyone staring at you."

I laugh in spite of the throbbing pain in my ankle. "I don't see how that's meant to make me feel better."

Mum smiles at Liam tenderly. "Hey, he got you laughing, didn't he?" *Just like Eric used to do.*

I hobble to my cabin with my arms looped over my parent's shoulders. They get me tucked up in bed while Jake parties on with his favourite people from New Zealand and any other country who wants to get sloshed with him.

Dad kisses me on the cheek. "You've got everything you need next to you. Water, phone. Don't get up."

"Have I wrapped your ankle too tight or does it feel okay?" Mum frets.

"It feels fine, Mum. I can't believe we finally used our first aid kit. Remember when Eric put it together? Remember he made you buy a purple box, just so I would like it? We bought band-aids and tweezers and all sorts of things for it. Remember he wanted to put a knife in there too?"

Dad nods bittersweetly. "I remember. He said he never understood why first aid kits didn't have self-defence tools in them. If you're stranded in the middle of nowhere, or if someone is after you, you need to have something you can defend yourself with. He said that."

I smile at the memory. Eric was always so concerned about keeping us safe. Especially me. *What if Bogart was real, how would you defend yourself, Buzzy? You need to be able to take care of yourself, you need to be able to hurt someone if they try to hurt you, no matter who they happen to look like.* But sometimes, he didn't seem quite as concerned. He didn't seem concerned at all. *You didn't hold your breath for long enough! I bet I can hold it for longer than you can. You can't release it until it feels like you're going to die. Ready? One, two, three. Hold your breath!*

Mum firmly ends the conversation, despite not participating in it. "Bea needs to rest, Mitch. Good night, honey. We'll see you in the morning. I'm sure Jake won't be long."

The combination of Panadol and wine quickly induces a deep slumber, until a heavy tap at the window snaps me awake. The clock says 1:18am, and the side of the bed next to me has yet to be slept in. Muffled music and distant voices establish my bearings. I haven't even been asleep for an hour yet. The celebrations continue outside. What a difference a new crowd makes.

I comply with my eyes' strong urge to close again, ready to return to the successful sleep I was actually having for once, before the tap at the window sounds again.

"Jesus, what time is it even?" I mumble, limping over to peep through the curtains. I expect to see a possum or a branch blowing in the breeze, not the object of my childhood disdain and adulthood obsession. But there he is. Right outside my window. The flawless full moon hovers behind him, tinted blue ever so lightly, and for just a split second, I question whether I am actually dreaming. "What are you doing?"

"Your parents locked up. Meet me out the front."

"No way! Jake will come back soon."

"He's bellowing out Run to Paradise with the rest of them. That's not usually the grand finale."

"Just give me a sec." I close the curtains and madly run my broken brush through the tangles in my hair. There's no time to change, so I hastily put a hoodie on over my singlet and pray that he doesn't laugh at my baggy, chequered pyjama pants.

Liam sits on the front deck, feet resting on the lone step. "Nice pants."

I roll my eyes as I squeeze down next to him. The header is narrow, only just wide enough for us both. Our shoulders unavoidably touch; our hips connect snugly. I tuck my lips together and remind myself that he has a girlfriend, that he doesn't love me, that surely, I don't really love him, that he's just someone I used to know and it's only his connection to Eric that draws me to him, that I'm wearing the ugliest pyjama pants ever and my actual boyfriend who I don't technically like, at all, could stagger home any second. "Thanks."

"Seriously, I like them. You look hell cute."

My body temperature triples. "Jake will be back soon. I'm sorry it didn't work out, meeting at the lake after the countdown I mean."

"If I wasn't looking at you when you sprained your ankle, I wouldn't have known why you couldn't come. I would have thought you'd stood me up."

He was looking at me. "It really hurts. I think it's just a little sprain though, it's not broken or anything."

"His name's Jake, right? Why didn't he come back with you?"

I consciously try to sound nonchalant. "Oh, well, I mean he knew Mum and Dad would look after me, I guess. He likes partying. He works at a nightclub. I'm sure he'll ask if I'm okay in the morning."

"You mean when he's hung over?"

"Can you just not? Please?"

"Why him, Beatrice? Come on, you can do so much better than that guy."

His self-righteous opinion on my love-life infuriates me. "So, you don't want me but you don't want anyone else to have me either? Is that it?"

He grips the slender temple of his glasses, rubbing his fingers on the gold metal. "I never said I didn't want you."

"Come on, Liam. What are you doing? Your girlfriend wants to marry you, and she's lovely by the way. It was glaringly obvious how into you she is. You don't need me."

"I know I don't need you. You're so desperate to be needed, you can't see how much better it is to be wanted."

"What is going on? It's the middle of the night, my ankle is killing me, and you're not making any sense."

"I'm sorry. I'm confused. I've *been* confused. It was

two years. I didn't see you for two years. It affected me more than I thought it would. I thought about you every fucking day. I didn't know if I was ever going to see you again, and that kind of killed me inside. I was trying so hard to tick all the right boxes, and then there was *you*. Always you in the back of my mind. You make me restless. And it's not that I don't want anyone else to have you, I'm not an arsehole. It's that you deserve the fucking world. You should be put on a pedestal and taken care of, loved, properly. Anyway. Did you get a mobile yet? Can we keep in contact and like, be friends or something? I just don't want to leave here and not have you in my life again."

I stare across the darkened sky, immaculately decorated with thousands of twinkling stars. I swiftly make a wish on the first one that captures my focus. It almost feels ungrateful, spoilt, considering I literally just got what I have always hoped and wished on stars for: Liam thinks about me. I mean something to him. There were times when I was certain I no longer meant anything at all to Eric. I guess part of me relied on Liam to make up for that.

"We can be friends. I do have a phone; I'm just not the best at using it."

"Let's swap numbers."

"Okay."

A satisfied smile creeps across his lips, adorably crinkling his eyes at the corners. "Okay."

If the revolutionary words in Eric's diary will change my life forever, will they change my connection to Liam, too? If it will cut the invisible thread that somehow ties us together, I need to hide the scissors.

"I don't want to read Eric's notebook yet. I mean, his diary. I think I want to wait. If I'm going to spend the rest of my life wishing I didn't know something, I'm not ready for the rest of my life to start right now."

"I completely respect that, Beatrice. I'll just bring it every year until you're ready, okay? And if I can't come up here one year, you'll have my number. So, the second you decide you want to read it, you can contact me and I'll bring it to you. No matter where you are. Okay?"

"Okay, friend."

He licks his bottom lip as if tasting his newly appointed title. Patting his knees, he stands and extends his hand. "Come on, *friend*, I'll help you back to bed."

I guess he liked the way it tastes.

New Year's Eve 2001

The first text message came from him. I refused to message him first. Even though I desperately wanted to. We wrote our numbers down on the palm-sized flip notepad that it seems every single cabin comes equipped with. I kept the piece of paper in my purse, folded into quarters, and looked at it every single day, willing myself not to contact him. I made sure to re-fold it precisely along the same creases so as not to make the paper more crinkled and hence Liam's handwriting more distorted. I glared at my phone, manifesting an SMS from him, refusing to be the one to initiate contact.

Our annual encounter at the lake had always been traditionally brief, and then I would spend all year wishing that there was some magical way that I could hear from him. Now that I had found myself in possession of a shiny, black electronic device that facilitated the possibility of contact, all I could do was stare at it in fear.

Two months later, after I had almost given up on ever hearing from him, my phone lit up, illuminating my soul with it.

> **Liam:** Hi Beatrice. Liam Sanderson here. If you can figure out how to reply, I'd love to hear from you.

Formal, with a hint of teasing. Very him. I fought the urge to send an instantaneous reply by timing my watch for ten long, torturous minutes.

> **Me:** Very funny. I do know how to text, actually. See?

> **Liam:** I bet it takes you five minutes to type each word. What have you been up to?

> **Me:** Seven minutes. You're not as smart as you think you are. Working at a newspaper. What have you been up to?

Liam: Doing what? Freezing the foot warts off the journalists?

Me: You're hilarious. You're never going to let that go, are you? I did like three months of that course.

Liam: It will be funny forever. What do you do at the paper?

Me: I'm just an assistant, like an office all-rounder, no one important. I organise interviews and do fact checking, stuff like that. Fumbling my way through. You didn't tell me what you have been up to.

Liam: Same as usual. Are you still with Jake?

Evasive as ever. His interest in whether or not Jake was still a part of my life fuelled me with a smug sense of victory. I revelled in having the upper hand.

Me: No.

I can be evasive, too.

Liam: Good. Hope you dumped him.

That guy really pissed me off.

My smile swallowed my whole face.

> **Me:** Did you really only message to talk about my ex?

> **Liam:** No. Just wanted to check that you're okay.

> **Me:** I am.

> **Liam:** Good. Talk soon.

We didn't talk soon.

Two whole weeks went by before I heard from him again.

But after I did, the messages came every single day, and I quickly grew addicted, bordering on emotionally reliant, as I tend to get with things sometimes. The world for me remained perpetually precarious, until my phone pinged. Sometimes he'd talk about the movie he and Laura were watching, sometimes he'd just send me a good night text, having had no time to message during the day. Yesterday he gleefully told me that the six pack of chicken nuggets he ordered came with seven in the box. The bonus chicken nugget made his whole week. It's a special feeling, knowing someone out there is just as excited to share the mundane moments with you as the amazing ones.

Laura sometimes texts me hello from Liam's phone and has mentioned that she wants to keep my number so that we can chat, independent of Liam. She wants us to get to know each other. Laura is a really lovely person, inherently likable. I hate her.

She reminds me of Mindy.

I'm still struggling with the guilt-ridden notion that my brother's childhood best friend is kind of becoming my best friend, too. I don't know if I am betraying Eric somehow.

I did in fact dump Jake, the morning after I hurt my ankle. For the first time in my life, I ended a relationship that I knew wasn't right for me. I dropped the charade and stopped ignoring the glaringly obvious fact that I wasn't the right person for him either.

"Are you seriously breaking up with me?" His eyes bulged from the shock, as if he had genuinely considered us to be in a happy relationship, even though both of us were clearly just choosing each other over being alone. "What the fuck? Why? Things aren't that bad?"

"They're not, but they're not that great either. Don't you want to be in a relationship that's *great*? Why do we need to just accept mediocre? We both deserve something that feels fantastic. Don't you think?"

"What's not fantastic? I treat you fine."

I had hoped that Jake would agree with me, shake hands and part ways with a spring in his step. I wasn't really prepared for a fallout.

"You're not a bad person, Jake. And I'm not either. But together, we're not great people. Most times I'd rather go play Scrabble with my parents than hang out with you, and you keep one eye on me and the other looking out for someone better. We're not right for each other."

"I'll play Scrabble with your parents too then." He

actually got upset. "Come on, please, Bea. I'm like thirty-five now. You're meant to be my safety girl."

I guess the panic of being alone made him oblivious to how gut wrenchingly offensive that was. Evidently the fear of solitude had also blinded me to the fact that I'd been dating a man in his mid-thirties. I'd only just turned twenty-one.

"I want to be someone's *girl*," my voice croaked, "minus the safety. We're never going to sing along to Willie Nelson together, and I deserve someone who wants me around because he loves me, not just because he can tolerate me."

"You know, you're not exactly swamped with options. I've been generous, sticking it out with you when I could get any girl I want in the club. Happy fucking New Year to you, too!" He slammed the door on his way out and found his own way home, probably with his new besties from New Zealand.

Even my ankle started to feel better after he stormed off.

I haven't missed him yet.

My job title is specifically Field Research Assistant. The bulk of my working day is spent fact-checking story proposals and sourcing newsworthy material from the community, and booking interviews with council members about plans they have no intention of implementing, like adding more shade at playgrounds or imposing a cat curfew. I accompany the journalists on their interviews and press record on the dictation recorder and then once back in my cramped cubicle in the bustling office, transcribe the recording for the journalist to write their article. But it's become an unspoken expectation by my superior, Terence, that I transcribe his interviews into actual articles.

Terence is heading towards retirement and hasn't really kept up with the times; he still thinks it's socially acceptable to tell blonde jokes in the staff room, directly to the blonde women who work there. He has two grandchildren and a third on the way. He has been married for forty years. Everybody knows all that. But what no one knows apart from me, is that Terence can't do his job properly anymore.

When I first started at the paper, I overheard the editor brand Terence's piece on the upcoming community spring markets *utter trash*. Joel is a twenty-six-year-old prick in a tailored suit that would cost a month of my salary. I imagined how humiliating it must have felt for Terence to be spoken to like that by someone young enough to be his grandson. Terence had thirty-five years of experience in journalism and his boss was fresh out of uni. The blatant disrespect pissed me off. But what really upset me, was when I found Terence huddled over his desk, quietly crying.

I've witnessed my parents struggle through unspeakably hard times. I've spied my dad crying privately in his shed. But this was different, because unlike every other time I've known something was wrong, I could fix this.

In my little cubicle, I set to work and wrote a new article for Terence. It was easy enough to compose. Instead of changing the gory details in Eric's stories to create upbeat happy endings, I changed Terence's tired, lacklustre words into an article worthy of publication. The familiarity of editing was simultaneously comforting and terrifying. Terence was sombre when I handed the new piece to him, as if realising something about himself that he wasn't quite ready to accept yet. But now it's just what we do, him and I, our strange little secret. He takes the interview, I write the article and then he changes two or three words for a pay cheque much more substantial than mine, and it's published in the weekly *Stay Tuned!* section of the popular read, credited with his well-known name and photo.

"Ah, bless, what would I do without you?" he says as I sneak his work into his office. I can't email it, that would leave a trail, he tells me. He always flips through the pages quickly while I'm there, as if making sure that I didn't try to cheat him. "It's all here, good girl."

Terence needs me. That's the kind of thing I get hooked on, no matter how lousy the pay is. Being needed feeds me more than an actual pay cheque.

> **Liam:** How's work? Still ghost writing for that washed up old journalist?

Liam keeps telling me to apply for the job that I'm already doing for somebody else. I don't know what I want to do for the rest of my life, but I do know that working at a newspaper isn't it. I have even less idea about what I want to do when I grow up now than when I actually was growing up.

> **Me:** There's more to life than money and public recognition. Ever heard of being nice?
>
> **Liam:** Nope. Pass on that shit. This might be the only time I'll ever say this, but Cat is right. You're being used.

Cat hates Terence. Her hatred for him brought out an aggressive side I didn't know she had. Designer clothes on the outside, impassioned misandrist on the inside.

"Fucking men in power!"

"Terence has worked hard his whole life," I reasoned. "It's not a big deal; it doesn't take me that long."

"Working hard his whole life doesn't give him the

right to use someone else so he can cruise along until retirement! I can't believe you're actually allowing a man to take credit for your work."

"He has a family. He just needs to get through another year or so."

"That's not your problem! Give me Joel's email. He's bloody toxic too but at least he might fire fucking Terence!"

"Cat, just no, just let it go. It's not a big deal."

"He's using you! It's a very big deal! Stop letting people walk all over you just because you're scared that they won't like you! Give me the email, or I'll break into the office and empty Cleo's cat tray all over Terence's desk!"

I didn't give her the email. Terence's desk has so far stayed clean but Cat does lecture me at least once a week about the patriarchy and self-respect.

Dad's knee has been playing up, so I'm driving us to the lake this year. Mum sits in the back and Dad rides shotgun as we sing along to On the Road Again, again. Dad calls Cat on my phone so she can be a part of it. She's staying at our house with her boyfriend while her apartment is being redecorated. I believe the look desired now is Scandinavian.

Liam won't be there. He's spending New Year's with Laura's family. Now that they're officially engaged, she wants him to get to know her siblings more. Laura wants a big wedding. She's narrowed it down to six bridesmaids but she's worried about offending some of her cousins, so thinks she might end up with eight. Liam told me he'd be happy just to do their vows at the lake, with me as his best man.

I park in the gravel driveway next to cabin 17. Pat and Joanie's caravan is just over from us, but I can only wave to Pat. Joanie must be inside.

Dad wants to break in the new fishing rod he got for Christmas and Mum is keen to start reading the new biography she got, so they head to the jetty together, hand in hand. Noticing that Dad hasn't rubbed in his sun cream properly, Mum smooths her hand over the back of his neck. I watch them from the deck of our cabin and somewhat aggressively squeeze half the tube onto my arms and legs, depressed at the thought that I will likely never have anyone notice let alone care whether or not my sun cream is rubbed in properly. I'm just gonna get skin cancer and die alone.

Grabbing my well-read copy of A Walk to Remember, I wander to a quiet spot by the lake, eager to lose myself in Landon and Jamie's tragically doomed love. At least they had a valid reason for not being able to stay together. I just drift from one shitty relationship to the next. Doesn't matter anyway: Liam is getting married. He'll spend his life having amazing sex and dancing with his wife in the kitchen and watching scary movies cuddled up on the couch. I will have to search forever to find someone who could possibly love me as much as I love Liam.

Still on the first chapter, someone pulls my attention away from the words on the page and the woe-is-me thoughts in my head. "Mind if I join you?"

I've never heard her voice before, not this close anyway. It's deeper than most women's. Pat has never ventured away from her caravan. I didn't think Pat or

Joanie ever did. Her presence feels unnatural; instantly hinting at the fact that something is wrong. "Sure."

Pat sits down next to me; raised knees wide apart. Eyes sunken and skin so dry it looks sore. "We were lovers for sixteen years. Nobody knew. She went back to her family, and I went back to my life, alone. The caravan stayed parked in my driveway, waiting. I tried to make it as nice as I could for us. Because it was our home, if only for four days every year. It was a glimpse of our make-believe, our what-if, wouldn't-it-be-so-wonderful life. A little taste of happiness. She told her husband she was visiting her sister interstate. We only lived on opposite ends of the city, a thirty minute drive from each other. We spoke on the phone, when we were both at work. We were so in love, but she was scared that she would lose her children, and neither one of us had come out. None of my friends think to ask if I'm okay, because I never told them that I was seeing someone, let alone a woman, who was married to a man, and that she got sick. She got so sick. The cancer spread everywhere. I've lost the love of my life and nobody knows." Pat's flooded eyes plead with mine. "Can you be the person who knows?"

Her pain leaps into my body, seizing my emotions. I can only listen as this broken woman, essentially a stranger to me, bares her soul, desperate for another human being to be aware of her heartbreak. Sometimes the only way to relieve your suffering is to let someone else *know*.

A crushing unity exists between Pat and I. Maybe if someone else knew for me, maybe if I had told, instead of appointing myself Eric's guardian even though I was a mere child myself, maybe, maybe he might still be here. *Maybe*. What a torturous word. What a cruel concept.

The words squeeze past the growing lump in my throat. "I'm so sorry."

She sobs into her knees, her whole body shaking. All I can do is put my hand on her back, and cry freely with her. I cry for Joanie. I cry for the heartache that Pat will now bear forever. I understand it painfully well. No papier-mâché volcano. No misplaced necklace or broken window, days or weeks later.

Nothing needs to trigger the raw, cathartic tears that stream uncontrollably down my cheeks. I cry for exactly the reason I want to, exactly when I feel it.

"I wish it had been me," she weeps. "Her poor babies. They're so young. Miller is just seven, Ellie is nine and Justin is twelve. They've lost their mum. It should have been me that got sick, me that died. I've got nothing, she had everything. Why her? Why couldn't they take me instead? Her life meant more."

The guilt of living can crush you. The guilt of being the one who is okay, the one who survived. I've tortured myself every single night, wandering the darkened streets, wrestling with the guilt that it was Eric and not me. I've said the same thing: his life meant more. He fought harder for it. I feel self-conscious, like I have to prove to everyone that I am good enough to be alive. That I was worth it. I know deep down that if it had been me who died, Eric would still be here. His diary will tell everyone that.

I scrunch Pat's shirt beneath my hand, wanting to hold her as tight as I can. I want to absorb even just the tiniest fleck of her pain so that she isn't completely consumed by it, isn't fighting it completely alone. I doubt she feels my effort, I doubt it makes a difference. But I sit by the lake and try so hard for her anyway, crying with, and for, the women who have taught me how to.

I wake up the next day just before midday. We all went to bed straight after the countdown. But for the first time since I can remember, I slept through the whole night. Nearly twelve hours of deep, healing slumber born from years of sheer mental exhaustion, perhaps finally enabled by the tears I shared with a woman whose name I don't even technically know. Or maybe because my mind finally sought rest instead of answers to questions it really already knows.

"I held my finger under your nose to make sure you were still breathing!" Dad jokes as I stumble into the kitchen like a bear awakening from its winter hibernation.

Mum tenses.

As if suffering a hangover, I shield my eyes from the excessively bright sunshine bursting through the open slots of the venetian blinds. "I think I'm going to go to bed early tonight. I'm still so tired."

New Year's Eve 2002

Liam: Are you here yet?

Me: About an hour away.

Liam: Edna's handing out half-price hotdogs. You're missing out.

Me: She must be in her 80s now. She's probably got dementia and doesn't realise. Did you and Laura get one?

Liam: I got one, she got two. I'll never understand how she eats so much and stays so thin.

Me: Just lucky. Some people get all the good things in life.

Liam: We've got a cabin right next to

the games room. Laura wants to play ski-hockey with you.

Me: I thought I wasn't allowed in the games room, remember?

Liam: I remember. Just tried to give you some space and keep you safe when Eric wasn't really around.

Me: I remember too.

"Jesus, Mitch!" Mum throws her arms forwards, bracing herself against the dashboard as the car comes to a sudden halt.

The koala responsible scurries off the road, disappearing into the bush.

"You okay, Bea?" Dad checks, before responding to the growing number of honks behind him with a finger gesture out the window. "Fucking koalas. Did you see? She was carrying a baby on her back!"

"I saw! I've never seen that before. Liam says the lake is quiet this year."

"I wouldn't trust anything that little upstart says."

"He's okay, Dad. He was a good friend to Eric."

"Oooh, I forgot to tell you!" Mum chimes in, predictably changing the subject. "Guess who I saw at the shops the other day?"

"Willie Nelson?" Dad jokes.

"No, dear. Ebony! She was in her full police uniform, looking quite intimidating. I think she was even carrying a gun!"

"She'd like that," I smile, "being intimidating."

I don't tell them, but I also saw someone at the shops the other day. Pippa. She walked straight past me as if she genuinely never knew me at all. Perhaps she didn't realise that she did. There was really only a fleeting look of recognition, that read more as if she was trying to figure out whether or not she did know me, and then a swift re-focus to the make-up section to her left. I wasn't sad or offended, but it was sobering to think that we're all another slightly-familiar face in the shops to someone. By the end of my life, imagine how many people will look at me and wonder *hmm, do I know her?*

Liam: I brought the diary, if you're ready.

Me: I am.

Liam: Laura can't wait to see you. She wants to talk to you about something. She won't tell me what it is.

Shit. I abruptly flip my phone face down onto the middle seat, but Liam's text still feels too close so I nudge it further away from me, all the way across to the other side of the car. Panic grabs me by the throat as if an actual person is attacking me. Laura wants to talk. She's going to tell me to stop being friends with her fiancé. I've overstayed my welcome and I'm a nuisance to them both now. I swallow the rising trepidation, preparing for my fate of a humiliating New Year's.

Laura hunts me down as soon as we arrive. If it's possible, she looks even prettier than she did when I first met her a couple of years ago. Her hair is longer, softening her sharp features.

"Beaaaaaaaaaaaaaaaaa!" she squeals, wrapping her

slender arms around my neck and planting a theatrical kiss on my cheek. "Mwah!" I squeeze my arms stiff against my sides but she doesn't pick up on my discomfort. "So weird to see you after so long," she babbles on, "even though we all talk all the time."

I knew it. She's sick of me being friends with Liam. I dig my heels into the grass, wishing my whole body would sink into the prickly surface.

Dad and Liam exchange a tense *hi*.

Mum's innate fear of conflict and disharmony compels her to separate everyone as a matter of priority. "I'll take your bag in, love. You kids go have fun." She steals my bag and ushers Dad into the cabin.

Embarrassed that Mum made me sound like a child heading off on a play date, I tuck my hair behind my ear and laugh awkwardly. "I think sometimes she forgets that I'm nearly twenty-three years old."

As if mirroring me, Liam smooths his hand over the side of his overgrown hair in slow motion, but most likely my pathetically smitten eyes and irrational obsession just process the first sighting of him in two years in that speed. "Come on, kids, let's go have fun."

I dismiss his dig at my mother. "Hilarious as always, Liam."

Suddenly shy, he frowns, as if confused. It occurs to me that I don't usually call him by his name. I think it occurred to him too.

I've gone this long without seeing him before. Survived this long without seeing him. But this time it felt different, maybe because we became so emotionally connected that the physical distance was a mere technicality. But right now, the distance no longer exists, and his physical presence is knocking the breath right out of me.

Laura loops her arm through mine and leads us to the games room. The three of us walk together in a row, down the same gravel path that Liam and I once trod with Eric. "Did Liam tell you I want to talk to you about something?" she blurts out excitedly.

I brace myself for intense humiliation. I'm about to be told to piss off and leave them alone, so they can be a couple and get married and start a family and live in peace without some annoying girl in the background who professed her undying love to her husband. "Sorry, I shouldn't message Liam so much."

Liam seems to choke on his own breath. "What? Where did that come from? I'm the one who messages you, anyway."

"When Liam first told me about you, I admit I felt pretty insecure." Laura's voice is so out of place here; it has a twang to it as if she is from another country, even though I know she's from Melbourne. I learned that the same day I told Liam that I was in love with him. "The way he spoke about you, so much protection in his voice, so much affection, I wasn't sure if I should be jealous or even more enamoured with him for caring so much about someone. I didn't know if he thought of you as a little sister, or a best friend, or a worst enemy! It was very confusing to me."

Cat said the same thing years ago when I enlisted her to be my private investigator. *Do you love him or hate him? What's the deal? Are you friends? What is he to you, I don't get it!* I have never been able to define what Liam is to me. What I do know, is that he isn't mine. "I think you are both so lucky to have each other. You have something really special."

"He's alright," she smiles, devotion splattered across her face. "I know he loves me. But what I wanted to talk about, was the fact that he also loves you."

I'm so aware of my eyes, popped open in shock. I make a conscious effort to squint to prevent them from bursting out of their sockets altogether. "What?"

I wait for Liam to say something but he seems content to remain silent. I expect him to freak out, but he strolls along somewhat stoically, hands in his pockets, as if everything is perfectly fine. Meanwhile, my body's flight response kicks in, whispering to me that I should run away. Liam isn't mine and I'm ruining his life.

"I'm sorry I made myself a third wheel. I'll leave you

guys alone."

"I'm not done yet," Laura laughs, squeezing my arm tighter. "Relax, everything is okay. I just wanted to say this. Love isn't only reserved for couples."

"I'm sorry if I've overstepped the mark or anything," I panic. "I know Liam and I talk a lot." I try to joke, "I guess I always did follow him around."

"You don't need to be sorry, silly. It's fine that you guys are friends. I just want us to be close too, because you're like a part of him, you're a part of who he is."

Liam clears his throat. Finally, some sign of discomfort. It's almost a relief to see him react, so I don't feel like I'm being ganged up on by the pair of them. "Laura knows about Eric."

"Oh," I whisper. He's told our secret.

"Anyway," Laura exclaims in her oddly deep south American accent, "we are all friends here, okay?"

I suddenly sense the condescending tone in her voice. "Okay."

"This is a safe place, right here, between us three. I can really help you. I'm studying psychology and I would really love to pick your brain for my thesis, when you're ready of course. The whole teenage suicide thing really ties in with it."

I only manage to maintain my composure for one game of ski-hockey before excusing myself. I am on the verge of exploding. Liam betrayed me.

"I should probably head back to my parents, spend some time with them before the barbecue tonight." Laura can find another guinea pig for her research.

"Come on, we've only had one game!" Disappointment brings out a squeakiness to her voice. "You won, now you've gotta whip Liam's butt! I'll play the winner!"

Liam, however, seems relieved that this uncomfortable play date, as my mother called it, has come to an end. "Her parents will crack the shits if she doesn't get back soon."

We both know that my parents would be proud of me for spending time away from them.

Back inside the cabin, Mum and Dad play Scattergories at the table.

"Sun is not a colour!" Mum moans.

"It is!" Dad retorts.

"Just because you couldn't think of a colour starting with s doesn't mean you can choose any random thing in the world and say it's a colour!"

"Alright, what did you put?"

"Silver, dear," Mum replies, deadpan.

"There's also saffron, sky blue, scarlet," I offer, sitting down next to Dad. "Or if you really wanted sun, you could have said sunset orange."

Dad smiles to himself. "You were always our little writer."

I scrunch my whole face in a subconscious attempt to stifle a rage brewing inside me. "I was not! I don't write. I never wrote anything."

"Mitch," Mum says firmly, shaking her head at him. "Okay, next round, you playing, Bea?"

I can't let it rest. Everyone handles me with care, as if I could break any second. Laura thinks I'm crazy enough to study. "If you mean those stupid articles at work, Terence writes them, I just spruce them up a bit."

"Which you shouldn't be doing. You know how I feel about that. I'll buy Cat the cat litter if needs be!"

Frustrated, I turn to Dad, pleading with him to explain what he meant.

"Honey?" he says to Mum, a much more elaborate question lurking beneath that one word.

Mum exhales, prolonged and seemingly laborious. "Just those stories you used to write, and Liam drew pictures for them, like they were little books. You were always writing stories."

The room closes in on me. "Eric wrote them. Eric wrote the stories."

"It's okay," she says softly, rolling the lettered dice. "W. Everyone got list seven up?"

"Eric wrote those stories, Mum."

"I know."

"No, you don't! Because you literally just said that I wrote them!"

Dad puts his hand on my thigh. "It's okay, baby. Be calm. We knew you were just trying to help."

"Eric wrote them!" The words incoherently splatter out of my mouth, drowning in frantic sobs.

Mum leaps up, rushing to my side of the table. She wraps her arms around me while Dad cups both his hands over mine, clasped together tightly on my knees.

"Eric. Wrote. Them." I hiccup as I gasp for air, desperately trying to suck it down into my lungs.

"Breathe, Buzzy," she whispers, "breathe."

Eric called me Buzzy. He was the only person who ever did. I know she wouldn't use his name for me. My subconscious is looking for him to make me feel better. Because he always did. When he was around, everything was perfect and normal and safe. But there were times when Eric couldn't be around, like when he would call me Bea. I knew in those moments that my big brother was slowly dying.

"I just wanted to create happy endings." My head flops down, weak from lack of oxygen. Mum instinctively catches me, pushing my forehead back before it bangs on the table.

"You did, do you hear me? You did a wonderful job." Her voice is adamant, insisting. "Eric's ideas were a bit scary and you made stories out of them. You made cute characters and sweet romances and no one ever got hurt." She wipes her face, quickly banishing the unwelcome tears pushing through. "It's okay. You didn't do anything wrong; do you hear me? We knew you wrote the stories; we knew you were trying to help him."

I clutch onto her arm, wrapped around my chest. "I don't understand. I don't understand anything!"

"You do, darling, you do." She cups my head and holds it close to her. "You do. You lived it. Nothing was your fault. Nothing was your responsibility. Just breathe. For now, just breathe."

So, I breathe. I breathe even though it feels like I literally can't, until I'm certain that I can.

An unspoken awareness that we are collectively falling apart because of me haunts my family for the rest of the day. Mum and Dad know everything, I realise that. I know everything, they realise that. The enormity of what I realise will only sink in for me when I read it in Eric's actual words. It's time.

We don't go to the barbecue. Dad conspicuously drives us into town to get pizza and we watch re-runs of The X-Files when we get back. We stay together to keep ourselves whole for just a little while longer.

Mum and Dad retire to bed about an hour before the countdown, but I have no intention of sneaking out tonight.

"Mum? Dad? Are you asleep yet?" I ask through the ajar bedroom door, possibly a mere forty-five seconds after they called out goodnight to me.

"No, baby," Mum murmurs. "What's wrong?"

"Just wanted to let you know I'm going to the lake

for a little while."

She sits up in bed and taps Dad in frustration when he doesn't do the same.

"What?" he gasps, snapping awake.

"There's not a big crowd, I just want to go for a little while, just for the countdown. I can wake you up when I come back if you want."

"It's late, Bea, it's not really safe wandering around on your-"

"That would be great," Dad interrupts, "if you could wake us up when you get back in."

Mum reluctantly concedes defeat. "Don't go too close to the lake."

"I'll be okay, promise. I won't do anything stupid. I just want to catch up with Liam."

Dad is already cuddled back into Mum's side, snoring peacefully.

"I trust you," she says softly as she gently lowers herself back down in bed to reciprocate Dad's cuddle. "Sometimes I just forget that you're perfectly safe now."

Mum must be about to fall asleep herself: she isn't making much sense.

"Thanks, Mum. Night. Love you."

" Love you more."

Pat waves from her deckchair as I venture past, as if she has been keeping an eye out for me. The glow from the lamppost nearby filters her caravan, and even Pat appears as if captured in a vintage photograph. A black dog with a grey face loyally lies at her feet.

Across the reserve, I spot Liam sitting under a tree with Laura and a few other people they've obviously made friends with. The aroma from the barbecue lingers in the air. There is a peaceful vibe to the sparse crowd. Apart from the nearby game of volleyball, everyone sits with their own small group, chatting and drinking away while Eminem's Without Me sounds from the speakers at a low volume. The families with young children must have gone to bed already.

Liam spots me too and stands before I reach him. The cool breeze pushes my shirt against my tummy, bestowing him with a massively unflattering view of my silhouette. I fold my arms low on my chest, mentally cursing the elements of nature as I approach him.

"Hey, how you guys going?"

Laura jumps up excitedly. "So healthy of you to come join us, Bea. That's a real step in the right direction."

My jaw clamps shut and I force out a tight-lipped smile. She's actually practising her counselling bullshit on me. "Thanks. Got to keep making those steps." I fear my sarcasm comes across as bitchiness, but I'm done putting everyone else's feelings before my own. At the cost of my own. "I was just hoping to steal Liam for a little bit."

"Oh yes, yes of course, go for it. He told me you two needed to catch up about things. Liam?" She almost ushers him away. No doubt she'll grill him later for all the details so she can write about me in her thesis. I wonder if she's made Liam wear a wire.

He kisses her cheek; swiftly, I notice, so it barely connects with her skin.

"I'll be back for the countdown. You okay here?"

"I'm fine, go."

Lighting a cigarette on the walk up to Liam's cabin, he has the audacity to scold me for smoking.

"I told you Cat was a bad influence on you. That stuff'll destroy your lungs."

"Cat quit ages ago." I expel the smoke dramatically slowly and relish the sight of it wafting towards him. I hope it makes him cough. "I don't need anybody to influence me, I'm perfectly capable of making my own bad decisions."

"I can see that."

I butt the cigarette on the porch of Liam's cabin while he goes inside to fetch Eric's notebook. Or diary. If I find out that he let Laura read it, I will never speak to him again.

The second he returns, I snatch it out of his hands. "I'll carry it."

He pushes his glasses back by the bridge. "Aren't you coming in?"

"No way, I'm not stepping one foot inside your romantic little love shack." I loathe myself for sounding so childish. I'm taunted by a manic desire to punch something. I'm sure I can literally feel my blood flow accelerate. I'm so angry, but I don't really know at what.

Liam is so calm and it's pissing me off even more. "You can keep the notebook. It's yours, if you want it to be."

I squint my eyes, unable to hide my anger. "It *is* mine. It always has been. You were meant to keep it safe."

"I did," he stammers, suddenly no longer stoic. A visible pain etches its way across his face. Good. "She didn't read it, Beatrice. I wouldn't do that to you."

"Whatever," I scoff, turning away from him, ready to go to the lake.

He reaches for my arm in desperation, holding onto

me.

"There's not enough light down there. You won't be able to read it. Come in for a little bit, Laura won't disturb us."

Nerves rampant, I face him; my eyes thickly coated with moisture, rapidly maturing into tears. "How could you talk about Eric with someone else, when I tried so hard to talk to you for all those years? You just didn't want to talk about it with me."

His glasses reflect the porch light overhead, blocking the expression in his eyes. I can't tell if he even cares at all. "Can we go inside? Please?"

Out here, overlooking the reserve aglow with fairy lights and the occasional mobile phone, we are not hidden from eager eyes keen to collect research for their thesis.

"Fine!" I huff, storming past him into his cabin.

The second he closes the door behind us, the world outside it ceases to exist.

It's quiet in here. So quiet. I swallow nervously and it

seems to echo around the room.

Protectively cradling my brother's journal in my hands, I lean against the kitchen sink while Liam fills two glasses from the tap.

"Here, drink. You'll get yourself all light headed otherwise."

I roll my eyes and take the glass from his outstretched hand, resting Eric's diary on the bench. "You don't know me *that* well."

His smirk pisses me off.

"I do actually. I know you better than anyone. You always get light headed when the world gets too much."

Furious that my eyes are indeed sore and my head fuzzy, I reluctantly gulp the water.

"Good," he whispers, satisfied with himself.

Sense abandons me, foolishly trusting that I can be alone to decide my own actions. I do not choose them wisely.

"How could you tell her about Eric?" I cry, hurling

my whole body into his. I thump the side of my fists against his chest as if banging on someone's front door, demanding to be let in. Over and over, my clenched hands slam into him as he merely stands there, infuriatingly composed. "How could you talk about it with someone else?" I barely recognise my own voice, strained against the restricting force of the inconsolable sobs that pour out of me. "I didn't talk about it with anyone! We needed to talk about it together! I asked you for years! Years! I tried to talk about it with you for years and you just left me hanging! You shut me out and you shared it all with her! You were the only person I could talk to about it! You were the only person who knew!"

My trembling fists surrender to exhaustion, resting against the buttons of his mascara-smudged shirt. He wraps his arms around me and holds me tight to his chest, as if intentionally providing a safe place to cry. In his embrace, I am shielded from the world. From the truth.

He rests his chin on top of my head. "You gave me your heart once upon a time, and I kept it." His whisper falls on my hair, sending a warm calm through my nervous system. "I can't ever give it back to you. It's mine. It's the best thing anyone has ever given me. I will keep it forever."

I sink my face deeper into his body, inhaling his scent. "You confided in her, over me."

"I didn't, I promise you. I only told her that Eric killed himself. She just got obsessed with it, analysing how it would impact us both growing up. I didn't tell her about Bogart."

Hearing the name, spoken by someone other than Eric, outside of my own mind, shoots dread down the length of my body. I pry myself back from his chest and look up, catching his intense gaze. "He died," I gasp. "Bogart died. Eric killed him."

"Yes."

"Because Bogart wanted to kill me."

"Yes," he utters, the answer visibly paining him.

"My brother tried to kill me."

"He was sick, Beatrice. He wasn't always Eric."

My mouth opens and closes slightly, attempting to release speech, but nothing sounds. I grab the diary off the bench and open to the middle page; splattered with big, bold, messy handwriting I don't seem to recognise.

Bea got a shock when she picked up the hot metal buckle. Stupid little fairy. Her skin didn't burn. She must have dropped it too quick. So disappointing. I wanted to run it all over her body just so I could hear her sweet cries, revel in her winces of pain. Next time. There's always a next time.

My hesitant, shaky hand turns the page.

The sleeping fairy's mother came into the room. I was so close. Wasted opportunity. I was hypnotised by my own euphoric thoughts of choking the life out of the fairy's defenceless body. I took a step closer to the bed, but the mother ruined everything. The bitch stood in front of me! The audacity! Doesn't she know who I am? She blocked me from the fairy. She will pay for that one day. But not yet. For now, I forced my friendliest smile and politely told her to go back to bed. She dared to challenge me. I punched her square in the eye. I can still feel the sting of her flesh on my fist. Bliss.

Vomit rises up my throat but I swallow it before it

reaches my mouth. My eyes close themselves, independent of my control; refusing to see any more. But I have to. I blindly turn the page and cautiously open my eyes to the relieving sight of Eric's own handwriting.

Bogart, if you're reading this. I'll never let you hurt her. I am stronger than you. You will never hurt my sister. Got it? I will never let you win. If I have to take myself out in order to stop you, so be it. You will never touch my sister. You will never harm her. Not while I'm alive to protect her. And if the only way I can do that is to not be alive anymore, I hope you suffer on our way out.

Immediately underneath, in handwriting that impossibly does not match Eric's, Bogart replies.

You are already losing, pathetic child. Every day, you know you can feel yourself less and less, and me more and more. The only scar you have from that day is me. Your sister will die at my hands. She will suffer. I will squeeze the life out of her with your own two hands.

"I wanted to talk to you, too." Liam is crying, and it feels so unnatural I can't bring myself to look up at him. "I didn't tell Laura any of this. I promise. We were children, you and I, Beatrice. Just children. All I knew was that sometimes my best friend was different, not really himself, someone else. Someone else who would boast about wanting to hurt you. So I tried to keep you away from him whenever I was around. I didn't know how to talk about it, for a long time. I know you needed to, but I couldn't. I had so much guilt. Eric told me he would kill himself. Maybe I even believed him. Maybe I let him. He showed me the blue rope; told me he would do it if he needed to. I should have told your parents, or my mum, or just anybody. But I was just a kid. I didn't really understand the severity of it. I believed him when he said he would kill himself if it came down to that, but I didn't believe it ever *would* come down to that. I couldn't talk about it with you because I didn't know if you really understood what had happened either, and I was terrified that you would blame me. And, and I guess I didn't want to change the memory of him for you."

I pick at the top button of his shirt, my cheek against his chest, glued there by the saturation of my tears. "But why did Bogart even exist in the first place? Doesn't something traumatic have to bring something like that on? Nothing happened. Eric and I had the same childhood."

"He saw something, Bogart told me. Eric had no memory of it; Bogart took it from him."

"Memory of what? I don't understand."

"When the car dropped on my dad. Our mums were spending the day together, and Dad forgot his lunch, so we all took it in for him. He was a mechanic at the dealership. He was working underneath a car when it fell on him. I'd run off to his office to see if they'd got any more notepads in yet, because I loved to draw on them. They had the car yard's logo at the top and it made me feel like I worked there too. Mum came with me and you followed her. You used to think she was so pretty and wanted to dress up in her clothes when you came around. Eric and your mum stayed in the garage, talking to my dad, well his legs really, he was underneath a car. He couldn't reach a tool and Eric reached under to hand it to him. But the car wasn't jacked up properly and it collapsed, pinning my father and Eric underneath."

"I didn't know any of this," I whisper, finally able to look at him.

"Bogart told me he was pinned under the car for an hour, waiting for the ambulance. The car was right on my dad's chest, and the jack was jammed. Dad was the only mechanic there, and Harold was out in the yard with a customer. Your mum ran to get him but they couldn't lift the car off. Bogart said my dad didn't die straight away. It was only right before the ambulance got there. Eric watched him for an hour; watched the blood drool out of his mouth. Saw the colour leave his skin. His eyes didn't close, they got bigger, and they stared at Eric. So yeah, I guess a five-year-old child, trapped with a dying man might be entitled to have some trauma. Bogart took that away from Eric, but then slowly took over Eric altogether."

The muffled countdown to the new year creeps in from outside the cabin. I liked that spot on Liam's chest. It feels like it should be my spot from now on. I rest my head there again, desperately wanting to close my eyes and sleep. I want to sleep. But I just listen to the numbers as they get closer and closer to one.

Happy New Year!

New Year's Eve 2003

"Jesus, Mitch, what have you been eating? You weigh a tonne right now!"

Mum and I flop Dad down on the bed, having dragged his drunken body back to the cabin. It's not even eight thirty yet. He really overdid it this year.

He's been quiet these past couple of weeks. None of us have openly acknowledged the ten-year anniversary of Eric's death, but the silent dread has been lurking behind each of us like a shadow.

When I was little, I loved the time between my birthday in March and Eric's in May, because for those few months, we were the same age. I still think we are sometimes, before I remember. It's natural to think that my older brother is turning twenty-five in a few months. It's not to think that my older brother is still fourteen.

Mustering the strength to do one final, exaggerated heave, I flip my father's heavy legs up onto the mattress, twisting his body so it lands somewhat vertically in the bed.

Mum slips off his shoes and lovingly drapes a blanket over him. "He's not good on the red. I shouldn't have let him drink the red." An obnoxious snore omits from his mouth as she tucks his shoes neatly under the bed. "He needed to do it though, I guess."

"Today was always going to suck," I whisper needlessly. I could play the trumpet right now and it still wouldn't disturb his slumber. He has so much alcohol in his system I doubt he'll wake up for two days. He'll have one hell of a hangover when he does though. I reinstate my normal speaking volume. "I think the anniversary hit him hard."

Mum doesn't feel the need to whisper either. "I'm not ready for bed yet, but I don't want to go back out there. Your father belting out The Lamb Chops theme song was probably enough for everyone to wish we don't return tonight."

"He did sing it pretty good though!"

The visualisation of my father gleefully and repeatedly reciting the classic children's song, paired with the immense relief that we successfully made it through the day we have all been quietly dreading, manifests into mutual, uncensored roars of laughter projected from deep inside our bellies.

Mum dabs her sleeve under her eyes, halting the tears that have formed. "He really would have kept on singing it forever!"

'Tears of joy' doesn't really make sense to me. How can crying mutually express happiness and sadness: they are completely contrasting emotions. The fact that they can both be symbolised by the same characteristically human response baffles me. I may not understand it, but I like seeing these tears from Mum.

We're still chuckling minutes later, enjoying a game

of Scrabble at the table. I catch Mum looking at me a lot, almost every time I'm studying my letters, like she's on the verge of saying something. She doesn't though and I don't push her to. Maybe one day she will. I can't imagine how she could even begin to express what she has been through, what she has been dealing with for all these years. Her son trapped underneath a car. Realising that he became someone else after the accident, and then trying to love him even though at times she was terrified of him. What a torturous love that must have been.

Terence finally retired. I don't do his work for him anymore; I purely do my own. Work is lonely like that now. No one really needs me. I'm just replaceable. Invisible. Irrelevant. I sit in a puny grey cubicle, headphones on, transcribing interviews, fact-checking stories and the informants, researching new leads. It fills the hours, but not my mind.

I've started looking around at different jobs, just to see what's out there but I never really get grabbed by anything. I'm saving up a deposit for a house, so I need to have a secure employment history anyway if

I have any chance of the bank giving me a loan. I kind of need to get myself set up.

Liam and I still talk a lot, even though he's on the other side of the world now. He moved to London. I've been okay. I finally understand someone: Liam needs time out in the world. And I need time in mine.

Our trauma bond neatly evolved into a secure friendship that remains impossible to label yet comfortably undefined. He is a constant in the timeline of my life; the painful past, the healing present and the hopeful or hopeless future.

He and Laura aren't together anymore.

"You and I are two lost souls," he told me on the phone one night while I was travelling up and down the fire escape of Cat's apartment. "I think that makes us look to the wrong people sometimes to feel found."

I hadn't gone to sleep yet. It was still early. I didn't often wake up in the middle of the night these days, but I liked walking before bed. "Is she okay? Was she heaps upset?"

"You should ask if *I'm* okay, bitch!" he laughed from his end of the call.

"Yeah, but you're never really okay and you've told me before that guys don't like that question!"

I could almost hear him smiling.

"She was okay. To be honest, she was weirdly okay. Like she enjoyed going through the process of a break-up. I think she wants to tally up some bad experiences and milestones and shit like that to make her a better psychologist. You know when you get the feeling you're being watched? I had that every day, but the feeling that I was being studied. I didn't really get it until I saw her interact with you."

Mum wins Scrabble by thirty-four points. "Close to my personal best! I'm going to call it a night my sweet Bea," she says, sliding the letters off the board into the box. "You heading to bed, too?"

I stretch my arms above my head, releasing the tension in my shoulders. "I'm going to go for a little evening stroll but I won't be out late. I think I'll be asleep before the countdown tonight. That'll be a first. I must be getting old."

"Not too much of the old, remember I've got twenty-four years on you." She kisses the top of my head and smiles down at me warmly. "I love you."

"I love you, Mum," I instantly reply.

I walk the long way down to the lake, avoiding the celebrations. It's loud this year. Crowded. Too much noise, too many people, just too much of everything for me tonight.

It rained for a little while this afternoon. The subsequent humidity has enticed the mosquitoes. I swat one as it lands on my knee below my denim skirt. The grass feels only slightly damp, so I don't mind sitting on it. The lake ripples in the moonlight, delicately dancing to the distant sound of a song I don't recognise. I sit close to the water's edge watching in awe as if in the front row of a ballet intended only for the most affluent of spectators. I almost feel under-dressed.

I watch the lake and it watches me in return. It

always has. It watched that night ten years ago, when Eric stepped off the branch and surrendered his life to a blue rope. I was in the audience too but as a child, I had no idea what I was really watching.

Only moments before, Eric had crept into my room, too eager to tell me his new story about Bogart. Except it wasn't Eric, and it wasn't a story.

That night, Bogart tried to kill me. This person who looked exactly like my brother, but who sounded so scary and looked somehow, illogically completely different, picked up a pillow and held it over my face. I tried to scream but the fabric was in my mouth, pushed down so brutally hard, I was certain I tasted blood. My tongue was caught between my teeth that were on the verge of snapping and my eyeballs stung from the pressure threatening to burst them in their sockets.

Time for you to sleep, stupid little fairy. Get some sleep now.

I felt my consciousness slipping away. I kicked my legs about furiously, desperately, frantically, as if jolting myself with a defibrillator to stay alive. I thrashed my torso with all my might, attempting to push off the possessed stranger straddling me. I fought. I fought so hard. He was killing me. I was dying.

Until suddenly, I wasn't.

The pressure on top of the pillow weakened and for just a split second I was certain that it was a cloud and I was in Heaven. But then it lifted from my face, and I desperately sucked the air down into my lungs, my skin saturated in sweat and tears. I stared into Eric's eyes looking down at me so alarmed, so petrified.

Eric had come back.

"Stay in bed, Buzzy! Do you hear me? You have to stay in bed!" His voice was his own again, only it was scarred by defeat and shame. "No matter what you see or what you hear, just let it go, Buzzy. Okay? You have to trust me. You have to let me handle this." His salty tears dripped onto my cheeks. "Please promise me, Buzzy; promise me that you won't try to stop me. Please promise me."

My lips trembled and I shook my head furiously.

"Stop it, Eric. I don't know what you're saying. I won't tell anyone, let's just go to sleep. I won't tell anyone. You were never here."

"He is getting stronger than me, Buzzy. I can't be here when I want to be anymore. I can't be here when I so fucking desperately need to be. Promise me you'll stay in bed. Promise me! No matter what, promise me you won't do anything to stop it. You need to let me take care of Bogart once and for all. Please. Let me save you, Buzzy."

My eyes pleaded for him to take it all back. Stop talking. Change his mind. But his mind didn't only belong to him.

"Eric, you're scaring me," I wept softly, sitting up. I wrapped my arms around his waist and squeezed as hard as I could. I remember being glad for once that I was chubby and he was lanky. Maybe I could hold onto him that way. I outweighed him. "Please stay with me."

"I will stay with you forever."
In that brutal moment, even as a mere child, I knew

that he meant in my heart only.

"Please! Please stay with me."

But Eric already felt himself slipping away again.

"It's okay, Buzzy. I'm going to protect you. I really have to go now." He gently pried my arms off of him, gazing at me quizzically, as if trying to think of a way to magically make me feel better one final time.

That's when he offered his firm hand, palm-down. The special handshake. With my big brother.

For the first and last time ever. I shakily placed my hand on top of his and relished the sensation of his hand turning over in mine, joining us in handshake. He let me set the pace, following my painfully slow execution, indulging me in my ambition to make it last forever. When our fists exploded like fireworks, his mouth mimed *I love you, Buzzy* but no sound came out.

I stayed in bed for as long as I could, just like he had made me promise. I lay stiff for minutes, or maybe it was just seconds. In my purple nightie, I carefully crept out of the cabin to witness my brother wrap a blue rope around the branch of my favourite tree, mere metres away, and loop his head through the opening tied at the other end. My bare feet dug into the wooden planks of the cabin's deck, blistering my heels as I witnessed Eric deliberately step off into the grim air. *Promise me you won't do anything to stop it.* I didn't scream. I didn't move. I just watched. For the longest time. When I could no longer stand to see his legs twitch, I pinned my eyes to the lake so I wouldn't break my promise to my brother.

Eric faced away from the cabin. He did that for me. He knew that I would think he was hurting himself, but he was really just putting an end to Bogart hurting me.

What I realised too late, was that the only way he could end Bogart was to end himself. When he stepped off that branch, I let him, just like he told me to. He was just getting rid of Bogart. I expected Eric to get up afterwards, because they were two different people. But tragically, they were trapped inside the same body.

I was relieved when Bogart was gone. He had scared

me for a long time. I had woken up to a pillow pressing down on my face before. Heard the threats many times. For as long as I could remember, I had lived in fear of when Bogart would come back. When Mum screamed that morning and the men rushed up to Eric from all directions, I knew he never would.

And then my heart sank, realising that Eric was gone too. I had disconnected Eric from Bogart. I watched as Dad tried to revive him, waiting for him to wake up after taking out Bogart. But that's not the way it works.

My phone pings.

> **Liam:** I don't know if I'm a few hours early or a few hours late, but Happy New Year. Let's catch up when I come home.

I smile gratuitously at the lake, as if it had smiled at me first. I absorb the serene beauty; ripples of black water ablaze with the light of the pearly moon. The motion makes me still. I bet the sun sets just to be closer to the lake too. Here, you can rest.

For the first time in four months, I release the words that shock has so far rendered me incapable of acknowledging out loud. The lake will be the only thing in existence apart from me that knows.

"Maybe I'll wait until Dad's not hung-over to tell them that I'm pregnant."

Part Four

New Year's Eve 2004

Dad waves his arm out the window, ushering on the beeping car behind us. "Just go around me!" The 4WD accelerates past, quickly swerving back in front of us once it has passed. "Was that so hard?"

Mum turns around, fretting. "Everyone okay? Jesus, Mitch."

"What? What'd I do? He was the moron beeping!"

"Because you're doing fifty in an eighty zone!"

"We've got precious cargo on board!"

Mum pat's Dad thigh before resting her hand on its traditional spot there. "And she's trying to sleep, so let's not give everyone cause to beep us!"

I stroke Gracie's chubby, rosy cheek and rest my arm

on the side of her capsule. "I might make On the Road Again her bedtime lullaby, it really does the trick!"

"We'll be at the diner in about twenty minutes," Dad says, looking at me in the rear view mirror. "If she's still asleep, I'll wait in the car with her while you ladies run in and have breakfast. Just bring me back a muffin or something that I can eat on the drive."

"It's okay, Dad. I don't want her to nap much longer anyway. The paediatrician said she shouldn't have more than two short naps a day at seven months."

"Seven months," Mum reminisces, "gosh it feels like only yesterday that she was born."

Mum is right, it does feel like only yesterday, but at the same time, it feels like forever ago too, if that's even possible. I just can't imagine a time in my life where my daughter didn't exist, where *I* existed without her, and yet somehow, I did for twenty four years.

I went into labour at midnight, nine days early, and Gracie was born almost sixteen hours later. Cat and

Mum were in the delivery room with me, holding my hand on either side of the hospital bed.

"You're so beautiful and smart and skinny and talented and appreciated and loved," Cat cried, squeezing my hand tighter than I squeezed hers. "You're doing so well. I don't know how you're doing this, but I'm so proud of you and I am going to love your daughter more than a real Aunty ever could."

"You are her real Aunty. Gracie will be so lucky to have you," I panted sluggishly.

Mum dabbed at the sweat on my face with a soft white towel. "Before I get too attached, you're settled on Gracie? You've changed it on me twice already now!"

A giggle managed to find its way through the pain ripping my body apart. "I know." I smiled to myself, recalling the drama my brother and Liam used to go through when deciding on names and trivial details like colours for the stories we came up with. "She is Gracie. Gracie Eric Moore. The family gem."

Mum gasped, hearing the definite name for the first time in its entirety. "Gracie Eric," she whispered to herself. "Gem. Wait until your father meets her, Bea. He's going to be smitten with her, you know that."

A sharp contraction suddenly claimed hold of me, echoing my scream across the bare, grey concrete walls. There were no windows. I had no concept of the time of day. It felt like I had been held hostage in an underground prison for days, a cold yet stuffy dungeon, tortured for information I didn't have. Cat frantically listed every complimentary adjective she could think of and Mum leaned in close, blowing softly on my forehead. "Just breathe, baby. Just breathe. Breathe through it."

The door to the room pushed open and two ladies with plastic watches pinned to their crisp white shirts entered. A blue mask covered the lower half of their faces. They had come in and out four times since my labour started, just to see where I was up to by the looks of things. It was explained to me that one of them was a student on placement, but I was having a contraction at the time and pretty sure I told them both to fuck off.

"That looked like it was a big one!" They stood at the end of the bed, peeking under the sheet draped across my raised knees. "You're crowning," the senior one confirmed. "Your baby is ready to come out now. I need you to push for me, really hard."

All the pre-natal appointments had been with the nurse up until this point. I had never actually met the person who was in charge of the delivery. This woman was about to be the very first person to see my baby, before me, and I hated her and her stupid white shirt for that.

"I can't!" I roared with sheer exhaustion. I sulkingly pulled Mum's hand up under my chin and rested my cheek, clamping her hand in place. "I can't do this anymore! I can't push anymore. I'm done. I just want to go to sleep. Yep, I'm going to sleep now." How could a human body withstand this much torture and still be alive?

"You're so strong," Cat affirmed, her bottom lip trembling. I think she cried more than even I did that day. "You are capable and brave and mighty and your hair is so thick and long and I've always been jealous of your eyelashes and you just need to bring all that together and do one more big huge push."

I shook my head furioulsy. "No! I'm not doing anymore! I've had enough! I'm going to sleep!"

Mum wiped away the sweat-plastered strands of hair on my forehead. "You're nearly done, baby. You're at the finish line."

"Sssssshhhhhhhhhh, I'm sleeping. Sleepy byes time."

"You need to push," Mum desperately tried again. "Gracie needs to come out now."

Depleted, I closed my eyes. "I'm done. You can all stay up if you want, but I'm going to sleep! Good night."

"Push, damn it!" The medical student's adamant demand from between my legs snapped me alive. "Your daughter *needs* you! Push! Push! And then we'll celebrate with pink marshmallows."

My daughter *needs* me. I squeezed my mum's and Cat's hands so tightly our arms shook under the pressure. I heaved my whole torso forward and pushed all my remaining strength and energy down my body, powered by a scream so forceful it would leave my throat hoarse for days. "Pink marshmallows? What the fuuuuuuuuuuuuuuuuuck!"

Despite the hours of agony to expel her from my body, the moment Gracie entered the world was ironically sudden and abrupt. The doctor delicately placed a naked baby on my chest, lowering my hospital gown off my breasts so she could lay on my bare flesh. "Meet your daughter."

It was as if a whole person had just appeared out of thin air. I don't know what I was expecting to come out of me, but oddly enough, a baby wasn't it. Overcome with emotion, I wept.

"She's an actual baby! Is she real? She's really mine?"

Mum dropped my hand and crouched on the floor in a blubbering mess.

Cat's grip tightened. "You are so strong and calm and amazing and inspiring and your eyelashes really are the best."

I could barely feel Gracie on top of me, the weight of her body a mere tickle. I remember thinking her skin looked as if it was two sizes too big for her.

The student delicately placed a blanket over us. "You did so good. You're going to do so good."

My heart was still racing from the stress of the delivery and I was sure that I was halllucinating. "Mindy?"

She lowered her mask and smiled. "I couldn't believe it either when I saw your name on the board."

"You're a doctor?"

Her eyes welled. "Well, not yet. Maybe in a few more years. But I did just help deliver your baby."

Mum regained composure and shakily stood from her puddle of tears. She looked down at my chest, at the tiny little human in the throes of a deep slumber. Gracie must have been exhausted too, having just completely revolutionised my entire world.

"Happy Birthday, sweet girl. You really are our little gem. And Mindy? Gosh, if this isn't the most unbelievable coincidence. Can I go get Bea's father? Is he allowed in?"

Mindy smiled *yes*.

Cat gently lowered my arm down next to Gracie, yet to let go since the delivery began, and kissed my baby's crinkled forhead gently.

"If it's okay, I'm going to love you and spoil you for the rest of my life. I'm going to write songs for you," she whispered, before leaving to get some coffee and fresh air.

Mindy moved a chair next to the hospital bed, level with my shoulders. "She loves you."

I cupped my hands around my baby's impossibly tiny bottom. "Gracie Eric, I love you, too." Looking at her was like stepping into an elusive square of sunshine on an otherwise cold and gloomy day; when the glow caresses your face and warmly cocoons your whole body in a silent moment of sheer peace and priceless warmth.

"Gracie does love you, but I meant your friend. She loves you."

I smile reflectively. "Oh. Cat's very special to me."

"I just noticed, because, well, I've carried a lot of guilt regarding our friendship, and I wish I would have known how to handle things and be a better friend, but I ghosted you."

A lump rises up my throat. "We don't have to talk about that, it's okay. We were only little, like seven or eight. I don't think it counts as ghosting at that age. And you tried to be nice to me towards the end of high school but I was a bitch to you.."

"I have to say this, if that's okay. What are the chances I would end up delivering your baby? It's like I've finally got a chance to do this, and I've wanted to for so long. When I was old enough to realise, I hated myself for just dumping you as if you weren't the best friend ever to me. You were my first friend, really, and you never forget your first friend. The thing is, I got scared, really scared, when Eric put that voice on. Even his eyes changed, like he just became a different person. And then that day under the clothesline, I don't know if you remember it, but we were playing in the backyard and I ran up to Eric but he was in that strange mood and he told me that he would hurt you if I kept hanging around. I told my mum and she said I wasn't allowed to come over anymore, and I wasn't allowed to play with you at school. She thought he was bad news. It only really clicked with me when I was studying, that maybe he was sick. I just wanted you to know that there was nothing you did wrong, towards me or towards your brother. You were a good friend. You were a good sister. You're going to be the best mum in the whole world."

I've lived my life almost in direct response to Eric and Mindy leaving, thinking it was me, something I did, or didn't do. I changed who I was to make people stay. Scared to show the real me, because then it really would have been my fault, it really would have been personal, when they didn't want to be around me anymore. I thought people left because they didn't love you, but maybe sometimes they leave because they do.

"I just had a baby. And Mindy delivered it." I marvelled at the shrivelled creature laying on my chest, brand new to life, and succumbed to an overwhelming sense of gratitude and disbelief. "Isn't life just a bit absurd," I proclaimed through gentle tears.

We arrive at the resort hours after lunch, because Dad drove so damn slow the entire way. We were beeped constantly, but he refused to go above fifty kilometres an hour with the family gem onboard.

Mum and Dad unwind with a glass of champagne on the deck of the cabin. "Bea, aren't you joining us?"

Cradling Gracie against my chest, I bend down so Mum can kiss the top of her head. "I will, I just want to show Gracie around and introduce her to someone."

I haven't bought a pram yet. Gracie is getting heavier to carry around everywhere so I probably should, but I like holding her close to me. Keeping her close to me.

I instantly recognise Pat's caravan out of all the others: it's the one that looks sparkling new every year. It is parked close to the barbecue, which has already gathered a merry crowd.

The old lady from the canteen, Edna lays out a tray of sausages ready to be cooked, a bowl of salad and even seafood on ice. "I've made wraps too, I'll run back to the kiosk to grab them," she tells the man lighting the gas. All these years, I never realised she contributed so much food to the party, let alone at all.

Edna would surely be about ninety now. It seems that she lives for these New Year's Eve gatherings.

Gracie kicks her chunky thighs out in glee as a lone ibis strolls along gracefully. "I hope animals like you better than they like your grandad!" I tease.

I was expecting Pat to be sitting outside, but it looks like she is in her caravan. Hesitantly, I knock on the door.

It opens almost straight away.

"Goodness," she smiles. "This is the nicest surprise I've ever had."

An instant reassurance finds me. "Hey! Sorry to

barge in on you. I just wanted you to meet my daughter."

Pat lovingly strokes the fine hairs on Gracie's soft head. "She's beautiful."

"Would you like to hold her?"

"Oh," she almost gasps, "yes, I would like that very much. Will you come in?"

Accepting her invitation, Pat steps aside to let me pass. The retro vibe that seems to have eternally dominated her personal style is just as prominent within her annual home on wheels. Gracie smiles a gummy smile and takes to Pat warmly, but she is pretty good like that. She's not a fussy baby.

I sit on the velvet cushioned bench at the kitchen booth; beneath the orange curtains I've only ever seen from the outside.

Pat sits Gracie on her lap, jigging her knees lightly to keep Gracie entertained. "Would you believe I've never held a baby before?"

"Wow, really? I wouldn't have guessed that, you're a

natural. She's the only baby I've ever held too."

"Do you mind if I ask, is the father around?"

"Nah, but that's okay. I made the mistake of getting back with an ex for just one night. Turns out so-called theatre actors can be pretty convincing when you're feeling a bit lost and vulnerable."

Of all the bars in town, of course work held my boss' retirement party at the very one where Jake poured the drinks. I successfully avoided him all night; hiding in the beer garden behind Cheryl from the accounts department. Foolishly, I failed to limit myself to one glass of wine. By the third, I was desperate to pee.

I ventured past the bar on my way to the loo with my head held low, practically kissing my chest. But as it turns out, I wasn't as inconspicuous as I had hoped.

Suddenly right in front of me, Jake eyed me from head to toe with smug confidence. "I do miss those curves. I bet they miss me, too."

A series of recent, unfortunately-timed events caused me to smile suggestively in response. Cat's boyfriend had proposed to her and here I was, cluelessly wandering through life, still living with my parents, binge eating my feelings away. My boss was retiring and that meant I would be stuck doing my own dead-end job, when what I really wanted, I realised, was to keep doing his. So damn it, I smiled that bad smile at my loser ex-boyfriend which meant that we both knew I would be going home with him that night. I was in and out of his unit in twenty minutes, and that includes the fifteen minutes of small talk before getting undressed and then dressed again.

Terence retiring pretty much changed my whole world. It gave me direction, and it gave me a daughter.

At the other end of the caravan, the old black dog lying on the bed sleepily rolls over onto its back, stretching his legs to the roof. Gracie points at him and giggles that insanely adorable giggle that belongs to all babies.

"It doesn't matter, she only needs you," Pat affirms.

"I did tell him of course, but he wasn't really

interested. Just means I get her all to myself."

"What about that boy that comes up here every now and again? He used to hang out with you when you were little kids. Well, I guess he's not much of a boy these days. I forget I've watched all you kids grow up. And forgive me for saying, but he turned into a mighty fine-looking man! And I don't even like men!"

Hearing Pat's laughter induces my own. "Liam? He moved to London. He needed to disappear for a while, and it was healthy for me that he did."

"Does he know you had a baby?"

"No, we do still talk though. He checks in, almost like to make sure I'm still alive. Wasn't really the sort of thing I was going to tell him over the phone." The orange curtains flutter upwards from a rare gust of wind. "But that's okay, because he knows where he can find me when he's ready to come home."

New Year's Eve 2005

"Mine favourite!" Gracie revels in the smooth surface of the rock held tightly in her little hand. Painted mustard yellow with sprinkles of gold glitter. I remember I wanted it to look like sand, back when I added it to my collection fifteen or so years ago. Gracie rummages through the shoe box to choose another, pulling out one with black and white stripes. "Lollipop!"

"That one was meant to be a zebra!" I laugh affectionately.

Gracie quickly tucks a handful of rocks under her dress, draped over her crossed legs as she sits on the pillow of grass beneath Nature's Ladder.

"The rocks belong here now, my precious gem. I've

held onto them for too long. We can put them around this tree. It was my favourite when I was little like you. You can put them around the tree and it will make the tree happy.”

Gracie slaps her hands on her knees and cries in frustration, holding her dress down tight. “No!”

“Help me put the rocks around the tree, Gracie,” I instruct her firmly. “Then you can sit on your purple scooter and I’ll push you around. You’ll be able to stand up on it one day and ride around on your own!”

My distraction works and soon a ring of painted rocks from my childhood are hugging the trunk of the tree that signalled the premature end of it. A sense of closure engulfs me and I smile in a silent moment of elation. I was always good at making up happy endings. I never dreamed that I’d be able to make up one for myself.

“Pretty tree!” Gracie claps.

“It can be again now.” The gentle warm summer breeze carries my voice to the leaves. I hope my brother heard it.

Back in our cabin, I cut up some watermelon for Gracie's supper while she sits on a plastic mat squishing the colourful contents of several tubs of play-doh into a singular brown blob. Mum and Dad have their own cabin.

"Nanny!" Gracie squeals, hearing a knock at the door.

"That's odd. Maybe Nanny and Granddaddy decided to say goodnight to you before they head off to the barbecue."

Expecting to open the door to my parents perhaps make my reaction to the sight of someone else somewhat dramatic. "Liam! What the fuck?"

"I've knocked on nine doors to find you. I was starting to panic that maybe you weren't here this year."

It has been three years since those gold-framed glasses were stood in front of me. I want to rip them off his face and clutch them to my heart.

"You didn't tell me you were back in the country! Oh my god! You're here! How are you here?"

"Well, the idea was to surprise you. I see it worked. Are you going to invite me in?"

Disbelief renders me immobile. I'm caught in a dream, unable to process this moment as reality. "I don't think I can move my feet. You're going to have to go around me."

He laughs as he squeezes himself through the ajar door, sliding his body torturously close past me. My eyes level with his shoulders, fixated on the muscles straining against the fabric on his forearms. I'm relieved I can't seem to move; I would surely throw myself at him if I could.

The shut of the door shakes off my stupor and I manage to pivot slowly towards him. But it seems I'm not the only one rigid with shock.

Liam stands perfectly still; arms stiff by his side, transfixed on Gracie as she vigorously squashes a ball of red play-doh between her palms.

"Are you babysitting or did you kidnap a toddler?"

"No," my voice croaks, "she's mine."

"She's yours," he affirms softly to himself.

Liam approaches my daughter as if approaching an alien life form; full of trepidation and innocent curiosity. "What are you doing?"

"Making ladybugs!" she delights in telling him as she twirls a tiny piece of black play-doh between her fingers. "Loveliness of ladybugs!"

Liam smiles to himself, fondly remembering a moment he had long forgotten.

"You're pretty clever," he says, sitting down next to Gracie; rampant with intrigue and fascination. He pinches off some play-doh himself and starts rolling it between his fingers. "Did you also know that ladybugs are meant to be good luck, and if one lands on you, the number of spots it has determines how many years of good luck you'll have."

"You're clever as well!" she marvels.

"I see you taught her not to talk to strangers," he smirks at me.

Gracie demands his attention before I can think of a witty rebuttal. "Make loveliness together."

"You want me to make ladybugs with you?"

She nods her head enthusiastically. "Make a family!"

Never one to show much emotion, his shaky voice breaks character. "I don't really know how to do that, but maybe your mum and I could figure it out together."

I consciously try to shallow my breathing; aware that my chest must surely be rising and falling in noticeably rapid motion.

Exhausted from an evening of squishing things and meeting a new person, Gracie falls asleep without struggle at seven thirty.

Liam is entranced, looking down into the portacot as if genuinely unable to pry his eyes away. "I can't get over how little she is. You made a tiny human. Is she a good sleeper?"

"Usually. I'm not sure how she'll go with the fireworks tonight, but she would have been asleep for a few hours already by then so hopefully she just goes straight through to morning."

"What time does she wake up?"

"About six thirty."

"She doesn't like, climb out of this thing, does she?" he asks, adorably clueless.

"No, dear."

"It's just, I didn't book any accommodation. I was kind of hoping I could stay here with you."

"What if I had booked a cabin with a boyfriend?"

He shifts his stance uncomfortably. "I took that risk. I had of course considered that possibility, but you would have told me if you were seeing someone. I probably would have just camped out in my car. I didn't consider the possibility that you'd have a baby though!"

"Shush," I tell myself, anxious my laughter will disturb Gracie. "Do you want to go sit outside? I just can't leave the cabin, obviously."

Out on the deck, overlooking the celebration, Liam

pours us each a glass of wine. He requests to keep the baby monitor next to him. "It's pretty cool how you can hear her when she needs you. I could have done with that when we were kids."

"It wasn't your job to protect me."

"Oh yes it fucking was. And now I'll protect her, too."

I glide my bottom lip between my teeth, trapping a squeal. "We both can."

"Will you come see London with me one day? You'd love it there, if just for the trees. They are something else, something almost regal. Everything looks so prim and proper, perfectly neat and orderly, and then there are these giant, lush green trees that are wild and free, and yet somehow, they're almost too perfect too."

"I do like trees."

"Let's take Gracie there."

"What, now?" I tease.

"No, not now. But while she's young. Let's make sure

she has the best childhood ever."

"Are you moving back here?"

"I'm already here. I worked non-stop when I was in England, and when I wasn't working, I'd just go for a walk and look at the trees and think about you. I just needed to be somewhere no one knew me for a little while. And then I felt okay to come home again. To you."

"I'm sorry I didn't tell you about Gracie."

"I'm not. It was the best surprise ever."

"You really like her, huh?"

He smiles shyly. "It's weird. I feel drawn to her, maybe because I'm connected to you. I just feel like she's always been here, waiting for the three of us to be together. I've still got your heart by the way. You gave that to me. It's mine to keep."

I return his shy smile. "I didn't ask for it back."

"Good. Because you won't get it."

A roar of cheer erupts from the party over on the reserve. Seems everyone got pretty excited when the next song came on. But here on the deck, an air of tranquillity shields us from the ruckus.

That's the thing I love the most about here: the contrast. It's just as possible to find peaceful isolation as it is to be engulfed in the bustling excitement of a popular holiday spot. Two worlds existing at the exact same time.

And the other world waiting back at home…never really stops existing.

I guess it never did.

The end

www.ingramcontent.com/pod-product-compliance
Lightning Source LLC
Chambersburg PA
CBHW050957210726
48287CB00004B/1259